*Cape Breton is the Thought-Control Centre of Canada*
RAY SMITH

*A Night at the Opera*
RAY SMITH

*Going Down Slow*
JOHN METCALF

*Century*
RAY SMITH

*Quickening*
TERRY GRIGGS

*Moody Food*
RAY ROBERTSON

*Alphabet*
KATHY PAGE

*Lunar Attractions*
CLARK BLAISE

*Lord Nelson Tavern*
RAY SMITH

*Heroes*
RAY ROBERTSON

*An Aesthetic Underground*
JOHN METCALF

*A History of Forgetting*
CAROLINE ADDERSON

*The Camera Always Lies*
HUGH HOOD

*Canada Made Me*
NORMAN LEVINE

*Vital Signs* (a reSet Original)
JOHN METCALF

*A Good Baby*
LEON ROOKE

*First Things First* (a reSet Original)
DIANE SCHOEMPERLEN

*I Don't Want to Know Anyone Too Well* (a reSet Original)
NORMAN LEVINE

*The Stand-In*
DAVID HELWIG

*The Iconoclast's Journal*
TERRY GRIGGS

# THE STORY OF MY FACE

# The Story of My Face

KATHY PAGE

BIBLIOASIS
WINDSOR, ONTARIO

**Library and Archives Canada Cataloguing in Publication**

Page, Kathy, 1958–, author
The story of my face / Kathy Page.

(reSet series)
Originally published: London : Weidenfeld & Nicolson, 2002.
Issued in print and electronic formats.
ISBN 978-1-77196-295-7 (softcover).—ISBN 978-1-77196-296-4 (ebook)

I. Title. II. Series: Reset books

PR6066.A325S76 2019 823'.914 C2018-904460-8
C2018-904461-6

Readied for the press by Daniel Wells
Copy-edited by Allana Amlin
Cover and text design by Gordon Robertson

Canada

Published with the generous assistance of the Canada Council for the Arts, which last year invested $153 million to bring the arts to Canadians throughout the country, and the financial support of the Government of Canada. Biblioasis also acknowledges the support of the Ontario Arts Council (OAC), an agency of the Government of Ontario, which last year funded 1,709 individual artists and 1,078 organizations in 204 communities across Ontario, for a total of $52.1 million, and the contribution of the Government of Ontario through the Ontario Book Publishing Tax Credit and Ontario Creates.

PRINTED AND BOUND IN CANADA

Thou shalt not make unto thee any graven image, or any likeness of any thing that is in heaven above, or that is in the earth beneath, or that is in the water under the earth . . .

(Exodus 20:4)

# 1



I look up from the map and see a tall woman in a padded coat, standing about two metres from the car, staring at me. Her shopping bags are on the ground, but her arms hang straight down at her sides as if she were still carrying something heavy. She stares hard. I don't like it, but the fact is I am a complete stranger in this unpronounceable speck of a place, Elojoki, that seems to have been dropped in the middle of flat and freezing nowhere, roughly 200 kilometres south of the Arctic Circle. There are four shops, one road, a scattering of low-rise buildings, high winds, ice and conifers for miles. It would be odd if I didn't attract attention. Besides, I have spent the last twenty-five years learning how to cope with stares. I can catch a stare lightly and turn it into a smile or the beginning of a conversation; also, I can push it back hard enough to hurt—

But this woman goes on and on staring even when she sees I am looking straight back at her and it's clear to me now that this is not a simple, curious stare. It's as if she is trying to do something to me, to make something happen, just by looking. Her jaw is slack and the whole of her face has gathered around her eyes. I could just drive on, but something makes me want to break the stare before I go. So I wind down my window, smile, point ahead and ask, even though I already know:

'Is the church this way?' My voice is bright and ordinary, slow, but competent in its handling of the foreign sounds; my breath billows and sinks heavily in the air between us. The woman neither replies nor moves. I abandon Finnish, try Swedish. Finally, I shrug, open my hands, and set off on the last few hundred metres of my journey. The woman, I see in the mirror, has turned around and is still watching me.

Elojoki has a history. That's why I'm here, so I'm going to need to make allowances. But right now I'm just too tired to do so. A delayed flight, the drive—the last hour of it the worst: mile after mile of narrow, icy road hugging the course of a frozen river—the trees to either side a green so dark they might as well be black. And now the staring woman. Right now, the whole trip, which I've worked towards for years, seems ludicrous: a woman of forty-four, not married, nor even attached, searching for a long-dead man. In Elojoki.

Yet here I am. Just to the other side of the bridge is the church, set on boulder-strewn ground a few feet higher than the rest. It is squat, wood-built and ship-lapped, painted grey-blue with a shingled roof and a small spire. Seeing it—its foreignness, the fact that it has survived—lifts my mood a little. Beyond it is a bell tower, the cemetery. To the right, behind a thicket of leafless birch trees, is the *pappila*, the long, atticked house that came with the pastor's job. It's empty now. Somewhere behind that, I guess, is the smaller guest house where Tuomas Envall lived when he first arrived here, and where, by sheer luck in the timing of my application, I am going to live too. All I have to do in return is give a public lecture on my findings before I depart.

Heikki Seppä, a tall man with a slight stoop, emerges from a Jeep parked outside the *pappila*. His official title is Local Officer for the National Board of Antiquities, Department of Historic Buildings and Sites, but since we met last year when the arrangements were being made, there is, mercifully, no need for introductions. A quick handshake, then he takes the rucksack and book-box and leads the way, warning of slippery patches on the path.

The house is just one room, lined and floored in wood. There's an old-fashioned wood-burning stove. Triple-glazed windows look out in three directions. A large table sits in the middle of the space. There is also a rather short-looking wooden bed, a rug and a cupboard and dresser, both old. The kitchen area and sink are under the east-facing window; a table-top fridge, a microwave and a vast, white plastic and glass coffee-maker have been brought in. Plumbing, new windows, background heating and electricity, along with the bathroom extension at the back, Heikki explains, were added quite recently. The Envallist rift with the official church was widening, and funds to update the *pappila* were not forthcoming, so the pastor moved in here just before he left altogether. Next year, when restoration begins, these modernizations will all be stripped out, and the corrugated roof will be replaced with authentic shingles. 'So you are just in time!' he tells me.



It is very important for me not to attempt to use the stove and not to smoke in this house, nor allow anyone else to—he speaks in English, slowly, almost perfectly, making the sentences first in his head. As he speaks, he opens and shuts the doors of the cupboards, fridge, microwave, glancing inside each, then closing them again, seeming pleased at their emptiness. He takes me in with small, easily bearable glances.

I tell him I don't smoke and certainly won't let anyone else do so.

He hopes I will be warm enough, and not too lonely in a quiet, out-of-the-way place such as this.

'The house is perfect,' I tell him. 'I am so very grateful for the opportunity to be here, to read the records and talk to contemporary villagers about the stories and memories handed down to them, to study their beliefs, that even if there were discomfort involved, it wouldn't bother me at all. As it is, I could not ask for more—'

'Good,' he says, running his hand over grey-blond hair that is thinning and cut short, 'I'll leave you to it.' He makes for the door, remembering at the last moment to give me the key.

When we shake hands again—this time without our gloves—I notice how large his are and that the little finger on his left is missing, which I didn't notice before. A tiny connection between us, a physical similarity. A good sign, perhaps.

Later, showered, wearing my dressing-gown and slippers, I make coffee, sit down at the spruce table (which is contemporaneous with Tuomas Envall, but, according to Heikki Seppä, not original) and stare out through the north-facing window. The evening is somehow bluer than at home.

I think in an idle, disconnected way of the years of work that have brought me here. First the languages, acquired night after night in the language lab, progressing rather as does a climber on sheer rock, inching up with crampons and ropes. Then research, contacts, grant applications, the sabbatical year, the laptop, maps. I have a brief, vivid picture of my office as it was before I packed—the books on the shelves, the maroon chairs with foam sticking out from the cushion seams, the sun coming in through broken Venetian blinds—and then I think of my least and most favourite students. After all, it's only three days since I cleared out my papers and books. That afternoon, I had my party, with colleagues and their partners and a fulsome speech from the Dean. Daffodils were in bloom, the grass was bright green.

Now, I'm thoroughly elsewhere, and I don't think I shall miss getting my slides in order or holding forth about Religion and Society, The Idea of God, The Paradoxes of Belief and so on. I turn off the desk lamp, switch on another by the bed, and close the three pairs of plaid curtains. The bed is just my length, and agreeably soft. I stretch out on top to begin with, aware that I promised to phone my mother and also that I should clean my teeth before I let myself sleep. The blue between the trees drifts into black, and silence sings around me. Perhaps half an hour later I'm still there, staring at the ceiling in a pleasant state of suspended animation, when there's knocking at the door—tentative, but still quite loud enough to make me jump out of my skin. Then it grows louder and urgent. I find myself standing behind the door (which doesn't have a chain), my heart racing as I watch it shake in the frame.

I'm more or less paralyzed, completely unable to find the right words in either language—

'Who is it?' I manage eventually to say in my own.

'Let me in,' the person outside replies, also in English. A native speaker, or as good as. A woman. Then the knocking stops, as if she knows I'm going to obey.

It's very dark. All the same, I can see that this woman outside is the one who stared at me in the village, now wearing a ski jacket and a hat with flaps over the ears. A white blob of a face, not young, no make-up. She's breathing hard. Either she's in trouble, I think, or she is trouble... In my handbag, on the table behind me, I have my mobile. But I wouldn't know who to call.

'Who are you, please?' I ask again as a gust of freezing air pushes between my skin and the dressing-gown, then past me into the warm room behind. 'Is something the matter?'

'Let me in,' she repeats in a low, flat voice that's almost familiar. And what else can I do? Chase her away?

So she walks past me into the room, a tall woman, heavily built, smelling faintly sour. She pulls off her hat, sets to work noisily on the fastenings of her jacket—a waterproof, breathable affair—which she throws over the back of one of the two chairs. Underneath she's wearing a dark-purple jumper, too-tight jeans, fur-trimmed boots. She sits down, one hand on each large knee, and looks up at me, her brown-black eyes burning beneath prominent brows. And suddenly, even after all that's happened in more than thirty years, I know who she is.

'Christina!' For a brief moment I'm lost in the sheer pleasure of recognition. Of course! Look—she even has her hair parted the same way, straight down the middle, though now it's cut in a jaw-length bob, and then it was pulled back tight in a ponytail—

'Why have you come here?' she asks, as I too sit down.

'I've come to research the life of Tuomas Envall,' I say.

'Weren't you satisfied with what you did to us last time?' Her voice breaks up as she speaks, and then she is sobbing, still staring at me, her face all blotched, red and wet, her hands fisted on her knees—

'You've come to destroy us,' she says.

I can't believe this is happening. I certainly can't believe what she's saying, or that she's saying it to me. I can't begin to work out what to say back nor what I could hope to achieve by saying it. If I wanted to convince her, I'd have to start at the beginning and explain everything from then to now, and even then... In the end, it's a gesture that comes. I point, using my bad hand, at my patchwork, asymmetrical face, a blotched parody of everyone else's, which was the absolute best that could be done back then. I ask:

'Isn't this enough for you?'

And then I tug the lapels of my dressing-gown wide open, so that she can see the rest.

'Christina, look—' I say. 'I am the one who was destroyed.' And she does look. I can see the small movements of her eyes as she takes it all in. Yet somehow, it seems, she manages not to see, because when her eyes return to my face she can still meet my eyes and say:

'You deserved everything you got. Only God Himself knows why He had mercy on you.' This statement, so extraordinary, so utterly crazy-wrong, makes me want, almost, to laugh. At the same time, my heart is galloping, my mouth is dry, I'm terrified—it's like blinking and finding, when your eyes open, that you're on another planet entirely. 'You blew us apart,' she says, 'scattered us. Families were broken. And now you've come to take our past away too. Why? Why won't you leave us alone?'

The last I remember of Christina, we were girls of thirteen. Her mother was on her side and Barbara was on mine. Now, of course, we're alone.

I close my dressing-gown.

Neither of us says anything for quite a while. Her eyes are bloodshot, her skin waxy. She doesn't look well at all.

Maybe she's remembering too. On one of Christina's upper arms—the right one, I think—there may still be a small roughly circular mark, which I made with my teeth. I remember biting hard, her screams, the salty taste of her, and I remember standing, later on, in the field, high as a kite on the entire situation, and refusing to apologize. But that was nothing, in the scheme of things. And it was way back then, before.

Maybe—surely—she didn't mean what she just said. Could it be something she heard someone say years ago, frozen inside her and releasing itself now?

Should I offer her a drink?

I don't.

'Christina,' I begin eventually, my voice oddly steady but fragile at the same time, 'I can't touch what you believe, even if I wanted to. But I am most certainly allowed to think about it, to explain it to myself, and to write about it too'—and then my own rage leaps out, and I conclude my appeal to reason with 'any fucking way I want!' and slap my hand so hard on the table that everything in the drawer jumps, and her too—

Well, now she's looking. Now she sees.

She puts her elbows on the table, her forehead in her hands, thrusts her fingers through her lank brown hair, pulls at it, and makes small, odd noises in her throat. It goes on for a long time. I sit and watch.

How come I am feeling stupidly sorry for her? Sorry enough to say:

'You really shouldn't worry. It was a long time ago. Is there someone I can call for you?' She shakes her head without looking up. Well, pity is one thing, but also I think this is my moment and I must make the most of it: right now, I can move her on. If I don't, she could be here all night.

'I'll drive you back, then,' I tell her, throwing off the dressing-gown, pulling a sweater on, then trousers, boots, coat, hat, gloves, the lot. I help her into her things. She's gone limp and quiet. I put my arm around her and guide her to the car, as I would with someone physically infirm. I drive with exaggerated care and smoothness, in silence, so as to preserve things in the state they are. We pass through the centre of the village, and continue on for several kilometres—the farms are getting farther apart and I'm beginning to feel uneasy when at last she tells me to stop. There's a gate, a yard, a cluster of lumpy buildings, a light burning still in one of them. I lean right over her to open the car door, but she doesn't get out.

'I came here over twenty years ago,' she says, quite calm now. 'Married young: wanted a fresh start, I suppose. We had five children in ten years. Then Jukka died. Well, of course, half of my family are on the Island, and the rest of them are all over the place—I don't even know where two of my brothers are, and anyway, I can't uproot the boys. . . Well, you know where to find me,' she concludes. Then, at last, she climbs out and pushes the passenger door to without closing it properly.

My hands are shaking as I check the locks on the door and windows of my little house. She's crazy, I tell myself, but it doesn't really help. I still can't believe what was said to me, and I can't believe what I did.

'You certainly deserve this,' I tell myself as I pull the bottle of Finlandia from the fridge and pour a good half-tumbler of the thick liquid—far more than I'll be able to stomach and at the same time not enough to stop my mind running over and over what's just taken place.

I could have—should have—guessed that someone from back then and there might be here, now. I just didn't think. And it is the oddest feeling to know, after all this time, how I appeared to one of them back then: to know what Christina felt I was doing, rather than what I remember as happening to me. To think that someone whom I would have said was only on the farthest edge of what took place, feels herself to have been so changed by it, by me—what am I to make of it?

This is not what I expected. But all the same, I've travelled this far and can't turn back. There's no choice but to stay, here, in the very same room where Tuomas Envall must have unpacked his trunks and sealskin-wrapped parcels: I can almost see him trying to light the stove, rubbing his hands together, singing softly to himself. And yes, Christina has also sat at the table over there. There's grit from her boots on the floor.

The vodka is thinner now and I take it in bigger sips, feel it cast me adrift. I climb into bed, set the alarm and turn out the light.

# 2

By ten the next day, having driven south for three hours in semi-darkness first through mist and then falling snow, I am following the curator of the Regional Museum, Ilsa Numminen, past a vast floor-to-ceiling window (through which can be seen more snow blowing into clots, and beyond it the sea, frozen in shades of pewter and white), on and down a broad set of stone stairs. Ilsa is a slender woman in her late twenties: flawless pale skin, thick, blonde hair cut short, eyes huge and unexpectedly brown. Her nails are manicured and polished, a thin gold ring with a chip of diamond sits on the third finger of her left hand. Well, she'll do anything but meet my eye. I can't blame her. Normally, when meeting someone for the first time, I make things easier for them by naming, right at the start, what stands between us. I'll say something simple like, 'I expect you're wondering about my face? I was in an accident.' Here, I missed the chance when the director was so lengthily introducing me and my project. Also, the encounter with Christina is having its effect. So all in all, it feels too much of an effort, and I leave her to struggle with the problem as best she can.



She stops at the bottom of the stairs to explain that this, the main building—stone-built, harbour-fronted—is where

Tuomas Envall grew up as a ward of his Uncle Runar and Aunt Eeva. The door to our right leads to the regional archives, which contain a few documents pertaining to Runar's business, his wife's housekeeping and so on; I can inspect these later on. Now, if I am ready, we will view the collection. Her voice, high with nerves, echoes in the stairwell above us.

On Wednesdays, the museum is not open to the public until the afternoon. The polished boards creak and shift secretively around us as we move through empty, dim rooms, past the collections of labelled artefacts and documents: baby bottles made from horn and leather, painted chairs and wardrobes, a life-size model of a tarpit, hanks of berry-dyed wool, bales of plaid cloth, tiny-looking clothes, fish hooks. There's a room full of several hundred brightly painted chairs, another full of clocks, a whole boat with life-sized models of seal hunters.

Ilsa pauses at a glass stand to gesture at a photograph of a family: eight children, arranged in order of height and dressed entirely in black. It's not of direct interest, but what does fascinate me is the sheer number of tiny white buttons on the black clothes, the fact that none is missing and every single one of them is done up. Well, Ilsa says, she is not sure exactly what these particular people believed, but it would be repressive, certainly. There were many revivalist sects at this time... There was Lars Laestadius, of course. There was Paavo Ruotsalainen and the Awakenings. People had visions, spoke in tongues, were desperate for salvation. In her opinion, such extremes arose because of social insecurities related to the nationalist struggle, the decline of the shipbuilding industry and so on.

She herself is against all rules and regulations, if I don't mind her saying so—

'Not at all,' I tell her. 'Please don't assume,' I add, feeling that the borrowed language makes me more formal than I would otherwise be, 'that a person who studies such things, or is even fascinated by them, also believes in them. Certainly not in my case.'

Our eyes meet briefly and she colours a little, then gestures that we should move on, past wood-turning lathes, a reconstructed one-room cottage (no chimney, a hole in the roof), a vast collection of matte-black earthenware. All this, I think, tucked away here. Walking or driving through, you would never guess; the cold, I suppose, drives the past so much indoors.

Upstairs is a contrast: prosperous urban rooms, stuffed with porcelain, gilt and upholstery. In the large room called 'Nineteenth Century,' Ilsa raises one of the blinds and points across the room at a family portrait.

'There is Tuomas.'

'I had no idea there was such a thing!'

He is perhaps fourteen or fifteen, posed standing behind his seated Uncle and Aunt. His guardians are both robust and substantial figures. While Runar bursts out from his tightly buttoned waistcoat, ruddy and whiskered, Tuomas's face is as white as his shirt, his gaze inward, absent. You would never guess what he had gone on to do, how much suffering, both physical and mental, he caused.



'As a young man,' Tuomas wrote in his posthumously published *Notes* (an incomplete account of the discovery and development of his faith which, along with everything else he wrote, I have read and brought with me), 'As a young man, I was beset by enthusiasms and notions of all kinds. My Uncle considered high and low what might be done with me. He called me frequently to his office to discuss the matter—'

What about Runar Envall's office? I ask, 'Do you know where that was?'

'Oh yes,' Ilsa tells me—her mouth is a little looser now, there is at least a possibility that she might, one day, smile—'the office has been preserved as part of the exhibition.' She leaves her station by the window and beckons me on into a panelled room; three windows look out onto the frozen harbour, dark shutters folded tidily between them. By the far wall there is a massive desk, behind it a tub-shaped rotating office chair. By one wall, a low table with a globe, a selection of chairs. Oil paintings on the walls, maritime, a grey marble bust of Napoleon on a pedestal. The room has a smell too—

'Polish?' Ilsa suggests. Tar, I think, mixed with cologne. I stand still in the room, breathe it in. So, I tell myself, Tuomas, a young man now, but looking roughly as he did in the portrait, came through this door, and perhaps stood exactly here, hesitating before he took one of the smaller wooden chairs . . .

'May I?' I ask Ilsa, who inclines her head ever so slightly.

Silently, the chair accepts me. Its narrow armrests are at just the right height. Uncle Runar, I imagine, would sit behind his desk to conduct the talk, and surely he was a confident speaker, able enough to pause between or even in the middle of sentences, perhaps to perform some small, unnecessary, physical task that had taken his fancy—arranging his seals in a row, trimming a cigar . . .

'You are interested only in the useless and troublesome things of life,' he told Tuomas, 'in those questions which most of us prefer to ignore until we are absolutely forced to consider them. You have no head for figures; you lack the stomach that seafaring requires. As for the law, you have none of the mental discipline it entails . . .'

And at this point, I imagine Runar would lean back in his chair, place his hands on a stomach encased in the latest design of waistcoat, lower his chin to his chest and look out from beneath his eyebrows. Not an entirely unfriendly gaze, but one which it would take strength to meet.

'Well, there is no point in wondering how this has come to be. What can be done with you?'

Tuomas wrote later: 'It was not to begin with a powerful sense of vocation that took me to my studies, but a sense of it being the only possibility. It became possible for my Uncle and I to agree that of all my unsuitable enthusiasms, the spiritual was most likely to offer a respectable living. I would become a minister of religion. The years of study, six, maybe seven, at Turku, Runar would pay for . . .'

I imagine them: a solid man, a fragile one, his brother's awkward, leftover son, standing by the window in Runar's study, with the blinds drawn against the light. The pair of them shake hands to celebrate the decision. Runar's solid face cracks briefly into a smile. Then he turns aside, lights a cigar and peers around the edge of the blind. He is waiting for the last ship of the year to come in. French goods. Porcelain, furniture, perhaps even some ladies' clothes.

Then they are gone, and here I am, sitting in the *maakuntamuseo*.

'You may take a photograph, if you wish,' Ilsa offers, despite the prohibitive signs that she knows I can read, and then, timidly, she smiles.

After the tour we have strong, black coffee together in the deserted museum cafeteria, with its rows of tables and sprigs of juniper in tiny vases, more huge windows looking out on to the frozen sea. She tells me about the town where she grew up, where, apparently, it was possible for her mother's generation, when ice-skating on the sea, to see through the ice and the still, chill water below it, right down to the bottom of the harbour, where lay the wrecks of merchant ships scuttled during the Crimean War. Later, they were salvaged, and she herself never had the experience. The story of this, she believes, is what gave her an interest in the past.

It is far too hard—too complicated—to tell Ilsa what has given me mine, so I just thank her and shake her hand when we say goodbye at the top of the stone steps.

The Volvo is already an inch deep in snow. I wipe the windows and switch on, wait for the engine to warm up. Twenty minutes later, I pull clear of the town. I am one of just a few vehicles on an empty, well-made road, going back to Elojoki: straight ahead, then right. . . I slip on my airport-bought sunglasses against the glare, lean back in my seat.

I am, it strikes me for the first time, setting out for Elojoki at almost exactly the same time of year as Tuomas did. His studies were completed in October 1861, and he set out for his first job, as assistant to the Pastor, on 20 March the next year. Though, of course, he first came from Turku to Pori, to Närpes, to Vaasa and on—I guess it would have taken him over a week, even in a two-horse sleigh. I imagine him to be wiry, as a young man, rather than slight, with light-brown hair and a thin, alert face, clean-shaven, green-eyed. Beneath his fur-lined coat, perhaps he wore the new black robes and short two-tailed tie that marked his profession? He would have added high side-pieces to the sleigh and he'd sit straight-backed on top of one of his boxes of books, holding the reins in gloved hands on his lap. One sheepskin beneath him, another over his knees, more still wrapped around his legs and feet. The road ahead, marked here and there by posts, would be barely distinguishable as a smoother, icier kind of white.

Of course, late March is not the best time to travel, nor quite the worst. The days are lengthening. This, apparently, is a particularly late spring; his was more or less average: the sun shone more often than not and the thaw had begun. Icicles at the edges of roofs dripped themselves to nothing. Sheets of water formed by day over the ice, transforming into low mists at dusk. Perhaps six more weeks would pass before the last of the snow disappeared and the earth's frozen moisture oozed up from below, broke the backs of the roads and flooded them in mud, just as the gleaming ice to his left-hand side became honeycombed with air, soft, treacherous, so that every way of moving around was difficult, if possible at all. It would be two months or more before the sea finally melted clear. Nonetheless, this was the beginning of spring. The sea-ice glowed, opal and milk beneath a vast and cloudless sky. The twigs of the birches were reddening; already on some of them there were catkins and tiny aromatic buds. They would grow redder and redder over the coming weeks, and then, suddenly, be covered in green. By then, the skylark would be calling.

I try to avoid looking at Christina's farm as I pass, but can't quite. It's one of the older buildings around, and I'd say it needs some attention. A truck is parked in front of the house. Two young men, her sons perhaps, are talking to the driver.

At the supermarket, small quantities of imported fruit and vegetables, looking oddly alien—too bright—are neatly displayed by the entrance, and everything except yogurt is very expensive. I pack my basket full all the same, wishing I'd got a trolley instead.

'The Researcher,' says the plump, thirty-ish woman at the checkout. She wears bright-red lipstick, a big smile. 'From England. It is a bit cold here, eh? But at least you will not starve!' A label pinned to her overalls says 'Katrin.'



'Natalie,' I tell her. She nods, still smiling, as she packs the goods into my bag. What else does she know about me? Again, it's something I didn't consider. But she's friendly, so I ask whether she knows of anyone who might be interested to talk to me about how things used to be in the village. Katrin thinks for a moment, jots down a couple of names.

'I'll speak to them. And the school,' she says. 'You should visit that. It's closing down, thank goodness, so we'll get an ordinary one at last. I've been driving my two children forty kilometres twice a day ever since we came here.'

I'm scarcely through the door when the thin trill of my mobile jumps into Tuomas's house, diffident but angry: it is, of course, my mother.

'I've been worried sick—' she tells me.

'Sorry, I'm fine. The museum's fantastic,' I tell her. I describe the snow, the sea-ice, the particular colour of the sky. My mother doesn't travel much. Even when younger, she wasn't interested. She was wild, but she had her adventures at home, and then, when everything changed after the accident, I was the perfect excuse to stay there for good... It's a shame: I'd really like her to be able to see this odd, far-flung little place, at least in her mind's eye. But on her part the interest just isn't there.

'Do you know how long it will take?' she interrupts.

'I can't say yet. When it's warmer,' I tell her, 'you could come over and visit me. You could come by ship. It would be wonderful.'

'I don't want to,' she says. 'As far as I'm concerned, they're all just way up the creek. What I want is for you to get on and live your life—'

My mother has always opposed this trip, and she has been against, in a lesser way, many of the steps that preceded it—in the first place, my sudden, seemingly perverse desire to insist on education, though she eventually admitted I was right about that; then the obscure nature of my first degree, the even obscurer thesis. It is as if she was aware, long before I was, where they would lead: here, to Elojoki. I know all this, but it isn't worth going into.

And naturally, I don't tell her about Christina's visit: she'd probably come straight out and drag me home.

'I am living my life,' I tell her, 'I promise you. There are different ways to do it,' I remind her.

'Sometimes I think you are doing this to punish me,' she says, coughing violently, making no attempt to muffle it, so as to let me know she is smoking again, because of the stress I'm putting her under. But I won't be blackmailed.

'No, I'm not,' I tell her.

'Have you got everything?' she asks, hoarser still. 'Did you pack enough of your cream?'

'Absolutely,' I tell her. 'Please don't worry. You? The flat?'

'All right.' She blows her nose loudly.

'Take care,' I say.

'You too—' and she adds, suddenly mucus-free, utterly perplexed: 'But Natty, what on earth do you think you are doing there?' She hangs up before I can even try to explain.

# 3

It's not been the easiest of arrivals, but perhaps that's appropriate, since Tuomas's wasn't either. 'I knocked on the doors and was sent away,' he says in his Notes. 'But I stayed. The Parish turned its back on me, but still I stayed. I had Work to do here, though I was still far from knowing what it was.' 

The pastor's house, or *papilla*, is basically a large bungalow, though there is a row of tiny windows in the attic, one above each of the larger windows below. Right in the middle of the long side there are steps to a large wooden porch, which has double doors and generous windows to either side of them. This is a kind of extension to the main hall—I haven't been inside yet, but you can see right through. There are low cabinets under each window, symmetrically placed lamps, three doors leading off in the principal directions, a striped rug on the floor. Tuomas must have stood in that hall, with the elderly maid, Ulla.

She told him the pastor was out and took him to the sitting-room, where he waited so long that he fell asleep. He woke to find standing over him a huge man in equally huge black robes, perhaps the oldest man he had ever seen, white-haired, white-eyebrowed, bearded: the pastor. His hands were curled into arthritic fists and his eyes, asymmetrically surrounded by irregular, elephantine folds of skin, seemed to both dissolve and burn at the same time. The pastor said nothing, but reached out and took Tuomas's letter of recommendation from the Bishop, then carried it away into his study and closed the door.

Eventually the old woman came back.

'Tuomas Envall, the Pastor of Elojoki has asked me to tell you—with respect, since he is sure that the mistake is not of your making—that he does not require assistance. He will make this clear to the Bishop. Meanwhile, there is a house in the garden where you can stay. The stove is lit. Your meals will be taken here.'

First, he cleared a path through the compacted snow and ice of the pastor's garden, and each day, after his private prayers and meditations in the little house, he took himself along and into the main house for the first meal of the day, at which he would enquire as to whether there had been word from the Bishop, then repeat his willingness to help in any way, however humble. Day after day, Esko Lehtinen, who clearly had something wrong with his throat (yet did nonetheless manage to make himself understood, in a voice half-whisper, half-shout, to others, and in church), looked past him and said nothing. Likewise, the house servants, the employees of the church, the tenant farmers, those members of the congregation whom Tuomas was able to meet—all of them refused to exchange with him more than the absolutely necessary formalities... The information he gave about himself fell into a huge void, any question he put forth would be sent away, like a stray boat accidentally hitting the riverside, with precisely the necessary force.

So Tuomas put up some rough shelves. He fixed a rail to hang his clothes from. He unpacked his possessions from their boxes and bags, considering carefully where each thing should best be placed. He had good writing equipment, and his books included not only theological texts, but also works of scientific speculation, poetry, history—but relative to what he'd have as a pastor today, or to what I've brought for a few weeks or months, his other personal possessions were few: two recorders, treble and descant; a silver watch; his pre-ordination clothes—well made in good fabrics. A tiny woollen hat, unworn, knitted in a cream-and-red pattern, made for him, so his Aunt Eeva had said, before his birth, by his real mother. This he hung from one of the four wooden pegs by the door, where I now keep my selection of weather-proof coats.

The disintegrating leather bag which he unpacked last of all yielded the contents of the bottom drawer of his closet at home: unused stationery, old notebooks and a wooden box—a forgotten, boyhood thing containing six cracked pans of watercolour paint, the blue, black and the green much used. Later, in his Confession, he would describe this box as if it were Pandora's: 'It was to take me as far away from God as I have ever been,' he wrote; 'it was my Apple, and no sooner was it in my hand than I began to devour it; I was in the desert not even fourteen days, and I acquiesced—'



But I imagine that at the time, it was with a gentle kind of pleasure, half surprise, half déjà vu, that he opened the wooden box, then felt again inside the leather bag that contained it and discovered there also the small sable brush that exactly fitted the groove cut between the two rows of paints...

What I think is that if Tuomas had a real mother and father—or just one parent, or even a brother or sister—then, once he had realized that the Pastor of Elojoki did not want him, he would have simply stayed the night and left in the morning. But as things were, the way that Elojoki refused him, and the way that he survived it, were to utterly change Tuomas. And maybe, without knowing it, that's what he wanted and what he came here for.

As for me, according to my proposal, I am to write a scholarly biography of the founder of one of the least known but most interesting post-Lutheran Finnish Protestant sects, the kind of book that about ten other academics will read but which will get me a few trips abroad and just possibly, one day, a slightly better job.

But perhaps what I am really doing, and have been doing ever since the accident happened, is telling the story of my face, in which Tuomas Envall plays a part. Ever since that time I have been putting the story together and taking it apart again, casting and recasting it in a way that is, when you think of it, oddly appropriate to the subject. I've been pulling small details out of memory and finding others attached to them. I've imagined what I cannot know, I've read, adjusted my imaginings, thought events through from other people's point of view (though clearly, I missed Christina's!). And of course, the story of my face is bound together with other stories: the story of a marriage, of a mother and her son; of the birth of a dream; of the archaeology of an accident. It is also a love story of sorts.

I have to tell it and I don't yet know where it ends. But I do know that my part of it begins on a spring afternoon over thirty years ago, when a red-haired girl with a face that was perhaps already extraordinary, but in a quite ordinary way—*when I*—first saw Barbara Hern.

# 4

I'm thirteen. I'm wearing my school uniform and I carry a green duffle bag, first properly, with the cord across my chest, then in my hand, grazing the ground, then clasped with both arms to my midriff. It's a spring afternoon and I'm walking in the avenues, where bright green borders of grass separate the pavements and the roads. I'm walking and I'm noticing things—such as whether or not each house has a garage, and, if the doors are open, what make and year of vehicle is inside. 

If someone were to ask me what my name is, I'd lie: 'Mary,' 'Elizabeth,' 'Jane.' If they asked, 'What are you doing, wandering like this?' I'd say, 'I've taken a shortcut and got lost' or 'I've accidentally dropped my key down a drain so I'm waiting for my mother to get back from work.' Depending on what I thought of the person asking me, I might just say, 'I'm only looking around,' and that would be the closest to the truth. But the 'looking around' is far too serious a thing to be dismissed with '*only*,' and in any case, it is not so much looking round, or even looking for, as *waiting*.

I've been waiting for a long time, though I've forgotten that I'm doing it. I only ever knew for a brief, burning moment. I'm waiting for the right person and the right place. When those come together, fit like a key into a lock, then the other person will know it too.

I walk past carefully maintained gardens, their lawns glowing, their flowers heavy from last month's rain. The houses are detached or semi-detached and stand well back from the road. It's hard to make much out. Here and there I glimpse the dark shapes of furniture, a picture picked out by a patch of falling light, a vase of flowers, a figure bustling from one room to the next. I fill in what I can't see with imaginings and memories. I enumerate, as yet with a kind of detachment, the many ways in which this well-tended place is different from home. Sandra, my mother, is not one for chores, so long as her clothes and sheets and the bathroom basin are clean.



I hear voices and follow them across the road to a corner house. The front door is ajar. The garage doors are also open, and likewise that of a caravan parked in the driveway next to a Hillman Minx, quite new, dark green, with glittering chrome. Beside the vehicles, a bespectacled woman with long brown hair pulled back into a thick ponytail crouches on her haunches, trying to pick up something small from the gravelled driveway.

Standing, she reveals herself suddenly as very tall. She is wearing, unconventionally for the times, men's blue dungarees over a pale short-sleeved blouse, but even so, the curves of the body underneath show through. A short, bearded man stands close by, cutting a length of wood into sections.

'Hello,' the woman calls out to me. Her voice is breathy, almost over-enthusiastic, playful and solemn at the same time. She holds me in her gaze and walks over to the driveway gates: wrought iron painted a pale blue that matches the doors on the garage and the porch. Close up, I can see that she's not wearing any makeup and that the skin on her face is dryish and faintly lined; she's older than I thought at first, and while her eyebrows arch gracefully over the thick lenses of her glasses, her eyes, each differently magnified, swim rather sickeningly beneath them. Yet her mouth is wide, and as if it had taken over from the eyes, it is involved from moment to moment in a series of subtle evaluating and expressive movements. She is not beautiful, like Sandra, but then again, she is not plain like Aunt Sue. She is somewhere in between, or something else entirely.

'Look,' the woman says, holding out the soft inner side of her arm. A ladybird toils up the pale slope of skin. When it reaches the joint, she takes it on to the finger of the other hand. 'My first this year,' she says. 'Do you like them?' I've never thought of liking ladybirds or not.

She collects the insect on her finger again, and puts it this time on my arm. To begin with, there's nothing, but by the time it's halfway up, I'm sure that I can feel it walk, each footfall separate.



'What are you going to do with it?' My throat's tight. My voice comes out with an exaggerated rise at the end; the ladybird takes to the air in a heavy blur of wings.

'How long have you been standing there?' she asks in turn. 'What's your name?' Her voice is smooth; it fills you up, like milk.

'Natalie,' I tell her: the truth. I hold the word up like an empty cup.

'I'm Barbara.' She unlatches the gate, opens it.

'Do come in and see—'

Just before I step into their garden, I look quickly away from Barbara, across at the man, who has stopped working on his bit of wood and is looking right back at me, then I glance up at the house beyond. There is a small round window, right under the roof. The rows of tiles lift up and over it, like the skin of an eyelid, and someone else is up there, I'm sure, watching us.

'John, this is Natalie.' The bearded man puts the sanding block in his pocket, offers his right hand.

'How old are you, Natalie?' He uses an awkward, over-solemn tone clearly reserved for strangers.

'Thirteen,' I tell him. The three of us stand there for a few seconds, facing each other.

'What are you making?' I point at the strip of wood. Almost everything I say at this age is a question. Once I have an answer, I'm ready with another one. 'Are you going on holiday, then? What's it like inside the caravan? Where are you going? Is it far? How fast can the car go? What do you do when you go on holiday?'

'I'll fetch Mark,' his mother says, when she can get a word in.

'Who's he?' I ask, glancing up at the window again.

# 5



He hangs back, glowering at me; a big, tall boy with a slightly plump face and brown, curly hair, surprised-looking eyebrows that don't quite match. He's wearing grey trousers, a white shirt and, pulled loose, a blue-and-yellow tie: St. Joseph's. I can see him taking in how I'm growing out of my green-and-white striped dress, my scuffed shoes, the duffle bag. I can see how life stretches ahead of him, a huge expanse of calm water, grey-green under a blue sky (what's beginning now will change it, though not quite so much as it will change things for me).

'Manners, Mark!' Barbara says. So he holds out his hand, then, when I'm slow on the uptake, puts it back in his pocket.

'I'm doing my homework,' he says to her, not me.

'You weren't when I came in,' she tells him. 'Can you help me bring some chairs outside? Will it be all right for you to stay a little?'

'Oh, yes,' I say.

She brings a jug of orangeade, a plate of biscuits. 'Home-made,' she explains. 'Take a few.' John wipes his hands on his overalls and we all sit down. Mark stares and stares, half hostile, half something else I don't quite understand. He's looking at my skin. Until now, people's skins have just been there, have existed in various shades of pale or dark, smooth and creased. But this thirteen-year-old skin of mine seems to strike him as utterly extraordinary, a different kind of thing entirely. It's as near to white as healthy flesh gets, but not at all translucent, a kind of thick white. My nose and cheeks are dappled with light, gingerish freckles—it's the same on my arms and in the V of my dress—and these seem to be suspended to varying degrees under the surface of the skin, adding to the sense of its opacity. Here and there is a single, much darker mark, right beneath the surface. I look out from inside this covering as if from something I'm wearing, head to toe—not really part of me. As if, I guess Mark thinks, I'm not human, but pretending to be—

He's afraid of me: I'm pretty sure of it.

'What school do you go to?' he asks, colouring up.

'St. Anne's,' I grin quickly, as if at some private joke. My green eyes come close to meeting his but don't actually do it—like the questions, this is a habit of mine. I bite into my shortbread, catching crumbs with my spare hand, and look from him to Barbara and back again, completely ignoring Mark's father—I can't see the point of him.

'Mark's at the boys' Grammar,' Barbara prompts.

'What's your favourite subject?' Mark asks. I chew, swallow, brush at my dress.

'Cooking,' I say eventually, to Barbara. 'Can I see inside the caravan, please?'

'Show her, then, Mark.'

I like the caravan straight away: the fold-down table, which his father is mending, the tiny cooker under its lid. I want to know where they each sleep, and why there is an extra bunk, and where things are put and kept. I tug at the maroon velvet curtains on their plastic rails, laugh, open them all again. I've been following the moon mission and the caravan reminds me of a spaceship. 'What do you do when you're away in the caravan?' I ask him. 'Where is the toilet? What sort of things do you eat?'

'Baked beans,' he tells me, flushing again. He's been standing at the door all this time, looking at his feet.

Outside, Mark watches me take yet another biscuit from the plate perched on top of the toolbox, and another one to hold while I eat it. I'm always hungry. Even if I'm not, I'll eat something nice, something homemade, just for the sake of it. I eat fast, in large bites, yet at the same time neatly, hoping to hide my desperation to be full.

'Can I see inside your house now?' He's too surprised to answer. Besides, I didn't really ask him: Barbara is just behind, touching up a scratch on the caravan. It's her I'm interested in. He's just in the way.

'Take the chairs in with you when you go,' she says. 

'It's just a kitchen,' he tells me. White tiles, cooker, square red Formica table, bent-ply chairs with red seats, the metal sink with some plates stacked up to dry. 'There's nothing to see.' I want to look in the cupboards but he says no, and, taking another biscuit, I decide to move on, opening doors for myself. I glance in the dining-room, continue through the hall to the lounge, a large cream-painted room running from front to back of the house. It makes me laugh.

'Why is this same green carpet everywhere?' I ask him. 'It's like grass.' I point to the back, where the lawn, just the same shade of green, seems to come right up to the French windows. 'You could play crazy golf in here!' I tell him.

'No, it is not like grass,' he says, deliberately speaking with great correctness, sounding every part of every syllable. Who do you think you are? I think.

'There's not very much in this room, Mark.' I turn around on the spot to take it in. 'There's nothing here, except this carpet-grass. Why?'

'If you say so—' Mentally, he's enumerating the contents to prove me wrong: two tan sofas, three dark-yellow armchairs, a tiled fireplace, a round wooden coffee table with a white cloth and a vase of garden flowers upon it; cupboards to either side of the chimney breast, above one of which are shelves of hard-back books; above the other a record player and radio. A huge, thriving spider plant in the front window; a hybrid of bag, box and table which his father made for his mother's sewing and knitting things.

'No photographs,' I say, 'no knick-knacks, no thingamabobs. No pictures. Nothing on your walls at all. Not even wall-paper!'

'We don't hold with those things,' he replies.

'What do you mean, "hold"?'

'Have you finished?'

'I want to go upstairs.'

'It's only bedrooms,' he tells me.

'I want to go, anyway.' He's not used to people who break the rules. I can tell he wants me out of his house, out of his mind too—but I don't think he knows how to do it. He's not used to fighting.

'No,' he says. 'You can't.'

'Who says? Whose bedrooms? I'll ask your Mum.' I'm already through the open door, back in the hall, beginning to climb the stairs.

He catches up with me at the door to his parents' room, grabs my arm at the elbow. He grips it hard. He must know it hurts, but I give no sign of feeling any pain, so he grips even harder: it's a game I could win, but I can't be bothered to.

'Just look,' he says. 'You can't go in.'

The room faces to the front of the house, its large windows screened first with plain nets, then with curtains in a creamy white.

The walls are painted a pale blue, with carpet in a darker shade. The woodwork, bedspread and mats at each side of the bed are white. There are two small wooden tables with identical white lamps, and home-built wardrobes on either side of the chimney breast. No mirror. The room is bright, but it has a sad feeling to it. Later, I'll find out that once a month Mark's mother spends most of the day in this room, with the curtains closed. She's explained to him that this is due to the early onset of the Change of Life, an event which means he will never now have a brother or a sister, as had been his parents' plan when they chose the house; ideally they would have liked at least one more of each... But for now, I just feel slightly disappointed that I don't like the room more.

'Okay,' I tell Mark, 'I've seen it now.' He lets go of my arm and leads me across the landing to a medium-sized room painted a startling, rich yellow, with the window and skirting a bright blue-green. 'The Guest Room,' he says. There's a three-quarter-size bed, made up and covered with a green candlewick spread, and a utility chest of drawers.



To the other side of the bathroom, a larger, pink-and-pale green room looks out over gardens to the back. It contains a single bed, a wicker chair and matching small table with a drawer. The iron and ironing board are just visible inside in a corner cupboard, and a sewing machine, attached to its own special table, stands in front of the window. Next to it is a pale-green paraffin stove, currently serving as a plant stand. Besides sewing, the room, with its deep windowsill, is used to overwinter plants. The smell of geraniums, laced with the faint tang of the stove, hangs in the air.

'This room—' I say after a moment or two. 'It could be a very nice room. Whose is it?'

'No one's. You can't go in,' he reminds me.

I will one day, I think at him. It's my room.

'What's up those stairs?'

'It's private.'

'Show me, though—' I grab his damp hand in my dry one, pull at him. 'Up those stairs, it must be—' He has no idea how to stop me. But he's lucky—Barbara comes into the hall below and calls out for us to come down.

It's getting late. 'Won't your parents be worried?' she wants to know.

'No. They've gone out,' I say more or less truthfully, adding: 'to the hospital, to see my Gran—' which is an outright lie.

'I see,' Barbara says. She smells faintly of paint, and is carrying her overalls in a bundle. She considers a few moments, then makes the invitation: 'Perhaps you had better have your supper with us, then? Do you need to wash your hands? Show Natalie the bathroom, Mark. Then you can both set the table.'

I keep catching him looking at me. He blushes when I catch him but he doesn't stop. The thing is, I must seem even stranger indoors, close up. There are fine, faintly ginger hairs on my arms and sometimes, when the light catches them, he can see even finer ones all over my face, the very faintest trace of fur, especially just above my eyebrows and on my upper lip. Also there's a slight tremor to my lower lip, as if I were about to cry, yet at the same time, such a thing must seem impossible: I'd kill you first, spring on your back like a tiger. . . The dress I'm wearing is very dirty. There are stains on the front, as well as the kind of grey dirtiness that comes from not being washed often enough.

I copy the way Mark puts the knives and forks down, place mine absolutely opposite his, watch him fetch the cruet from the sideboard. I've never seen such things before.

The sun is setting as we take our places at the table. His parents are opposite each other and likewise, across a shorter distance, Mark and I. He's avoiding me now, looks instead at his mother, who just now reached forward for the serving spoon, then stopped halfway and sat back, waiting.

'God—' his father's voice is loud, full, but at the same time intimate, as if talking to someone well known, but temporarily concealed behind a wall or afflicted with slight deafness, 'God, you who made this world and all that it is, accept thanks from those you have made.' After this is a pause, then with a soft scrape Barbara removes the lid of the dish: macaroni in cheese sauce, topped with tomato slices, to be eaten with bread.

'Do you have a faith, Natalie?' Mark's father asks just as Barbara is handing my plate across the table.

'Plenty more later if you want it,' she says.

'Pardon?' I pick up my fork, start to eat—no one's ever told me to wait for others to be served. If they did, I'd ask them why. Mark's glaring at me again. 

'Do you go to church?' the father persists.

'Oh, yes,' I tell him brightly, a brimming spoonful of macaroni halfway to my mouth.

'Which one is that?'

'Saint Someone's. I don't know the name. I only went a few times,' I say. 'With school.'

'Do you know God?' Mark asks me.

'Let the child eat,' Barbara interrupts. 'She's hungry.'

'We do,' Mark says.

'What's he like?' I ask, knowing it's cheeky. I stare straight at him and speak with my mouth full.

'He is not like anything,' Mark's father tells me, stern but good-natured. He puts his cutlery down, presses the tips of his fingers together. 'He may be compared to any number of mundane things, and in this way we show our desire for union with Him. But in the end, He can only be known as He is, immanent in His creation.' He smiles warmly at me. I put more food in my mouth, look away. God is not what I'm here for.

'Natalie, you have such gorgeous hair,' Barbara says. 'What a colour!'

It's she, I later learn, who does the decorating, who brings home the tins of paint with their image-evoking names—Sunburst Yellow, Eggshell Blue and so on. Mark's father prefers to avoid the use of similes or metaphors—verbal imagery—in reference to the mundane.

'When you're older,' she says of my hair, 'it'll look wonderful in a knot. Does it come from your mother's or your father's side?' she continues easily. 'We always say that Mark gets his height from me and his brains from his father.'

'My Mum's is even redder,' I tell her. 'She's a real looker, everyone says.'

'You see, Natalie,' Mark's father cuts across, 'we are members of the Worldwide Congregation of the Envallist Church of Grace, called to worship the Immanent, and beware of Imitation. Our church was founded in Finland. That's why we have the caravan, so that we can go there every year.'

Caught between irritation and curiosity, I fill my mouth again, almost smile at him.

I help Barbara to wash up while Mark's father spreads a sheet of the *Envallist Times* on the table and cleans the family's shoes. Mark goes upstairs to finish his homework.

When he comes down again Barbara and I are sitting opposite each other at the kitchen table. A radio concert of piano music is playing. Clean shoes are in a row on the floor; John is nowhere to be seen. None of the three of us says anything for a moment or two. We just look at each other, sensing, each one of us differently, that something has changed.

The fact is that a few hours ago, before I arrived, the three of them—father, mother and son—were a family group living amongst people who differed from them. The distinctions between them didn't matter much. But from now on, where each of the Herns stands with regard to the other two will be different. Mark will feel separate from his mother, akin to his father because they are the men. Barbara and I are of another kind, unreliable, frightening.

A puff of cooler air, smelling of cut grass, pushes in through the open door. I catch Mark's eye, make him look away. *When she's gone*, he's thinking, *things will go back to how they were.*

He's got that wrong.

'You'd better see Natalie home, love,' Barbara says. I am so close; I could reach across the table and touch her hand.

Mark and I walk downhill, the hedges to our left, the road to our right, a progress marked by orange pools of streetlamp light, brighter then dimmer then brighter again. After a while, I ask:

'Why is it you don't have a TV set? Everyone else does. You rent it. They fix it when it goes wrong or give you a new one.'

'When television first came,' Mark says, 'some of our congregation wanted to allow it. You know how television works?' I shake my head. Of course I don't!

'It's because of a cathode ray tube, which is basically a variable pulse of electrons hurtling though a vacuum, then hitting a screen coated with compounds of phosphorus. It makes a glow where the electrons hit the phosphorus. The point of light moves quickly across the screen in lines—across, then off while it goes back across and down, then across again—like writing, but very fast—so fast that the human eye and brain reads all this *movement* as an *image*. We don't see the point of illumination move, because we can't see fast enough. But if we were flies, which see much faster, then we would not see an image, just the point of light moving across the screen. So, some people said that the image on a television screen does not, in any objective sense, exist—'

It's all Greek to me, but I'm amazed at someone being able to say so much at one time, in whole sentences.

'They were wrong, of course,' he concludes. 'The way an image is made isn't important. The function it serves is the thing. Whether or not it stands in for the Actual, is it or is it not a window for—'

'You mean you don't watch TV, not at all? You'll miss the Americans landing on the moon,' I tell him.

'I don't want to see it,' he says. 'I can read about it. I can listen to it on the radio—'

'I wish I was with them,' I tell him. 'You wouldn't catch me down here on earth, if I could get that far away. . . But have you seen what they eat? Dried things in packets. Nothing that makes crumbs, because they float about and you can't pick them up, then they might get in your eyes or your lungs and choke you. They have to pee in bottles—'

I stop, suddenly, on a corner. The estate is not perhaps as remote as the moon, but it's certainly a place Mark hasn't visited much. The pairs of houses are small and low, people don't do their gardens, but use them instead as garages. 'Don't come any farther. It's just up here.'

We are under the last streetlamp. Ahead of us is a good stretch where the lights are broken.

'Do you like girls?' I ask him. The orange light deepens the colour of my hair, paints my skin mottled gold.

'It depends on the individual,' he says.

'What about me?' I persist.

'I don't know you,' he says.

'Do you want to see me again?'

He'd like to say something so terrible it would make me vanish, but he's been brought up to be polite—

'No, actually, I don't want to,' he manages to say. *Don't ever come back*, he's thinking. *Leave us alone*—

I run straight across the road without looking first, disappear into the stretch of gloom on the other side, reappear at the next working streetlamp, making for the lightless corner house with a broken gate. I stand by the door for a while, as I always do, listening. Then, when I know it's empty, I let myself in. Feeling my way in the dark, I go straight up and into Sandra's room and look back down into the street. Mark has stayed put, waiting for a light to come on, for something to happen, for some sign that I'm really in the house. But I won't give it to him. I watch, invisible, until he gives up and turns back down the street. Then I go downstairs and turn on the TV.

This is how it begins. This is the afternoon that brings me, half a life later, here, to a one-roomed wooden house a stone's throw from Tuomas Envall's church.

# 6

Something woke me—a sound of some kind. I lie in the darkness for quite a while before realizing that it isn't darkness at all. Light is pushing bravely through the four sets of plaid curtains, those to my left—which I think is south—in particular. Outside it will be bluish and cold, but the curtain fabric warms it up, and I'd be quite happy to stay this way for an hour or so. However, my watch, when I find it in my dressing-gown pocket, says it is almost midday. So there's no option. 

It's on my way to the shower-room that I see the envelope pushed under the draught excluder at the bottom of the door. My name is type-written in capitals, underlined, with a full stop after.

Inside, the letter starts without any kind of salutation, and the capitals continue:

> I'M SORRY IF I SCARED YOU, BUT I'M SAYING PLEASE THINK. I WANT TO TELL YOU THAT I KNOW YOU HAVE SUFFERED, BUT THAT'S BECAUSE YOU RESIST THE LORD, AND THE FACT IS YOUR SUFFERING CAN BE A PEARL WITHOUT A PRICE IF YOU OPEN YOUR EYES. AND PLEASE,

> PLEASE DON'T COME HERE AND DO THE SAME THING ALL OVER AGAIN. LOOK WHERE IT GOT YOU LAST TIME—REMEMBER THAT. WELL, THEY WANT TO TURN EVERYTHING INTO A MUSEUM AND THEY HAVE ALREADY TAKEN OUR CHURCH AWAY HERE, BUT IT IS NOT THE ONLY ONE NOW AND WE DO STILL HOLD SERVICE HERE IN MY HOUSE EVERY WEEK. IT IS THE WAY. COME TO IT AND YOU WILL SEE. FORGIVENESS IS MINE, SAID THE LORD, AND IT CAN FALL ON ALL OF US LIKE MORNING DEW.

She doesn't sign her name either. My first reaction is that the whole illogical business about suffering drives me wild—but at the same time, something about the letter makes me want to take her two hands in mine and cry. Then I read it again and my blood runs cold. It's the lines in the middle: LOOK WHERE IT GOT YOU LAST TIME—REMEMBER THAT. Well, I'm scarcely liable to forget. So is she making a threat? It depends entirely on the tone of voice I use when I read it in my head. But the fact is, I'm sitting here, on my own, in what amounts to a wooden hut, and I still don't know who I should call if anything goes wrong.

Then, all of a sudden I'm back there, in the field. '*Sinner! Sinner!*' Christina is calling out, not in the sing-song voice kids usually use to insult each other with, but fast and hard, as if she were literally goading me with something sharp. Her fat face is angry-white, her brown eyes glitter, bird-like. I can still feel the surge of anger that pushed itself through me back then. She's certainly not going to stop me doing my work—but how can I make myself safe? Should I go to the police? Would they understand? I just don't know, and I push the letter back in its envelope and then can't even decide where to put it. More than anything, I realize with a shock, I would like to burn it, but that won't get me far, and in any case it would set off the smoke alarm. So in the end I have to rush my shower and go out with wet hair; I'm almost late for my tour of the church.

Because of weakened structural timbers, special permission has had to be given for my visit, and I, having made a signed declaration that I will not hold anyone responsible for injury to my person, have to be accompanied by both Heikki and the pastor of the next parish, who currently covers this one as well.

The pastor is already waiting by the gate, a thin, brisk man, Swedish-speaking, not given to conversation. We have to wait for Heikki before anything can begin. He removes the handwritten poster, stuck with masking-tape across the join of the big double doors. *The Faith is still alive! Give us back our Church*! it says.



Heikki moves it carefully to one side and attaches it again with the same pieces of tape.

Everything, even the roof and the outside, which looks like large blocks of painted stone, is wooden. Inside, there's no electricity, but light pours in through huge, clear, glass windows. The whole thing seems too big for such a small place, but I have to remember that people would set out the day before and travel for miles to worship. There's seating for four or five hundred people, including a gallery, painted in two subtly different shades of pale green. There's an organ, and accommodation for the choir. The roofed pulpit is reached by a small staircase of twelve steps. Between Tuomas's arrival in Elojoki and his climbing those twelve steps to preach his first sermon, were six hard months, during which time his perfectly ordinary Lutheran faith became a new sect, Envallism. Those months are the main object of my research here: what exactly led Tuomas to write that first sermon, *The Forgotten Commandment*?

'Let me tell you,' it begins, 'about Salvation—' It's a text full of poetry and passion, extremist, absolute. It's as different as can be from the run-of-the mill dissertation that Tuomas completed two years before. I've read it many times, searching in vain for clues as to what might have happened in the intervening time. Now, standing in his church, I can imagine the way the light fell through the window and lit him as he stood at the lectern. I can hear him, his voice warm and slow as he sounded each word out, giving it its due. I can see his eyes, the opal green of sea-ice, shining the same way.

'In this most fundamental of alterations,' he said, everything remained outwardly the same, yet was transformed inside. A flame burned inside the saved person, and its warmth could be felt 'with every breath and every step taken.' Did they, he asked the villagers of Elojoki, want to be saved? And if so, did they obey the Lord's Commandments as they should?

He read from the big Bible, Exodus 20:4: 'Thou shalt not make unto thee any graven image, or any likeness of any thing that is in heaven above, or that is in the earth beneath, or that is in the water under the earth . . .' He asked the congregation to look about them in the church, and to think of what was in their homes: it was clear how far and how deeply all of them, including and especially himself—he was not leaving out himself—had sunk in this respect. But God in his mercy had shown Tuomas Envall the error; he would show them.

An image, Tuomas told his parishioners, was 'a window through which the devil might climb,' and what they must do to prepare themselves for Salvation, to 'open the way,' was to remove from their lives all visual representations of any kind. By this he meant not only images of religious subjects, but images of anything at all: it was a small sacrifice, when compared to the ecstasy of Salvation, but it must be done thoroughly and wholeheartedly. God, he told them, required of the villagers of Elojoki that they rub down and paint over the flowers painted on their chests and trinket boxes, their spinning wheels and clocks, their cribs and chairs and cupboards; that they smash and bury their painted foreign crockery, however much it had cost; that they tear down any wall-papers patterned with flowers, leaves, fruit, ships and other such things and burn them, along with any paintings, prints and drawings they might possess; that they collect any carvings, including children's toys, that they might have in their homes; that they search books for illustrations and remove them, also to be burned; that they sift through their closets for items of clothing or other fabrics which, unlike the traditional village plaids and stripes, might have imitations embroidered or printed or woven upon them—these, however, need not be burned but could be shredded into thin strips and made into rugs—

The congregation, stirred, bewildered, stepped out into 
yellow autumn light, the first fallen leaves blowing about their feet, the sky achingly blue. Perhaps they were still undecided. But in the morning, the cherubim, crown and sun were sawn from the pulpit, and the poor-man statue from outside the door of the church. A party of men set to work in the vicarage itself. They made a great pile of papers and wood in the garden, to which Tuomas added his oil paintings and water-colour sketches and the illustrations from his many books. People came to watch, then one by one, went home to build up their own fires.

It was observed that the rich had more imagery in their lives than the poor, that many of the things to be destroyed were of foreign origin, and that imagery was not only a Popish but also a Russian thing. By the end of the week the repainting and repapering was done and the windows hung with new curtains in plain colours, traditional plaids and stripes. Tuomas, elected almost unanimously as the new pastor of Elojoki, took possession of the vicarage. In the weeks and months ahead, forgotten images would of course keep turning up and have to be individually destroyed, but in essence they were now ready, Tuomas said, to begin God's work, which he called *The Work of Love.*

The wood of the pulpit is warm to the touch.

'Look,' I call out, 'you can see the saw marks. And over there—what's missing from there?'

'It would have been a coat of arms,' Heikki informs me promptly. 'And there, on that wall behind the altar was once a huge painting of the crucifixion, commissioned from Holland especially by a local landowner, not long before Tuomas Envall arrived. You can see where it was fixed.'

'What I'm after,' I tell him, 'is what made him think of it. What *exactly* gave him the idea—' The pastor waits for us by the door, as if genuinely in fear of the weakened roof. When pressed, he says that he believes, given the recent split from the official church, that the building should be restored to the condition that existed prior to Envall's arrival. The Envallists, of course, do not.

'I am what you call a pig in the middle,' Heikki says as we close the door behind us.

We go back to the community centre afterwards. Maps and plans of the area and its buildings cover an entire wall of Heikki's office. His large, blond wooden desk, on the other hand, is polished and paperless. There is a computer, a pair of gloves and some car keys, a framed photograph with its back to me, plus the inevitable coffee cup and saucer: a filter machine sits on top of a filing cabinet in the corner, and I accept his offer of a cup for myself.

'There's a woman here from England,' I tell him. 'Someone I knew a long time ago. Christina. Her second name used to be Gardner but—'

'Kirsti Saarinen,' he tells me. He leans over the desk to top up my cup. 'I don't suppose you could take her back with you? That woman is a thorn in all our sides. Her sons too. She and her followers camped outside the church, singing, to try and stop it being closed. They object to everything—the restoration, the idea of the museum, the new parish boundaries. Naturally, they don't like the school closing. They complain about this new community hall, even as they book it for their weddings—'

So I tell him about Christina's visit. I say that she came at night and made wild accusations. I don't tell him what they are. I say she's sent me a threatening letter, but I don't show it to him.

'I had no idea she would be here,' I say. 'Do you think I should inform the police, in case she bothers me again?'

Heikki leans back in his chair.

'It is difficult for me to judge,' he says—and of course, I have told him so very little: it's either that or the whole lot, the Story of my Face, and likewise, it would be a problem if I did inform the police.



'She wants me to abandon my research,' I tell him.

'I expect that makes you want to do it even more!' Heikki says as he writes down the number of the nearest police station on a compliments slip and hands it to me.

'But most likely,' he adds, 'she is just unstable. Spring is the season for depression. You pull yourself through winter, and then, for a while, it just gets worse. The mud, the slush, still not much light—you'll see. I really can't tell you what to do about her. But with more important things,' he adds, 'I can help.' Next, he'll show me the parish records, take me around the main house properly.

He beams at me across the desk, ready to go—though what I want to do more than anything is to go home, lie on Tuomas's bed, stare at the ceiling and let my mind drift, without any interruptions.

'I need to write up my notes on today first,' I tell him, 'sort out my papers.'

'Of course,' he says, still beaming. 'Let me know when you are ready.' And then, rather abruptly, Heikki looks aside, picks up the photograph on his desk and holds it out to me. A white-blonde girl in a summer dress, unmistakably his.

'My daughter, Kirsikka,' he says. 'I am divorced. She lives with me on the weekends,' he adds. Beneath the smile, I can tell, he is looking at me carefully, weighing everything up, habituating himself. I know, because it's only natural (though that doesn't mean I should like it), and also because I have been here before. Not often, but once or twice: men whose dark fantasies I somehow fit, or who want to see what it could possibly be like, or think I must be desperate and so I'll put up with them, or that they'll have some kind of unpleasant advantage over me.

'You?' he asks.

'None,' I tell him, appreciating the fact that he doesn't make any assumptions, and at the same time angry at being asked because anyone with any wit might guess.

I get to my feet, shake hands. Then there's nothing for it but to go back to Tuomas's house, put Christina and her mad letter behind me and get on with what I've come here for.

# 7

While Mark, Barbara and I would all say that the story begins that spring afternoon when Barbara lifted the latch on the gate to let me in, John Hern, I'm sure, would have seen it differently. He would have said that the arrival of the letter, a week or so later, was the beginning of what happened to him. 

John Hern: a man quite able to argue the hind legs, bit by bit, tediously, from a donkey—but also one given to sudden ecstatic speeches about the nature of divine love or the experience of 'being in God's moment,' and then again, one prone to crying out in his sleep with nightmares. A man who sharpened his plane and chisel before putting them away. Who thought it best to err on the safe side and therefore grew a beard and knotted his tie by feel alone, and also drove dangerously, so as to avoid using mirrors—this even though Envall did not expressly prohibit them. Likewise, a man who made love to his wife with his eyes wide open so as to see only what was really there: the sag and stretch of their skins, the paleness, broken veins and other signs of their mortality. Who insisted that she do likewise, but nonetheless forgave her when at some point every time, her eyelids sank down and made her face in its way absolutely perfect, and then everything she was made of softened and gave itself over to what he was doing to her and what she was feeling, so that he could no longer be sure whether his own eyes were open or shut or where in heaven or earth he was—

John Hern: the only one of us not to survive what took place the summer after that letter came:

> With respect to your recent application to renew your passports I am returning your documentation since it is incomplete. You are aware that the office has in the past, entirely at its discretion and in a small number of cases, permitted certain exceptions on religious grounds to the requirement for passports to bear a photograph. As a result of Her Majesty's Government's imminent ratification of international treaties which bear directly on this practice, no such exceptions can now be made . . .

That same day, I make my second visit.

This time, I unhitch the blue gate for myself, walk up to the front door and ring. Barbara seems to believe me when I say that a water pipe has burst, so we've been sent home from our school. 'Mum's at work,' I add—the true bit.

I follow her through the hall to the tidy kitchen, where she serves me a glass of something she calls lemonade, though it has no bubbles, and a plate of biscuits, different than last time, very crisp, with a nutty flavour I don't have a name for.

'We had bad news today. A letter—' she says, watching me eat my way through them. 'So it's lovely to have someone to cheer me up. Bring those with you and come and sit in the garden.'

There are wooden chairs and a table in the shade of a large tree.

'What were you doing the minute before I came?' I ask, surprising myself. Even by my own standards it's an odd question, but she doesn't seem to care.

'I was upstairs,' she answers. 'I was just thinking. Feeling a bit sad—' She explains about the letter, how they were expecting it, but hoping against hope. There will have to be a big discussion about what to do. The fact is that they already have to use money, which has pictures on. There's at least an arguable biblical precedent for that, but nothing, of course, about photographs, and where would you draw the line? 'John says we must stand firm,' she says. It means that they won't be going on holiday to Finland in the caravan. 'Actually, for myself, I don't mind so very much. It's an uncomfortable journey. But Mark will miss it, and Mr. Hern,' she says, 'he's going to be very upset. His family came from the village years ago: one of them made that dresser in the hall. But for me, it's different. It's only since we married—'

An Envallist wedding ceremony, Barbara explains, is the one that matters, though not legal on its own. Hers took place six months after the registry office affair, out of doors, in a grove of spruce trees near a lake, not far from Elojoki in Finland. Her parents wouldn't attend, but her brother Adrian did.



'The sun shone almost until eleven-thirty at night,' she tells me. 'Afterwards, we ate at big tables on a wooden pier built out into the lake, smooth as glass. We watched the sun slip away behind the trees. It was perfect, except for mosquitoes, great big ones that brought you out in lumps . . .' She laughs, makes a face, scratches at an imaginary bite on her arm.

'The best thing with bites like that is to rub them with wet crystals of sodium bicarbonate. It stings, but takes away the itch. Leaves white powder on your skin . . .'

Has she got any more of these biscuits? I ask. It turns out that I've eaten the last one, but they don't take long to make, so we go back into the kitchen, and when Mark pushes open the front door, he smells baking and hears my voice. He comes to the kitchen, to make sure. My back is to the door, but I can tell he's there. Barbara is opposite me, her eyes settled, soft as butterflies, on my face. She doesn't see him either. She's just finished telling me about the registry office wedding, which only took ten minutes, and how after that she had to go home and tell her parents what she'd done, but they'd left her a note saying they'd decided to go to town, so she had to wait.

'Then what did you do—?' I love the way she answers questions, any daft question at all, letting me pull the details out any way I want. She never says 'Nosey, nosey, aren't you?' or 'Don't ask me!' or 'Cheek! Why would I tell you that!' No, she always does her best, searches for at least something she can say... I turn the end of my plait slowly around my finger, and wait for her answer.

'I just let myself in and made supper, because I hadn't eaten much all day—' And then again, whatever Barbara says, even if it's disappointing, I can always ask something else—

'What did you make?'

She breaks into a smile: 'Natalie! It's so long ago! I think you've got me there!'

'Please—' I can hear my own voice now, the way Mark must have heard it: that mixture of thinness and weight in it, the way it lurches from one moment to the next between happy-go-lucky and absolutely desperate, as if, right now, it would hurt me bodily if I wasn't given my answer. That voice, I know, passed the feeling of my wants wholesale into the listener's bloodstream. No one except Sandra could ignore it.

'Mark!' She gets up, kisses him on the forehead. I twist in my seat, frown. He pretends not to see me.

'A good day?' she asks.

'No.' He's reproachful—how could she forget the letter? 'Of course not.'

'Well, darling—there's lemonade in the fridge and Natalie and I are just waiting for some almond biscuits to cool.'

'I don't want any,' Mark says. 'I'm going upstairs.'

'Mark, Mark. Mark? Mark!' I make my voice just loud enough to pass through the door. I hear the creak of floorboards as he comes over, stands just inches away. There's no lock between us.

'Remember, you can't come in here,' he answers, not very loudly, using a dull, tight little voice; he can't be sure if I've even heard. He stands there, rock still, waiting for me to give up and go away. Instead, he hears a series of sharp intakes of breath.

'I'm crying, Mark,' I say, loudly. I'm not, of course. I've managed, somehow, to bring a kind of dampness to my eyes, but I soon forget to carry on the breathing. 'What are you doing, Mark?' I ask.

'Nothing,' he says, before he can think not to. I rattle the handle. He grabs it on his side to stop me. This, he must realize, is how it'll be from now on. He doesn't want anything to do with me. I don't want much to do with him either, but he's there, in my way. I may as well.



'You can't not do anything. No one can!' I tell him. 'I bet you're thinking at least. You must be, or you'd be dead.' He keeps quiet. I do too. After a while, he jerks the door open, but of course, by then I'm gone, back down the stairs to Barbara.

'Are you all right now?' Barbara asks, as we walk to the gate. She smiles back at the slow, serious nod I give her. The evenings are long now, she says. She supposes it is all right for me to walk home alone. (Of course, really she wants to walk with me, to see where I come from, but John is due home for his supper any moment now.)

'Give my regards to your mother. And don't forget the note. I do hope she likes the biscuits.' I nod again.

'Can I come back?'

'Of course.'

'When?'

'Whenever your mother says. You're always welcome.'

'But Mark doesn't want me here.' I'm testing her: what she's noticed, what she'll do. I lower my eyes, finger the brown bag of biscuits I'm taking home. My mouth waters.

'He's just used to being on his own. Or maybe it's the age he's at. You come just whenever you want.'

She reaches forward to tuck a loose strand of hair behind my ear and I know that she wants also to unroll the right-hand sleeve of my dress and fasten the buttons on the cuffs, though the left one is missing and, in any case, the sleeves are far too short and the cuffs need turning... Oh, how she longs to gently straighten everything up, a touch here, a touch there—and that's what I want too—but she stops herself. These things don't seem right to do before she has met my mother, obtained permission.

'Go on, now,' she says, 'hurry home.'

I straighten up, turn my head slightly to one side, tilt it at the same time, close my eyes—something I've often seen Sandra do. There's pretty much no choice for Barbara but to bend down and press her lips against my offered cheek. And then it's all right, I can go.

'God bless you,' she says, in that whispery-husky voice of hers which—even in memory—can relax my shoulders, make me fill my lungs, calm down and think that everything will, after all, be all right in the end. I leave her, standing in the front garden, with its evening scent of honeysuckle and old-fashioned roses, breathing it in and feeling lighter and braver, and at the same time tender—but also greedy for other stirring scents: the smells of a baby's head, of day-old, worked-in clothes, of wind-dried linen, sex, the ozone tang of her own blood at menstruation, at birth. Of strawberries, plums from the tree in the back garden, leaf mould, steam, windswept beaches—her own private, inimitable intimate relation to the world, the one thing that can never be taken away—

Afterwards, I imagine, she goes straight in to see Mark.

'What is the matter with you?' she asks. Mark shifts awkwardly in his chair, pretending to read, not answering. Hair is just shadowing his chin; he probably hasn't even noticed it yet. His brows are pulled down and he's wearing one of John Hern's expressions, a kind of angry implacability. All of a sudden he seems huge.

'I don't know why you are being like this, but the way you behaved today—looked through Natalie, didn't even speak to her, let alone whatever happened when she came up here—is not tolerable, and when I tell him your father will say exactly the same—' He's her son, but Barbara doesn't at all want to touch and tidy him. And he, sitting there so solid, so somehow other, wouldn't welcome it... How did they get like this?

'You're a good boy,' she says, more gently, as she sits down on his bed, 'but you've always been an only one. You can't know what it's like to be any other way. Your Uncle Adrian and I were very close as children. Even now, despite the problems, I do believe I could count on him if it was something important—Mark, you know how I did always want you to have a sister—'



'That girl isn't anything like any sister of mine would ever be!' he says. 'Don't be daft!'

Barbara is always bursting into tears. She cries regularly in Service, if the reading is sad, especially if there's anything in it about a child, barrenness, or motherhood. He'll notice her fidgeting in the chair next to him, and force himself not to look at her, though he knows she's groping for her handbag under the chair, in order to find a handkerchief. It's a quiet kind of crying to begin with. Her glasses mist over, her cheeks redden, shine with tears. Then she'll start to gasp and sniff. She won't be able to find the bag and he'll have to do it for her, pull it up into her lap, open the clasp. Later, when she's finished, the faint snap! of her closing the bag will interrupt him all over again.

'It was God's will. He took her,' he says now. 'Don't start crying now. Stop, Mum, please.'

When she's gone, apologizing, gasping for breath, feeling her way down the stairs, Mark pulls a box of weights out from under his bed. He's charged with a feeling of fight, a desire for violence. He wants to obliterate the interloper; he wants to punish his mother for the mess she's making, but of course it's wrong to even think this way, and anyway, he can't begin to think how. He wants to leave school, he wants to fight the Government, all governments, who support the commerce in images, advertising, news, art, billboards, neon, full-page colour spreads, TV sets, and who now have made it impossible for them to attend the summer congregation in Elojoki. He's sick of living like this. And then again, the feeling of wanting to fight has itself to be fought until every joint and bone in his body has pitted itself in stalemate against some other part. He loads five pounds more than the last time, holds the hand weights at shoulder level, lies back on the floor, sits up.

Heat shoots to the surface of the skin. His heart pumps. On and on he goes, up and down, up and down. His face and chest are drenched with sweat, his eyes squeezed shut. Tell me, please, he asks, a little scared of doing so: *I want to serve. I'll do anything. Give me a sign—*

# 8



WELL NATALIE: IT'S THREE WEEKS NOW. DOES BEING HERE BRING MEMORIES BACK FOR YOU THE WAY IT DOES FOR ME? DO YOU WISH YOU'D NEVER COME? I DO.

Yes. Yes—and also no. There are days the village—its mixture of concrete and dried-blood red buildings under a grey sky—looks to me like the absolute arse of the earth. At other times, when there's a little warmth in the light, or even actual sunshine, the layered views—twigs, treetops, sky—from the windows of Tuomas's tiny house seem all of a sudden infinitely various and beautiful.

Today, however, is definitely an arse of the earth day. The note from Christina jaundices my view and then again my face hurts badly from the freezing, gritty wind. I'm sticking to my resolution to take in as much exercise and daylight as possible. I struggle on along the main road, past the community centre and the supermarket, then turn right, avoiding newly iced puddles and looking up briefly to monitor my progress towards some squat, concrete blocks of flats.

Inside it must be thirty degrees: I have to strip off my cardigan and jumper, unbutton the neck of my blouse. Mrs. Lohi, who recently moved from one of the outlying traditionally built houses to a new ground-floor apartment, is, however, well wrapped. She sits in a bright-blue armchair with her back to the triple-glazed sliding doors that lead on to the communal gardens behind—some small birch trees, leafless, of course, a climbing-frame and sand-pit, currently covered by thick ice and a crust of pitted, ageing snow.

Mrs. Lohi is over ninety and every part of her face, cheeks, chin, the sides of her nose, is wrinkled, though as recently as last summer, Katrin says, she was still using a bicycle to go to her allotment on the other side of the river.

'My eyes are not good,' she tells me. 'I can't see detail anymore, just the shape of you against the wall. I am doing this by touch, someone pins it on for me—' She holds up the piece of cloth in her lap, appliqué work and embroidery, an abstract design in wheat, rust and muddy green.

'I'm having the cataract operation in June. I'm looking forward to it!'

Coffee cups and biscuits have been set out on a tray in the kitchenette; she sends me to fetch them.

'Katrin in the supermarket said that you might talk to me,' I remind her some time later. 'She said she would mention to you that I—'

'My memory is good,' she says. 'I know who you are, Natalie,' she adds, quickly. 'Kirsti Saarinen told me you were here the day you arrived.'

'What can you tell me?' I ask.

'I remember what my mother told me,' she says, looking, it seems, at the white-painted wall several metres behind where I sit. 'My mother's older brother, Eino, the carpenter, he was one of the first to leave Elojoki. You know that one of the pastor's jobs was to record those coming to the parish and leaving it, as well as births and deaths? And marriages, of course. It was the pastor who issued a letter confirming your identity, a kind of passport. So you'll find Eino's departure in the register, and all the rest that went, young men, mainly, or couples—a little while after the famine years, 1872 perhaps. You can see all the deaths too. And in the other register, the names of all the strangers who turned up from other places, even worse off than we were. Times were very hard. It was when things began to improve that some people felt they had the strength to go and seek out somewhere new where, they hoped, such things would not happen. No one wanted anyone to go, but at the same time, it couldn't be condemned.

'So Eino went to see Tuomas Envall for his permit to travel. He came out of there, my mother said, with tears running down his face. There was a service and a parade to see him off. He took work on an English ship. He was aiming for Canada, but the ship stopped at Ipswich and he met a woman, married and settled there. They had four boys and a girl. All five of them kept the faith, and had their own families. Others followed.



'The Summer Congregations began in 1880. I can even remember Eino myself, because he used to come back when he could, and then, of course, his children and grandchildren visited too. Somewhere I have a spoon that he carved for me. I watched him do it. I can find it for another time, if you are interested. It means nothing to my grandchildren. I'm thinking that I'll give it to the museum they are going to set up here...

'My mother always said that when Tuomas Envall looked into your eyes and you met his gaze, the feeling was of a kind of warmth beginning in your heart and spreading out to your very fingertips and the ends of your hair. She believed that we were all living in an earthly paradise, here in Elojoki. That's how she felt. She believed that until the day she died.'

'And you?' I ask, when the silence has begun to stretch a little. 'What do you believe, or think?'

Mrs. Lohi's hands, big-knuckled, crab-like, have fallen still in her lap. She takes her time to consider the question.

'I too have been very happy here,' she says eventually. 'I observe the faith and I still go to Service when I can. The prohibition has never troubled me. Of course, it may simply be my nature to be happy, wherever I am . . . well, I don't care which.'

She smiles, raises her hands. There's the faintest glint of gold, lost in the rolled flesh of her ring finger. She will be interested to know what conclusions I come to, she tells me, waiting on her walking-frame while I re-layer my clothes in the hall. She will let me know if she finds the spoon.

So, Christina, the fact is that at times I'm very glad to be here. Sometimes, oddly, I feel almost as if I belong here. I'd like to know what it is that you hope to achieve by all this. Surely you realize by now that I won't—

Each time a letter comes I'm tempted to actually reply to it, rather than just frame a few sentences in my head. If I think of her as she was when we were children and compare it to what I've experienced of her now, then it is clear that, while back then she seized on others' transgressions and took pleasure in having an outsider to blame, now it's far deeper than that, a matter of desperate need. Exactly what loss or hurt does hating me like this protect her from? When driving past her house, especially last Sunday, when I saw other cars turn in and park neatly in the muddy forecourt, I've found myself thinking it might be best to stop, go in and—well, what? Have a look around. See where she's ended up. Talk? But I do know that that would just draw me further in, and I don't want that. So our conversation must be indirect and unspoken.

I do not need Christina's warning not to 'do the same thing again.' Let alone the physical damage, it's not as if I don't have my own regrets: the dishonesty of my means, for example. None of it would have happened as it did without that. Though saying that, I trip myself up, because if none of it had happened, where would I be now?

# 9



It is the Sunday following the arrival of the Home Office letter and my second visit to the Hern family. The Suffolk Congregation—over thirty people—gather in the beamed front room of the Thorns' farmhouse. They sit on sofas and chairs gathered from all over the house—ladder-backed dining chairs, carvers, oak benches from the kitchen, a mismatched pair of Windsors, assorted painted Lloyd Looms from the bedrooms and landings, two nameless things with rush seats, some round three-legged stools. At the last minute a set of folding picnic seats in aluminium are brought in from the Thorns' caravan. Even these are not enough, so all six Gardner children make do with cushions on the floor.

Mr. Thorn settles himself, facing the congregation, in an armchair just to the side of the cloth-covered trestle table that serves as an altar. He looks carefully around the room. His big, bony hands lie on his knees like sleeping dogs; the two huge vases of delphiniums on the table burn blue behind him. There's a fat candle with an invisible flame. At his feet, a square of light is cast from one of the windows.

'First, we will wait in silence before the Lord,' he announces.

Silence, according to Tuomas Envall in his Meditations, is 'a substance, an absence, a place, a thing, a liquid in which God can be found by willing and observant seekers.' It can be a steady flow of small, perfect droplets counting out the minutes.

Sometimes, it sparkles. Sometimes it swallows everything up—a winter lake darker than the sky. Sometimes it starts shallow, hardly there, and drop by drop, ends up deep… Mostly the Silence at the beginning of the Envallist Service lasts an entire half hour, but occasionally, if interrupted by inspired speech, it can be very brief indeed. Once, Mark remembers, Joanna Weston spoke for the entire half hour of her response to the passion of Christ, which she had called 'a lesson in the inner and inimitable experience of the flesh, proof of its worthiness, however sin-drenched.' The words tumbled from her mouth, like acrobats across a stage, dazzling with their motion, their cleverness, the years of meditation and thought that had gone into making them. Afterwards, it was the feeling of them you remembered, rather than exactly what she had said.

Today, the Silence is saturated, heavy, and it is in part to escape from it that Mark's eyes begin to feel their way around the room. This is a place he has visited once every six weeks or so since he can remember: the low ceiling, the panel-work on the walls, the small-paned windows set behind foot-deep sills, through which he can see the flat fields of cereal crops and bright-green beet. Spurts and sighs of wind part and flatten the wheat, then evaporate, leaving it momentarily intact.

Inside, it is still. From the back row, next to his father, Mark can see only the backs of heads, some erect, some bent low, hair in shades of brown and blonde, cut or tied this way and that. Older heads show a gleam of scalp or are dulled by oncoming grey. Anna Herrick's thick hair, gathered into two loose plaits and then coiled and pinned to the back of her head, is completely white and has been as long as Mark can remember. He took free piano lessons from her when he was small, but he wasn't one of the few that she chose to take on to higher grades. Back then her seriousness about music had frightened him, but now that her face has come to fit her hair, he's curious rather than scared.

Broad-shouldered Mr. Gardner and the Gardner boys have thin, straw-coloured hair, crew-cut by the barber now and then, home-trimmed in between. The three Gardner girls, Christina, Mary and Eva, wear theirs in single thick plaits, as does their mother, Josie, though hers is considerably less neat than theirs. Mostly, the girls and women have plaits. Susannah East and her mother are unusual in their chestnut-brown curls; Mr. East and Mr. Thorn almost identical in their cropped salt-and-pepper bristle, thinning on top.

In the middle row, Tim Anderton and his twin brother Peter, about Mark's age. They'd be indistinguishable, but for the fact that Tim wears his hair cut very close, whereas Peter's grows down further, turns up where it touches his collar. They have an older sister, Fay, who abandoned observance as soon as she got to university and refused to attend church (her parents and the grandparents who live with them were to blame, some people say, for being over-strict about things like skirt lengths and shoes). Fay's hair, Mark remembers, was long, bright blonde; it fell over her face when she leaned forwards, individual strands attaching themselves not just to the shoulders of her own pullovers in wintertime, but also to those of whoever sat next to her. Later on, you'd find those shed hairs clinging to you, shining out against the dark cloth. Her mother, Elsbeth Anderton, wears her hair loose, as her daughter used to—perhaps still does—kept from her face with slides, but it's not blonde now, if it ever was. She is tiny, unhealthy-looking, with a sallow skin and over-bright eyes. Next to her, in a pencil-thin ponytail is poor Susan Cameron, who began to lose her hair in patches when her husband left a year or so back. He simply did not return one night from work. Months later, adding insult to injury, he sent a postcard from New York—

The silence is thicker than ever, like a liquid about to freeze. The delphiniums burn in their vases. Pollen falls on the table. And suddenly, Mark sees in his mind's eye an island. A mountain, fields, sheep, cows, houses—all clustered around the harbour. Glittering sea, wheeling gulls. The words arrive in his head, like writing, voice and music all at the same time:

'We will buy an island, and live on it,' the voice, half his, half not, says. 'We will build an Envallist church from blocks of stone. It will be in the windiest, most exposed part of the Island, on a headland or a spit or a cliff looking out over the sea. It will be a thick-walled room like this one, with a stone-tiled roof and plain-glass windows giving views of the sea and sky. My father and I will make the seats and the altar. Next to the church will be a bell-tower, the way it is in Elojoki . . .'

He hears the ringing sound of a bell, rushed to his ear then snatched away by the wind. The congregation will walk to the church over the fields and through the gardens. . . The people in this room, the Gardners, the Johnsons, the Lattens, the Teals, the Thorns themselves, he sees them walking towards him, as clearly as he has just seen the backs of their heads, as if they were all of them already there.

Then a small movement catches his eye: one of the delphinium florets has fallen onto the white cloth. He looks down into his lap, feels his skin tighten with fear.

He knows that what he has just experienced could be a vision, like those of Ezekiel, or Isaiah, even that of John. Sometimes, he reminds himself, as with Mary's husband Joseph, a vision can take the form of a simple statement of fact or an injunction, or at other times, as with Jacob's ladder, it can be an Unspeakable Aspect of God symbolically revealed, or then again it can be a prediction of the future expressed obliquely. . . In scripture, even the dreams of non-believers are sometimes vehicles for God's word and will, even when the dreamer himself doesn't understand or can't remember them—

It could be a vision. On the other hand, what he has just experienced could be a self-induced piece of mental imagery, the very worst kind of temptation, which means that the devil is within him.

He closes his eyes and tries his hardest, but even though he grows tense with the effort of wanting it, he can't make the Island come back. Maybe this is a good sign, because if it is the kind of man-made image that can be dwelled upon, falsely venerated and so on, then it would come from inside him, and so surely he would be in control of when it appeared?

He looks up again. There are the backs of heads in front of him, there is the blue of the delphiniums—a concentrated royal-blue inkiness, an iridescence that verges on purple towards the centres of the individual flowers.

Mr. Thorn glances at the clock.



Someone should speak! Mark thinks. Then saliva floods his mouth and he swallows it down. His heart bangs in his chest. No—he thinks, please—and Mr. Thorn's eyes, moving from face to face, meet his. His mouth fills up again and, as if pushed, he stands.

'I believe we should find an island and buy it, then live there, all of us,' he says aloud. 'I have seen a vision of this in my head. We need our own place, away from the world of Imitations. So we can live right, yet still remain open—' The congregation turns to look at him. Suddenly they are all there—the faces implied by the backs of heads, their many pairs of eyes all angled so as to touch his face. They want him to continue. But as suddenly as the words have come to him, they pass, leaving him with a dry mouth and shaking legs. He grasps the back of the chair in front of him, then, keeping his eyes fixed on Mr. Thorn's as a drowning swimmer might hold a rope, he sits slowly down. His father embraces him, grasps the back of his head and pulls it down close to his own.

After the reading, they all go outside to sit on the recently mowed grass, eat squares of communion bread and then the

Sunday meal. The older people have chairs brought for them, the rest sit on the ground. A warm breeze lifts the edges of the cloths and rugs, the women's skirts. More of the blue delphiniums are growing in a packed border against the barn wall. Edith Thorn, neat in her ironed Sunday blouse, reaches her hand over and rests it on top of Mark's.

'You've spoken what is in many hearts,' she says, smiling. 'We shall talk of these things a great deal in the Summer Congregation. What you have to say will be very important indeed.'

It has been more or less decided, she explains, that because so many are unable to renew their passports they will hold the Summer Congregation near Hunmanby on the East Coast. Arrangements are being made with a landowner to use several of his fields for a week. Privacy is guaranteed, a water supply, chemical toilets, rubbish clearance. The price is reasonable... 'Are you feeling all right?' she asks, touching his forehead gently. 'Why not lie down?'

He follows her back into the house and upstairs into a shady room, allows her to bring him a glass of water. Certainly, he thinks, sipping it and watching the curtain being gently sucked in and out of the window, something has happened to him. He recalls the story of Tuomas Envall, holding the hands of the dying man. Of course, it was not so great a thing as that, but perhaps it was an experience of the same kind—'a kind of white heat that does not burn.'

'At least,' Barbara says on the way home that afternoon, 'there won't be that ferry journey to deal with. I've never liked it much. And another thing—everyone will speak the same language, which is surely a good thing.'

'You seem almost pleased,' Mark tells her, his judgement of her clear in his voice. Although his earlier intensity of emotion has gone, it has left behind a kind of strengthening residue.

'I'm just making the best of things, darling.' She has clipped sunshades onto her glasses; her arm trails outside the car window, catching at the tips of comfrey and vetch in the narrow lanes.

That evening, while he's in the kitchen and his parents sit over the remains of supper, he distinctly hears her tell his father that she would like to invite Natalie to the Summer Congregation.

'The red-haired girl?'

'She's an only child.'

The gaps between these remarks seem long, and the connections between them weak, as if the real communication was taking place some other way.

'Has she shown any interest?'

'She does so like to be with us—'



After another long pause, his father asks, lightly, 'What about her parents?' The wrong question, Mark feels. He goes back into the room; they've moved their chairs closer and are holding hands on the table, both hands, fingers interleaved. His father gives Mark an odd, almost sheepish smile.

'Don't,' Mark tells them. 'Don't ask her.' They stare at him.

'She'll spoil things,' he announces with all the authority of having earlier spoken in Service 'what was in many people's hearts.' He addresses his father, banishing Barbara to a dim presence at the edge of his frame of vision: 'She'll drive us apart—' he announces, and feels as he says it as if the girl is on the verge of materializing in the gathering darkness and any minute will be in the room with them again, looking around, greedily taking it all in for some incomprehensible purpose of her own—

'I've no idea why he's like this,' Barbara says. 'Maybe he's jealous.' With her thumb, she makes tiny stroking movements on the back of her husband's hand.

'I'm not—I just know,' he tells them. 'She's beginning to do it already—'

Barbara interrupts: 'Is this another vision?' she asks. 'Shouldn't we welcome a stranger who seeks us out? Christ Himself turned no one away. Didn't He say—'

'Please—' Mark's voice gets lost in his throat, emerges thin and high as if whatever made the proper sound had slipped out of place. Both parents smile, then stop themselves. 'She wants something. She'll just take it.'

'What might that something be?' his father asks. 'Could it be the Lord's Grace?'

'Whatever it is,' Barbara says, 'even if it's just some company, can't we just give it to her?'

John disentangles his hands, clasps them together. He closes his eyes, pulling the pale lids down like blinds, so as to hear more clearly the inner voice. Mark has no choice but to look hard at his mother, pushing hopelessly at her for some kind of acknowledgement of her duplicity, for a last-minute withdrawal. It's hopeless. He's appalled, but not surprised to hear his father eventually say:

'It must depend, of course, on what her parents think. So long as she enters into the spirit... Well, we do have four berths, after all—' He reaches for his wife's hands again, looks up to her face, watching and unconsciously copying with his own smaller, redder lips, the smile that's growing there.

The next morning a letter addressed to 'Mrs. S. Baron' nestles in Barbara's best, cream-coloured handbag. Her face is smooth and plump, as if she's slept particularly well. Her green skirt and matching short-sleeved blouse are homemade as ever, but smart. She hums to herself as she lets the blue gate swing closed behind her and sets off briskly down the Avenue. The May blossom and ceanothus are finished and the last of the flowers lie in faded pink and blue drifts on the pavements and grass verges. Laburnums are out now, and peonies.

Few flowers grow in the estate. No. 88 is a flat-fronted, pebble-dashed semi with the Council's maroon paint peeling from the front door. From the other side of the road she watches a stringy, bullet-headed man hack at the tangle of brambles and columbine which spills over the front fence and reaches higher than the ground floor windowsills. His efforts are vigorous but have little effect on the sheer bulk and tangle of vegetation. As she watches, he throws his shears down and begins pulling at the bushes with his gloved hands. The down of thistles and dandelion clocks clots the air. Barbara crosses the road, stands by the fence.

'Excuse me—are you Mr. Baron?' She repeats herself several times before he notices.

'No—' He faces her, sweating hard, hands fisted, the creases of his face black with dust. 'Not to my knowing!' He adds, 'I'm just the gardener, me.' At this, he makes an explosive noise in his throat, halfway between laughter and a cough. His forearms are scratched and bleeding, his eyes still bright with effort, angry, she guesses, with the bushes for taking more out of him than they should.



'You've got your work cut out!' she tells him. 'This is where Mrs. Baron lives, isn't it?' The tattoo of a snake, she realizes, is winding its way around and around the man's upper arm. She glimpses the head—socketed eyes, jaws agape, red mouth, split-whip tongue, and blinks, returns her eyes to his face; a flush comes to her own, takes hold, spreads. Anything can bring it on—

The man stares at her, grins. She can't look away, in case she sees the image of the snake again.

'I'm looking for Mrs. Baron,' she persists. 'Is she in?'

'Not so far as I know,' he says.

'If you don't mind, I'll just make sure.'

Stepping over stray lengths of bramble, she makes her way up onto the shallow porch. The windows of the house are opaque with dust. On a wire shelf beneath the panel of grimy frosted glass next to the door is a row of milk bottles, rimmed with algae. There's neither bell nor knocker, so she bangs on the door with her hand. Then she pushes her letter through the slot in the door.

'Thank you,' she says. The man watches her all the way back to the gate.

'Thank you,' he repeats softly as she closes it.

She feels him looking at her still as she retraces her steps, back across the road, up the slight incline, out of his sight, past more pairs of the same kind of house, finally, out of the estate...

The Barons, she tells herself, must have quite recently moved to the house from elsewhere. They're obviously struggling. Mrs. Baron works peculiar hours, and her mother, or one of their mothers at any rate, is ill. But they are doing their best, trying to tackle the place... It'll help them out to have the child off their hands for a week or so.

At the far side of the crossroads is a patch of grass and a wooden bench with a plaque on it. She sits down, eases the backs of her shoes from her heels, closes her eyes and begins on her prayers, which she missed earlier. 'Lord,' she asks, 'let me complete well what I have begun.' Next, she prays for John. In seventeen years of marriage she has certainly come to know the strength of his will. Sometimes she thinks it's too strong. Likewise, his loyalty to her. 'But,' she tells God, 'I do know these are things which will not change. As we grow older, they'll get stronger, squeeze out other, smaller traits. I'm prepared for that. I give thanks for my marriage,' she tells Him, turning her face, eyes shut, up to the sun, but doesn't mention to God that she feels especially thankful for the physical union between them: for being able, even at this age, even against his will, to lead this difficult man she chose for herself to a point of agreement where other differences don't matter one bit... She smiles, her eyes still shut tight, her hands neatly on top of each other in her lap, one arm threaded through the strap of the bag next to her.

'Let him not take things too hard,' she prays. 'And as for my son—please forgive him. He never normally complains,' she reminds God. 'He's pleased to do your will in all ways. He works hard—' She thinks of all those sports days and football and cricket matches she has attended, the sight of Mark diving for a catch or folding himself over the high-jump, the smell of cut grass, of sitting on the slatted wooden chairs or on a rug in the sun, the fragile paper cups of tepid lemon squash, the little twists of ribbon on their tiny brass pins, the almost smoked smell of his skin at the end of summer days. . . She sighs, shifts the position of her feet, and remembers the look he gave her this morning before he set off for school on his bike. 'Help him through whatever it is that he is suffering now,' she asks.

The good bit of her prayers is done now.



What remains is to give thanks for the time there was with the girl-child that He chose to take away from her.

'I don't want to say her name today . . .' she tells Him. She gives thanks for the memories she has polished over the years, kept, like a set of pebbles gathered from a brief beachside walk. The navy-blue eyes seeking her own out and holding them a long while, then, and only then, the slow, gummy smile. The constantly flexing fingers. The grip of that whole hand on her one finger. The fresh-baked smell of the top of her head. The thick but soft hair she was born with, brown (though now she's beginning almost to think of it as red). The way her face relaxed after her milk, the soft weight of her, sleeping.

'But,' she explains to Him, eyes still shut, frowning now, 'when a child lives, you don't have to carry your few pebbles away. It goes on and on. You just stay there on the beach.' Her hands clench up; she bites her lip—it's the thing in life she has to bear, this weight on her back, this hole in her heart. When she prays, so John tells her, she's supposed to thank Him even for that, for the silver lining that hides in even the darkest cloud of suffering, if only she could find it—and, she tells Him 'You know how I have tried—'

But now the possibility of ever carrying another child has halved and halved itself until it's too small to count, and now the girl has arrived at her gate—

'Now,' Barbara tells Him, 'now, after all these years, I think I've borne it long enough. Release me.'

# 10



'Children are very adaptable,' says Mrs. Peltoniemi, a faded beauty with a habit of nodding slowly at the beginning of everything she says. 'The fact is that this is a good education. Our children do well in tests. They have a strong analytical drive, wonderful memories—' she smiles, raises her hand in greeting to a well-wrapped group moving out into the playground. Certainly, the school is not so bad as it looked from the outside. It is painted in bold colours and decorated with wall-hangings in abstract designs, numbers, alphabets and so on. The children run and shout like any others. All the same, it's disconcerting: tiny classes of well-behaved, mostly blonde children, who have all been 'led by example' and, if necessary, 'turned away' from making images, and encouraged instead towards an enjoyment of geometry. Mrs. Peltoniemi watches me watch them.

'Parents and teachers respond much as they would with any other undesired or dangerous behaviour,' she explains. 'Ignore it, or make a sour face, shake their heads, perhaps withdraw approval for a moment or two. Of course, it's hard for an outsider to understand. Exceptional musical ability is common. Several studies have shown their powers of concentration to be higher than average. I'd say they are on the whole less troubled than the average child of our times. But, it seems, these qualities are not in demand—'

As I leave, the sound of a choir singing something contemporary with quarter-tones and long pauses pours out of one of the classrooms, hair-raisingly beautiful.

Afterwards, I emerge from the supermarket with my carrier bag of salad, smoked fish called pike-perch and some bread, and the first thing I see is Christina. She's coming the other way—we hold each other carefully in view, and all the time I'm thinking that I should say something to her but I don't know what. We draw level, then acknowledge each other with a bit of a nod: it's almost as if she'd never knocked on my door, never sent those letters. Then she stops and calls out my name.

'Natalie—we must talk.' I stop too, and turn back a little to keep her in view, but say nothing.

'Do you get my letters?' she asks, brightly, as if they were something ordinary.

'Yes, I do.'

'Good. I send my youngest, Pekka, to deliver them. You can never be sure! Though he's a good boy in the main. He went to that school you've just visited—' The look she's giving me is half hard, half considering.

I just stand there, keeping her in view.

'What do you think, then, of what I'm telling you?' she asks. 'Have I got through to you? I'm only trying to help, you know.'

Help?

'Actually, I'm considering whether to call the police,' I tell her. 'The people I've discussed it with think it unnecessary, but I still might. I don't want any of your letters, you see. I'd like you to stop, please.'

She raises her hands, palms out, at waist level, as if literally stopping me from coming closer. As if I was out of order.

And then she backs down completely, becomes, suddenly, all smiles. 'You must come for a coffee sometime. Have a chat,' she says, her voice eager, verging on warm; she makes a little wave and turns into the chemist's, leaving me standing there.

Perhaps from time to time she just runs out of whatever keeps her steady in the winter-time. Seasonal Affective Disorder is what Heikki Seppä was suggesting, but it feels more serious than that. Does she want to hurt me back? Does she think she can bring me into the fold, and that somehow that will make whatever it is all right?

At home, I eat my pike-perch sandwich, phone my mother. The afternoon stretches ahead of me. I find myself imagining Elojoki as it was in Tuomas's time. Such a very small place: the forest pressing at them from the west, the sea from the east, the huge sky arching and yearning above them—just one road passing through and no general shop until 1872. So it must have been relatively easy to control what came in, reject this, blot out a picture on a label with thick red ochre paint. Even though photography had existed for over twenty years and had already caused debates and controversies, though not, according to Tuomas Envall, sufficiently radical ones; even though exposures were growing shorter by the month; even though most towns had a photographic studio and soon most clergymen would feel it necessary to have their photograph taken—despite all this, at that time making and looking at increasingly realistic images was still a process which required consent and effort. And although the first motion picture presentation was not far ahead in time, it took place half a world away, in California.

At the same time as the means of making images grew more sophisticated, the means by which an image could be reproduced mechanically was also developed. The lithographic press gave way to photogravure, so that colour photographs could be printed. And even as early as 1926, television existed: the image of a man sitting on a chair in a shadowy room was transmitted through the air and picked up by a receiver in another room several metres away...

Tuomas didn't live to hear of this. 'A man never changes, but if he follows God, he becomes more properly himself,' he wrote, just before he died suddenly, at sixty-five, in wintertime, out of doors while chopping wood. His daughter Mustikka became for a year or so an unofficial leader of a movement which had now spread, albeit thinly, to the very south of the country and also as far away as Canada, Australia, South Africa and England.

Of course, I am drawn to my subject for personal reasons, but at the same time, I've come to enjoy it for its own sake. One of the things that pleases me most is the fact that a belief system such as Envall's has managed to survive against all odds, right up to the present day. This isn't sentiment—I admire it for its obstinacy. I appreciate it the way one can appreciate a good joke, or a particularly powerful irony, as evidence of the essential waywardness of our hearts.

At the same time, when I decide to turn in early, I find myself glancing towards the door to check that I've locked it, and that no letter has arrived.

I remember how once before I also kept watch for letters. I had pretended our telephone wasn't working, so Barbara told me she would write. When I found the envelope I took it upstairs to my room, opened it and realized straight away that I needed someone to help me.

# 11

Penelope Cole was not my teacher anymore but she was the one I thought would do best. She had her head down, marking, and I was so close to her that I could see individual hairs, the way the grey was made up of white and black. I stood by her desk, shifting my weight from foot to foot, and willed her to look up and smile. 

'Excuse me, Miss—'

She remembered me, of course. Teachers generally did: the extraordinary hair, the dull, almost inaudible voice I used when forced to read anything aloud, the way my writing was inconsistently peppered with childish mistakes and perfectly spelled longer words, my habit of staring serenely into space during tests, as if the whole thing was nothing to do with me, refusing to even try—Natalie Baron? Oh, yes—At the same time, because I would sit right in the front row, my eyes roving over the teacher's face, almost meeting her eyes twenty times in the course of a lesson, slipping away just before the moment of reciprocation, dragging away bits of her attention, returning again to her face as soon as she'd looked away—because of this, and because of my sudden enthusiasms (for a topic in History, say, or a particular experiment in Science) during which I would gather and hoard facts, shoot my hand up, begging to contribute, and because even when the subject bored me I was always trying to make it interesting, wanting to know something, anything, ready to ask a question, and because I listened to the answers given as if life depended on them: because of all this, I managed somehow to suggest that despite the missing homeworks, the blank test papers, the 'word-blindness' and the playing dumb—despite my making them want to tear out their hair—I might still be worth bothering with.

I stood there, with dirty fingernails, fiddling with the strings on my duffle bag.

'Yes, Natalie?'

'You look tired, Miss,' I said, softly, wiping the palms of my hands on my dress. It had recently been let down, but not pressed; the old crease still showed.

'I certainly am, Natalie,' Penelope Cole said, adding—not a secret, but nonetheless something she would not have said to any other child—that this was because her sister Josephine, whom she looked after, was particularly bad at the moment and needed a lot of attention during the night, so she had to do all her marking like this in the lunchtimes, instead of sitting in the staff room with the rest.

Whilst her sister clung to her dignity on a physical level, Penelope Cole, who could have been head of department, a good one too, was clinging to her very existence in the school as to the edge of a cliff. She was thin enough to feel the cold right through spring. Her face was wrinkled from all the talking she did, her cheeks rough-red from the wind; she cycled six miles to and from work every day, she never got enough sleep and now there were thirty-three exercise books to mark in forty-four minutes.

'It's about my writing,' I said. 'Will you help?'

'I really don't have much time, Natalie—' She gestured at her pile of books, but by now I had my grubby duffle bag right on her desk and was reaching down into it. 'Can't Mrs. Jay help?'

'No, she can't.' I gave her the envelope. It was addressed to Mrs. Baron, marked 'By Hand' where the stamp would be, and, naturally, had already been opened.

Miss Cole handed it back. 'This is your mother's. You shouldn't—' I removed the letter from the envelope, flattened it on the desk between us.

'She told me to ask,' I said, and brushed her face all over with my gaze—a tangible thing: close up like this, its effect on someone like Penelope was midway between pleasure and discomfort, like the edge of paper stroked on skin and enough, under the circumstances, to distract her from the possibility of a lie, the fact that really, she should be checking just in case. 'It's about me. It's an invitation.' Without being asked, I read it out to her and I read it well, although slowly, stumbling just a couple of times. Miss Cole leaned forwards and took the second paragraph in for herself, while she waited for me to get to the end of the first: 

> So naturally we are seeking your opinion and permission. We would be travelling by car and staying in our four-berth caravan, returning on 4 August. It is of course a religious holiday for us but no pressure would be brought to bear on Natalie and there is plenty of time to enjoy the countryside and play in the fresh air with other children.
>
> I do hope you can say yes but in any case it would be very pleasant to meet you and your husband, seeing as we see so much of your daughter. If you think that Natalie might come there will naturally be questions you want to ask. I am here any afternoon and my husband too in the evenings and Saturdays.
>
> Yours sincerely, Barbara Hern.

'Well read!' Miss Cole exclaimed. She reached for her pen. 'And how lovely to be invited!'

'The thing is,' I told her, 'my mother has a problem with writing, like me. Worse, really. Normally she just ignores things that come in the post. We can ask the neighbours but she doesn't want people to know our business. Do you see?' I asked.

'I do see,' Miss Cole said.

'She says I can go but I have to do the letter. If I write the answer out, she can just put her name at the end—' My face was slack, my eyes huge with the fear of disappointment. My voice grew quieter, thinner: 'There mustn't be any mistakes,' I told her, 'none.'

It was irresistible: Miss Cole moved the exercise books aside, opened her desk and brought out a sheaf of good-quality paper.

'Do your best,' she told me, 'then we'll go over it.'

By the end of the break we had the text fixed: a joint effort, as Miss Cole put it. I had, for example, taken up her suggestions that my mother should not address Barbara as 'Barbara' but as 'Mrs. Hern' and that it was better to say simply 'It is very kind' as opposed to 'It is very, very kind.'

On Tuesday and Wednesday, while Miss Cole marked, I tried to get the letter written correctly, and failed, differently, maddeningly each time. 'Dear' became the animal, 'holiday' accrued an extra 'l,' whilst 'arrange' lost an 'r.' 'Possible' mutated into 'possable,' then 'busy' wanted to rhyme with 'missy.' It was a long time since I had tried.

> Dear Mrs. Hern,
> It is very kind of you to invite Natalie to join you in Hunmanby. I am very happy for her to go on the holiday. It would be lovely to meet you but I am rather busy right

now. Hopefully it will be possible to arrange something nearer the time.

Thank you again for your kind invitation.

Yours sincearly,

I wanted to explode, to ball the paper, crush it, throw it out of the open window, let it vanish into the bright blue sky—but I knew I needed the thing; I had to get it right. I was trapped inside myself like some fairy-tale maiden with a seemingly impossible task: count all the grains of barley in a barn. Stitch a nightdress without using thread. Make a pair of giant's boots from the skins of sardines. Spin gold from straw. In the story, of course, there is always some kind of supernatural aid, a fairy godmother, and a small animal once shown kindness. But Penelope Cole was only a teacher.



'This is so much better than it was when we began!' she said. 'I'm very pleased.'

On Friday, Miss Cole said that she would write the letter out in her writing, very clearly, so that all I needed to do was copy it . . . also, she had brought me some special bond note-paper from home and sent me out to wash my hands before I began.

That day, Miss Cole had no marking to do, and she could have gone to the staff room and made a cup of coffee to go with her homemade pâté and salad sandwiches. But she stayed to keep me company while I worked, a letter at a time, leaving the pen in place on the paper while I looked to the text on my right, carrying the shape back like a bucket over-filled. I found it oddly calming and for minutes on end, was lost in the task. Miss Cole sat still at her desk and surrendered herself to the quirks and kinks of the way this particular part of the hugeness of time was flowing, its currents eddying and parting and reforming around the point of a child's pen on paper. . . She watched, and thought of the path of her own life, which seemed to her to fall into two parts, the shorter before, the much longer, harder afterwards. But still, at this particular moment, she felt she would alter nothing.

The wooden chair squealed on the floor. I came up to the desk with my pieces of paper, held carefully at the corners. There was a flutter of excitement in my stomach and I think we both believed that this time it would come out right. . . Even when the finished letter was on her desk, it did seem for a moment that we had succeeded—until Miss Cole, smiling as she bent over the letter, spotted, right near the end, an old enemy risen from the dead, 'hte,' and then realized that, as if out of sheer perversity, I'd invented a completely new mistake and copied the 'N' of my own name backwards. The very neatness of the handwriting made these trivial errors show up more than they otherwise would have. Miss Cole let out a sigh. Well, couldn't she have pretended? But she never had, not over anything important; it wasn't in her.

'The main thing,' she told me, 'is the progress you've made. And perhaps, if you just very carefully correct—'

'It must be perfect!' I told her.

'We can try again on Monday,' she said, and I gathered my brows into a slight frown, the expression of a judge about to pronounce, but waiting for one shred of possibly mitigating evidence. I reached out my hand, still smelling of the pink disinfectant soap dispensed in the school cloakrooms, and picked up Penelope Cole's fair copy of the letter. It was better than mine could ever be, because the writing looked grown-up, whereas mine was big and I pressed too hard.

'Monday will be too late. So can I have this?' I asked, and somehow, the spell was broken because all of a sudden Penelope Cole said, 'No.' She was sorry, but it just didn't feel right, she explained, for a letter she had written to be used out of school. She took it back, and put everything that was hers away in her register drawer.

'If it's so very important,' she said, 'surely your mother can make a telephone call?' Then she reached down and brought her lunch box up onto the desk. 'Hungry?' she asked as she spread a paper serviette on the desk and unwrapped the sandwiches.

I took one, bit into it, swallowed my rage along with the food. 'Why are they so heavy?' I asked. 'What's that oniony smell? Who made them?'

'Why do you still live with your sister?' I asked a little later on.

'Because I do.' Penelope Cole filled her mouth so as to prevent herself saying anything she shouldn't. 'My sister made this bread herself,' she told me. 'We're twins. We still both have the same eyes,' she added.

Child and woman, we watched each other. There were shifts of attention, comings and goings towards and away from the surface, the beginnings of things suddenly concealed. There was a refusal to meet the eyes, but equally, a refusal to go away. What is it, Penelope Cole thought at me, that you want? And I couldn't answer because I just didn't have a name for it. The two of us chewed and swallowed, looked and felt the shape of what couldn't be said.



On Monday, I missed my appointment to see Miss Cole. On Tuesday, she stopped me in the corridor. 'Oh,' I told her, before allowing myself to be swept along in the tide, 'we just phoned up, like you said.'

Miss Cole didn't know that this was the last time that she'd see me. But perhaps, because of her disappointment, the sadness that she must have felt when it seemed that the week of lunchtimes would add up to nothing, she took particular notice, just as people do when they are knowingly saying goodbye. The fuzz of hair, the general mottled pallor: the child, she thought, ought to look ethereal and almost does, but on second glance the impression is of an angel accidentally miscast in fleshier than usual human flesh …

Much later, after the summer holidays, after Aldrin and Armstrong had put soft, grey moondust in jars, left messages for other intelligent lifeforms, a flag, footprints, returned safely to earth; after Brittany, the ferry strike, storms, bad mussels and so on, Penelope Cole would have returned to school to find that all the children had as usual grown and some of them were gone, and new ones had arrived to take their places. Hearing the news about Natalie Baron, she'd have searched for the letter we had written together, and, of course, found that it was gone.

# 12

Barbara and I: we've mixed a dab of fresh yeast with sugar and water, watched it froth, poured it into the sifted flour and sugar. Now comes the beaten egg, the tiny purple-black currants, the misshapen cubes of candied peel. In the bowl, under its cloth, too slow to see, the dough grows. You must be patient, and you can't eat this kind of mixture because it would rise inside and give you a tummyache.



Barbara is telling me how she and Mr. Hern (as she calls him when she's talking to me) first met at a cycling club; how from the start she was struck by the peaceful expression on his face, which seemed at odds with the sudden speeches he made, the power and extremity of his beliefs. Then again he would always stop to help someone with a puncture or a broken chain . . .

'Please!' he called out to her, as they cycled through flat fields, Ely Cathedral (which he refused to visit) in the distance, 'Let's stop a moment—' There, sitting on warm, damp grass with the wheels of the bicycles still whirring, he took her hand and asked her to join him in 'Blessed Union.'

'Those were the actual words he used,' she says, 'and the whole of me said yes, although I asked for an evening to think it over, and of course I had to be converted, and have two weddings instead of one, and I knew my parents would never forgive me—' She frowns, shrugs, smiles, all at the same time.

So I sit at the now-familiar table, simultaneously drinking in Barbara's remembered past and the way she is now, for me: the way she leans forward when she talks to me, the fact that she interrupts herself to ask whether I'm too hot and to offer me a drink, the bubbles of excitement in her voice, the slow stretch of her lips when she half-smiles, thinking, perhaps, of something she might or is about to say—

'Why get married?' I ask.

'To have children,' she says, immediately. She pulls the cloth from the bowl and holds it out for me to see: a creamy wet mound of the stuff, alive, almost but not quite disgusting. 'Rub those trays with that butter-paper, will you now? We're ready.'

'Why have children?'

'For love!' she says. 'Why else, silly?'

We flour our hands, push it down, folding it in on itself. It sticks, peels off again. The smell of it rises softly up the back of my nose, fills all the space inside.

'You know, a baby's head has a smell something like that,' Barbara says, 'halfway between yeast and vanilla. And a bit like the cupboard where biscuits are kept.' She frowns slightly, tucks a stray strand of hair behind her ear: perhaps she's wondering what on earth is making her tell me all this. But she doesn't wonder too long, because she wants to tell me it as much as I want her to, and thinking too much might get in the way.

'The fact is,' she says, 'I thought it would happen straight away, but it didn't. We'd given up waiting and then one morning my stomach turned at the smell of the grill I'd lit for toast. A bit of chop from the day before was stuck to it and burning. A really tiny bit, and Mr. Hern wasn't bothered at all, you see, and that's how I knew for sure that I was expecting—'

Later on, she felt the baby moving around and around inside her, later still she could press with her hands and work out where its back, bottom, elbows and feet were. At first she laughs, as if it is the most amazing thing in the world. Then she takes off her glasses and wipes her eyes on her arm, but flour gets in them and she has to wash her face at the sink.

When I imagine having a back, bottom, elbows and feet inside me, I'm scared.

'It only happens gradually,' she says, as she inspects the dough. She reaches for a knife and cuts it into halves.

'Does it sometimes happen when you're not wanting it to?'

'I suppose it must.'

'Did you want a boy, or a girl?' I ask, and for a moment it is as if I am not there at all, as if something has suddenly frozen her. I know that I mustn't persist, or ask anything more. I sit, she stands, opposite each other. Then, when she comes back to herself we each tear our bit of dough into palm-sized pieces, and I copy how she rolls them on the table and coils them up.



So Mark was born, and Mr. Hern brought daffodils to the hospital. The baby was eight pounds, with absolutely no hair.

Hot air gushes from the oven, loses itself in the general warmth of summertime. Barbara's glasses mist over. She removes her oven gloves, fumbles open a kitchen drawer. It's full of pieces of old sheet, washed, torn into squares, ironed, folded. You can use them for all sorts of things, she says, for dusters, as bandages, paint rags, face flannels. We don't have them at home, and I'm almost angry as I watch her pick one of the softest pieces and rub her lenses dry, absorbed, away from me for a few moments. And yes, her eyes bulge and look in two directions at once, don't connect properly with what she is doing. It looks all wrong, it looks stupid—but at the same time it is as if she sees something wonderful when she looks back at me.

'There,' she says, 'that's better.'

I'm going to go away with Barbara tomorrow! It makes me so happy that my chest hurts, my throat stretches and my lips go soft—but also, I'm terrified.

There is a conspiracy between us. I can sometimes make things happen, but I'm not always in control. Neither of us understands. We obey the thing that is passing through us.

While the buns cool on wire racks, we drink the bubbleless lemonade under the awning at the back. Then, at about five, Mark comes back with blood on his shirt, saying he was in a fight. I watch, jealously, while she fusses over him, and I have to be more or less told to go home.

'Get to bed early tonight and sleep well. We'll call for you early,' she reminds me at the gate. 'Regards to your mother. Don't forget the note. Hurry, now.'

Of course, I don't go home. Where the Avenue meets the terraced road that leads into the Meadows estate, I turn right, then descend through smaller streets until I reach the allotments at the bottom of the hill. The sun is on its way down now and midge-clouds hang in the air. I push through the gate onto the main path, then turn off and make my way via the small borders between plots. Here and there people are still working. They've seen me often before and take no notice. I reach a plot with a green painted shed. I sit down on the bench underneath its window, tip the bag of buns onto my lap, six of them, coiled, dusted with sugar, all slightly different sizes. To begin with I unravel them, then I just bite straight in. I eat four, enjoying the way they turn heavy and sticky in my mouth. The two I can't manage I roll up in the bag and leave on the bench for the two soft-voiced men whose plot this is.

The third tomato plant in the row is mine. I inspect its spiky yellow flowers, which the larger man of the pair told me would turn into small green berries, then bright red tomatoes. Things in the garden take so long. I pinch out side shoots, as I've been shown. I do their other plants too, not quite so thoroughly. The tomato leaves give off a volatile, bitter scent which is almost animal.

I like it here, but I won't be coming back. The two men only talk about plants. However much I ask, they won't allow me to go home with them, won't even say where it is or what they are called. They tell me different names, stupid ones like Bill and Ben, each time I ask. They laugh between themselves at things I can't understand. Well, I don't need them anymore.

It's about half past nine, the sky almost dark, the shadows gone, though I can still see well enough to find some small snails, gathered in the damp under the plants. I press them one by one between finger and thumb, and listen to the thin shells collapse with a wet gasp.

When I turn into Margaret Close the sky beyond the orange streetlights is black and distant. I can see straight away that there's a light on in the front of the house, even though it's Friday, when normally they go out and sometimes don't come back. Once I reach the gate, I hear music. It's a disappointment since I don't have an alarm clock and have been intending to stay awake by watching the astronauts on TV, which is downstairs, where they are—they'll probably want it and they might be up all night.



I extract the key from my sock, slip into the hall and wait for my eyes to get used to the dark. A crack of light is coming from under the lounge door. I begin to feel my way up the stairs, aware suddenly of my hands being uncomfortably sticky, of grit in my shoes, the duffle bag cutting into my shoulder.

'Natty?' Sandra calls when the stair creaks. So I go down again, push open the lounge door. She is enthroned on the sofa. Her hair, brushed until it shines like metal, is piled on top of her head, making her look even taller than she is. A few strands stray about her face. The pink of her wide mouth is deepened with lipstick, her skin whitened with make-up, her eyes outlined with kohl. She's wearing a filmy blouse, a short skirt. Her feet are bare, the nails on her toes picked out in a pearly pink that matches her lips, her fingernails likewise. She's particularly beautiful like this, and terrifying at the same time. Doing herself up, she calls it. It makes her bolder, even less predictable.

Luke's next to her, one of his arms around her waist, the other holding a tumbler and a cigarette. Sitting with his knees flung apart, the way men do. Another man, drinking beer from a can, sits on the floor with his back against one of the armchairs. A friend of Luke's from the base: I can tell by the hair, and the build of him, and the way he sprawls, as if he didn't usually live in rooms. He stares fixedly ahead, his forehead tight.

There's just one lamp on, by the mantelpiece. The place doesn't look so bad at night. You don't really see the spills and burns on the carpet, the scuffs and dents on the walls. In the glow of the lamp, you can't see that the glass on the pictures is thick with dust; I myself never saw these things until I started visiting the Herns. It was just our house and I was oblivious to the smell of nicotine and the sound of my shoe soles sticking and unsticking themselves to the vinyl tiles on the kitchen floor. I used not to mind the sink being always full of cups and glasses. But now I do. It makes me feel sad. And you can't see out properly; the windows haven't been cleaned since before we moved in. 'You're welcome to have a go,' Sandra says. She's not one to bother what others think.

'Come over, then,' she calls out now, loud because of the music. Luke bought the hi-fi, after he stood her up once. I do what I'm told, stand in front of them. There's dough stuck under my fingernails, making a slight, half-pleasant, half-irritating pressure at my fingertips. I push one fingernail under the other, rake it out and slip the tiny pellet into my mouth. 'You don't have to stay out, you know, Natty!' she says, reaching out to give me a quick squeeze of the arm. I feel like a ghost of myself, but force a smile. 'Just know when to keep to yourself.

Sit here, now. I'll do your hair. You look a sight.' Her fingers tug at the fastening of the plait, pulling at the roots. 'Did you get some tea?' I nod, thinking: What's it to you? She sometimes puts on a show like this when other people are here.

'Shouldn't be out so late,' Luke chips in, 'at her age.' He's never minded before.

'So where were you, then?' he asks me. He's got no right to. He is nothing to do with me, so I don't answer. Something makes me glance over at the other man.

'Mike,' he says, catching me look. I go on looking as if I hadn't heard. They're all the same, men. I know what they're like under their clothes, between their legs. Just after we moved in here I saw, by accident, when I was sent home for still not having any games kit. I never talked to the man, never even knew his name, but I saw everything about him. His backside was hairy, white with dark hairs, carrying on up from the legs and so was his back, though there was a stripe above the hips where it must have been rubbed off by his belt. He was in Sandra's bedroom, on the bed, with her blue-white calves flung over his shoulders. I saw his cock coming out of more messy hair when he pulled it out of her—and more hair there too, on her, looking as if it had probably come from him, rubbed off somehow, though I know better than that, now that it's started to grow on me.

He let her down onto the bed and turned around to face me with it pointing at me. Stupid thing. The front of him was hairy as a doormat too, hairs all swirling like iron filings around his navel, and two tiny pink nipples, then on and up to the base of his neck, where it went in a sudden rush upwards like grass along the side of a fence. The neck itself and the face were shaved. They didn't seem to belong to the body.

'What are you staring at! Get out!' I lived there, not him, so he had no right to tell me to get out, and so I stayed. Then Sandra laughed and he shouted at her too.

'You'd better go,' she said, and I did, then.

You hairy-cock, I think at Luke.

'So where were you, missy?' he repeats. I decide to tell him, even though I don't have to, so as to save trouble:

'At the allotments.' I suck my finger, taste sugar again.

'She does go there,' Sandra tells him.

'What's she doing at the allotments? That's the point,' says Mike, the man on the floor. He's grinning mirthlessly. The pupils of his pale-blue eyes are tiny dots, the wrinkles around the eyes lighter than the rest of his skin. 'One day she won't come back,' he adds, matter-of-fact. 'That's the way it goes.'

'She helps out,' Sandra tells them both, 'don't you?' She's just pretending that she's bothered, pretending that she knows. But at the same time, she rakes her fingers through my hair, and each time they go through it I lean into her a bit more.

Then she rubs the scalp where it pulled. 'Better?' she asks. I put my face on her chest; the skin smells of cocoa butter and patchouli and she puts her hand on my back. Her heartbeat, a thing more like touch than sound, passes into me; I close my eyes and the day's tiredness rushes into me, overwhelming and delicious. For a moment, I almost forget the stalemate that's between us.

'Suppose I didn't come back?' I whisper into her skin.

'What?' There's martini on her breath.

'Suppose I didn't come back one night?' There's a pause, a moment in which anything could happen. She might hug me so tight it hurts. 'Don't you even think about it, Natty,' she might say. Then a tremor passes through both of us, the first quakes of the unstoppable laughter which comes out of her at moments which have the similarity of never being funny for the other person. The laugh flings her head suddenly back to allow itself out—the sudden whelp, the downwards swoop, the arpeggios that follow. It jolts me upright and awake. One side of my face is damp, the ear on that side stuck to my head. Sandra's eyes are brimming with the liquid that laughing produces, but underneath that they smoulder, as if they need their wetness to stop them from burning right up, as if that was what the laughing is for. Suddenly, I feel sick. Those buns, I think.

'I'd think myself lucky!' Sandra says, as the laugh leaves her, her face stretched by its passing into a broad smile, her voice hollowed out and rough at the sides. 'When are you off, then?'

Luke's smiling too. But the man on the floor isn't. He's been looking at me, in quick glances like sips of a drink, ever since we started talking about where I'd been.

'What's your problem?' Sandra presses her finger into my chest. 'I gave you a decent name, didn't I? And my hair. Looks like you'll get my physique as well. I could do with a comb here.'

'You borrowed it,' I tell her, 'this morning.' She reaches for her bag and roots half-heartedly through the contents.

'We'll do it tomorrow.' She sinks back on to Luke. Hairs are growing through the snake tattoo on his arm. His hand cups Sandra's breast and seeing it makes me angry and bewildered. 

'Say goodnight now and go up to bed.'

'Let her stay,' says the man on the floor.

'No,' Sandra tells him. 'She's only thirteen. And she needs her beauty sleep.'

'Can't I take the TV up?' I ask. 'I'm not tired yet.'

'All right,' she says, 'if it keeps you quiet.'

The man on the floor, Mike, wrestles the thing up the stairs, cursing our lack of lights. He's sweating hard by the time he puts it down near the door where the socket is. He stays crouching next to it.

'Where's your aerial?' he says. 'It won't work without a proper aerial.' I like him even less now and I don't answer. I fight the look he's giving me, give it back as much as I can.

I move my eyes from one bit of his face to the other: the brows, tensed; the pale eyes, set in shadowy sockets; his ears, exposed, too big. The line of his nose, not quite straight. The shadows of hairs under the skin of his jaw, dark even though the short hair on his head is fair. I stare him out.

'You'll go a long way,' he says at last. 'You've got your mother in you, all right.'

'Aren't you going to say thank you?' he asks. I want to shake my head, but restrain the impulse, stand there like stone.

'Don't I even get a goodnight kiss?' When I still say nothing he brings his hands together in a loud clap, so that I jump. Then he smiles, rises smoothly to his feet and goes, leaving the door wide open. I close it, turn the TV straight on, filling the room with the hissing it makes, turning the controls this way and that.

I remember how after I'd heard the nameless man leave, Sandra came downstairs and sat by me. She turned the sound off the TV and explained that what I'd seen, the thing men and women did, felt so good that they'd rather do it than anything else, and besides, it stopped them being at each other's throats.

I can't imagine wanting to do anything like that with any men. I don't like men and I wish they weren't around so much.

Most people are prudes, she told me. But really, the only problem with sex was that it got you bloody pregnant! It was her good mood that I responded to, rather than the meaning of the words, which I didn't really understand. I went to fetch her an ashtray from the kitchen... Fortunately, she continued, there was the pill now, but it made your tits even bigger. Sometimes men gave you a present or even wanted to marry you but that was the end of Free Love, sure as eggs is eggs.

'Well, there it is, Natty. It'll make sense when it happens. I've told you. Now forget it. Don't tell anyone else. And don't you dare ever come in my room like that again, or you'll feel it after.'

Then she said she'd get us chicken pies from the shop but she couldn't find her right shoes, so I went, and somehow that upset me far more than anything else. You have these nice ideas! I thought shrilly at her as I set out. The thoughts were loud as words. Maybe I even said them.

It's lucky, though, that I didn't say more just now downstairs, because whatever I have to do to make it happen, I will be leaving in the morning. I pull open the cupboard and find two pullovers from last year, some other tops, a pair of jeans, and push them into my duffle bag. I remember the letter Barbara gave me this afternoon. The flap of the envelope is only tucked in at the back. The paper vibrates in my hand, and I'm angry that I can't stop it happening. But I smooth it as much as I can and read, far more easily than I would have done just a few weeks back:

> Dear Mrs. Baron,
> Thank you for your letter. It has been lovely to have Natalie visit us on her way home from school, she has become almost part of the family. You can be sure that we will look after her. It's colder in the north, so she will need warm clothes even though it is summer, and waterproofs. We need to leave very early tomorrow, so will have to call for her at 5 in the morning, I'm afraid. But at least we will finally be able to meet each other, which I'm sure you are as keen to do as I am . . .

Barbara's other letter is in the shoebox at the bottom of the wardrobe. I take it out, fold the two of them together with the new one and put them back in the zip pocket of the duffle bag. Then I sit on the floor, watching the white dazzle of the screen, lean forward, move the hold button a fraction, and, miraculously, the snowstorm gathers itself into a picture of the cabin on Apollo 11. The three astronauts move in their odd, lumbering way around the tiny space. You can tell by their slow voices how very far away they are from everything on earth. Even though they will return, they have broken some kind of connection, I think, and they will never again quite belong with everyone else.

# 13



I've put on a pair of blue trousers and a checked cheesecloth blouse that Sandra bought too small by mistake, and when they come I'm waiting, wide awake, with my duffle bag, outside the front gate. The sleek-lined car and its boxy caravan draw to a halt, and I run to meet them before anyone manages to get out. A sweet tang of exhaust fumes hangs in the air.

'She had to do a late shift,' I say, holding out the twenty-pound note I took from my mother's purse an hour ago, 'but she said to give you this towards the holiday.' I manage to keep my voice normally loud, although I know that no one came up last night, and can see that the window downstairs is open: they'll all be sound asleep down there, I reassure myself. Barbara, halfway out of the car, stops, glances at her husband.

'Perhaps your father—' she begins.

'At the hospital.' I tell them. Still there's a hesitation, an inability amongst everyone, somehow, to take the next step.

'Isn't the money enough?' I ask. I hold it farther out, all but push it in her hand.

'We don't expect you to bring money, sweetheart,' says Barbara, as she accepts it for safekeeping, 'but where are your things?'

'Here—'

'You can't have very much in there,' Barbara says. 'I did tell your mother—'

'It's all in there!' I insist, shaking the bag at her. 'It is!'

'Haven't you got a coat?' Barbara asks, 'an anorak, at least. Wellingtons—' At this point, Mr. Hern leans towards his wife and puts his hand on her knee.

'We had better get going,' he says. 'She can always borrow things.' Finally, Barbara's face breaks into a smile.

'Open the door,' she tells Mark, who is sitting, stone-like, in the middle of the back seat. One of his eyes has blacked up since yesterday. He reaches over to pull the catch, then moves to the far side.

I pull the door closed with both hands. Their car smells of leather and Nivea cream; the upholstery bears me up.

Mr. Hern glances over his shoulder, pulls out.

We drive in silence to the roundabout, then back past my house and out of the estate. We overtake a milk float. Then we join the ring road. I shift around, cling to the back of Barbara's seat and pull myself forwards, thrusting my head into the gap between the front seats.

'How many miles is it?' I ask. 'How long will it take us to get there? How often do you have to fill this car up? How many stars does the petrol have in it? Where are we now?' I twist back suddenly to look at Mark. He's sitting with his long legs stretched right out to the base of the driver's seat, his feet tucked under it, a book on his lap. Its pages fan in the wind.

'What's it about?' I ask, but he keeps on pretending to read.

'He's keeping silence,' Barbara explains. 'To prepare himself for Monday. He's going to lead the service. It's a big responsibility.'

So I can talk even more. What's that thing over there in the field? I ask. What's the car's top speed? What time is it now? Is driving easy to learn?

On flat ground somewhere between Bury and Peterborough, I fall asleep and Mark feels the absence of my voice wash cleanly through his flesh, leaving it his own again... When he turns, he'll find me with my hands loose in my lap, my head pulling towards my shoulder and, just visible behind the swaying mass of hair, my mouth open. Later, my head will change sides. Later still, I've slipped against the window and turned my face towards it as if I too were looking out, though my body, melted into the corner, still points more or less forwards.

As we pull north of Newark and the first set of four fat chimneys comes into view to our right, I heave myself upright, open my eyes briefly, rub my face. Then I knead the seat like an animal making its bed, and collapse the upper half of my body onto it, face down, one arm under my head, the other reaching to the floor.



Mark gives up on the book, surrenders to the journey and the opening out of the landscape. In moments when the wind about his ears is less, maybe he can hear my breathing: a faint but insistent wet catch at the end of each exhalation.

'Are you okay?' Barbara asks him. 'Are you hungry or thirsty yet?' He shakes his head, even though he is hungry, because he wants to keep things like this for as long as possible: the bright sky, the shade in the back of the car, the wind about his ears and his silence, wrapped tightly around him, invisible, but strong.

Yesterday, Stokes had asked him: had he ever seen a woman's tits? They were on the field, at lunchtime. Had he seen the slit between her legs? Had he seen fucking? Stokes gestured with his hands, his own eyes squinting tight shut for a moment, before opening very wide in a parody of curiosity. There was laughter from his hangers-on. Minutes earlier, Mark had been practising high jump with Wright and Walker, but now they were gone.

'No,' he told Stokes. He believed it was a thing to do rather than watch. Nor did he wish to see a picture of it either, thanks.

There was a blur of print, then, as Stokes got his magazine out. Mark looked this way and that, to avoid the images, not succeeding entirely. Finally, when it was utterly impossible, he closed his eyes. Running would have offended his dignity, and if they caught him the result would be the same in any case. So he stood there. For a few moments there was nothing but a smell of his own sweat and the banging of his heart inside him. Then someone hit him, a couple of blows to the stomach which knocked air out but were quite easy to withstand. To begin with they seemed to find it hard to hit someone who wasn't looking at them and didn't respond. But as the minutes passed, they became accustomed to it, and began to make comments and give each other instructions: 'Who does he think he is? Jesus Christ? Give him one. Get him by the ear.'

Spit landed on his face. He felt it run down his cheek towards the corner of his mouth. Before he could wipe it away, someone went for his chin, jerking his head back. For a moment, he saw the sky, and even as he closed his eyes again, he knew it could not be for long. Someone stamped on his toe. A kick at the groin just missed. Then Stokes—he knew it was Stokes from the breathing, the way he smelled, everything—had him by the ears, head-butted him, kneed him. He began to struggle, pushed Stokes away, hit back. During the course of this, his eyes opened, though he saw very little, just the bits of Stokes that he was aiming for. Once started, he went on. He didn't feel Stokes hitting him anymore, not until afterwards.

'Got it?' he said to Stokes, the tang of blood on his tongue. He wiped his face on his sleeve, startling himself with the colour. Both of them had nosebleeds but Stokes' lip was split too, and while Mark could have gone on, Stokes, breathing heavily, was looking around for one of his lot to lean on. But in the midst of the fight, the bell for final assembly had gone, and the few people still outside besides themselves were distant figures converging on the main building. They were standing, Mark realized, amidst a flurry of torn pages. Most of the bodies were unrecognizable now, but he looked quickly away. Seeing was not the same as looking, but it could be the beginning of it.

They had better go inside, he told Stokes, and then realized that he would have to help him. Together, not speaking, they laboured up the steep rise that separated the fields from the school.

At the top of the steps leading into the main building, he pushed through the double doors, protecting Stokes as they swung back behind. He sat Stokes on a basin in the toilets, filled another with cold water and wiped his face clean with wads of wet toilet paper, taking particular care of the swelling around the split upper lip.



'You're crazy,' Stokes said, wearily.

'I won't have to put up with this forever,' Mark said, smiling. He felt as if he were only a little heavier than air, and some slight alteration in the atmospheric pressure would allow him to float upwards.

'I think what will happen is that we'll buy an Island,' he explained. 'That's the way things are going. Then this sort of thing'—he gestured at the wire bin full of bloodied paper—'won't happen. It'll have its own teachers, school and so on. Believe me.'

It was later, after talking to his father about what had happened, that the idea of the silence came to him. And now, wrapped in it, he smiles to himself, remembering Stokes' incredulous, bloodied face.

He tries to imagine what's to come. It's hard, because the memory of the Finnish congregations is so vivid. He knows there will be no village right by, and no river, no bridge, no birch trees, no red-painted wooden houses interspersed among the newer ones, no plaques where Tuomas Envall lived and died, no church, no orderly graveyard with just the names and the dates on granite stones, Matti Hirn's father and mother among them. There will of course be fields but larger ones, and no white nights; it will be thoroughly dark by ten o'clock.

This time he won't be running around with the village children, being shown their houses and animals, pointing at things, saying their names in Finnish. There'll be no cows to milk first thing and late afternoon, no games of hide and seek in the shady summer barns where some of the older girls sleep on the upper floors, no unsalted butter pressed into bowls or jars of berry jam, no rubbery, sweet-tasting cheese. This time they are not carrying with them rolls of cloth, pots and pans, cooking knives—gifts to compensate for their keep. There will be far fewer people of course, gathering in only the one group instead of several. All this is different.

But Mark too is different. He has had a vision. That is how God will use him, not in scientific research as he used to hope. He will be conducting Monday's service. The words, stored and refined during the silence he is keeping, will spring, inspired, from his mouth, and after that he will be in the middle of things, speaking and being listened to. During one of the meditations, it's possible that he might be given further visions: there is a still, open place in him, always ready for that, should it come. He can feel that place even now; he can feel that place even with me sleeping beside him in the back of the car, my head almost touching his leg.

And like this I do seem almost harmless. So he allows his eyes to rest on me a little longer than before. He sees how the tips of the fingers of the hand that's under my head poke through the intricate endless tangles of my hair, as if to find their way up to breathe—pale, smooth, full of sleeping nerves, and he finds his own hands suddenly restless. He closes Physics IV, returns his attention to the window.

Distant cooling towers stand to both sides, stretch into lines or settle to squat groups according to the angle of view. Pylons plant their feet in the fields, stride alongside the road. The traffic thickens, lorries mainly, some other caravans, cars.

We turn north-east, towards the coast on a narrower road. Now and then there's a pub with a painted sign. Some of the lorries, too, have crude images on them as well as words. Mark looks away when he sees them, looks instead at the real things God has made: the sky, the fields, the road ahead, or inward, at his own hands or his mother and father.

'I'll stop at the next lay-by,' John calls over his shoulder. 'Keep an eye on behind, would you?' Mark leans out of his window as far as he dares, the wind stinging his eyes. His father makes slow circles with his arm and in this way the Herns and I move almost imperceptibly from steady movement to a standstill, and I wake up.



The car shakes slightly each time a vehicle passes. A heat haze shimmers above the surface of the road. To the other side of it spread generous, undulating fields in different blends and textures of gold and green, dotted occasionally with livestock and broken up with stands of poplar, oak and copper beech. Above us, the sky is endlessly blue: it's the broadest possible daylight and yet on the radio a newscaster announces that Armstrong, Aldrin and Collins are approaching the point when they will go into orbit around the moon.

'It puts our journey in the shade,' Barbara says. 'Do you think they'll make it?'

'Yes,' I say.

'It's so very hard to imagine,' John Hern replies. 'So it should be,' he adds, opening the door, easing stiffly out of the car. He stretches, circles his neck, then climbs up the bank behind the lay-by and disappears.

'We'll put the rug on the grass up there,' Barbara tells Mark, 'if you wouldn't mind, and watch the world go by.'

My hair is a huge irregular mass, as if it had grown while I slept, the right side of my face is hot from pressing against my arm. The afternoon light is too bright and I squint until I'm used to it. Mark, smoothing out the plaid rug, watches me emerge from the back of the car. I can see that he's trying not to react.

Barbara pats the rug next to her, holds out a plastic cup. When I sit down she puts her arm around my shoulders, squeezes and leaves it there. We eat our sandwiches and watch the cars go by. All the time in Space, which is as black as the inside of my own brain, Apollo 11 hurtles silently around the moon.

# 14

The days lengthen, but there are still no leaves on the birch trees, just tiny buds. Patches of grubby snow and air-riddled ice persist in the noonday shadows of buildings and trees, in the hollows of the newly visible chocolate-brown fields. The very bareness of things forces me to see more in what little there is. I'm thinking that perhaps it was the same for Tuomas Envall at the beginning of those long, hopeless months before his triumphant sermon. Perhaps the season helped, pushed him to clean the paintbox he had found and to dampen and stretch a piece of paper onto a board. In any case, making use of the time between his reading in the morning and his silent lunch at the pastor's table, he had begun to paint, 'to accept the Devil's invitation.'



Time and time he'd painted the view from this window: the path, the trees, the pastor's house. Different days, different lights. Sometimes he filled a bottle with water, walked out through the village into the surrounding countryside, sketching barns, the boulders protruding from the slush-pools in the fields, the first buds on the birch trees. Soon it was impossible for him to pass a day without painting; the more he painted, the more it seemed he saw and the more of the day he spent doing it.

And then there came a day when I forgot to recite my psalm, and then another, and when I realized this, I told myself that I was simply celebrating the Lord's power and glory in a different way, and so fell ever deeper into temptation. My situation was difficult, and I was ill prepared for it, but instead of accepting what was, I sought to distance myself from it, to make it again in a way that pleased me better . . .

Easter came: the pastor continued to conduct the services, holding the congregation close to him still, just as he gripped the pulpit to keep himself upright. Increasingly, he would be absent for one or other of the day's meals, and Tuomas, eating alone at the long table, would hear him coughing and moaning in his bedroom.

There was no point in knocking on the door or calling out to him, Ulla said: just as he did not wish for an assistant, so also was the pastor adamant that he would not be seen by the doctor.

The river water melted, setting reflections free, but the landscape darkened overnight and the ground itself was still frozen. Tuomas, forced now to paint thinner and thinner to save the colours, tried to convey the way these reflections appeared as captive fragments of some other, brighter reality. Then finally the paints ran out and, deprived of his distraction, Tuomas wrote to his bishop, describing the situation he found himself in, apologizing for his lack of success and begging for advice.

No answer came. When the roads were better, Tuomas thought, he would ride there himself, though he was not sure what he would say. Indeed, it sometimes seemed that his tongue was fusing with the roof of his mouth, and moving it to pronounce words, even prayer or song, was a huge effort of will. By mid May, the roads were dry, but he didn't ride to the bishop. 'I stayed where I was,' he wrote later, 'and sent money to Oulu for more paints; I received pigment, linseed, turpentine . . .'

At home, my mother informs me, they are having a heatwave. People are going to work in shorts and bright-coloured dresses, lying in parks at lunchtime, buying fans. Here, the ground is still frozen. But villagers have begun to display on their windowsills little trays and pots of grass grown indoors from seed. Sometimes, on my walks to the supermarket or the community centre, I glimpse on a kitchen or dining-room table a vase containing a dozen daffodils or one or two bright and expensive Gerbera daisies.

When the sun is strong, a faint steam rises from the ground, and there's a rotten smell, somewhere between excrement and ethyl alcohol, which, I've been told, is last year's organic detritus concluding, in double time, the process of putrefaction interrupted by last year's frost: a true sign of the beginning of spring.



Tuomas's little house has its own smells: the resinous tang of the dry wood it was built from all those years ago, still in some way alive; fresh coffee and, later in the day, the heavy sludge of old grounds in the filter papers; imported apples and oranges in their bright plastic bowl; periodically, sheets, needing to be taken to a Mrs. Lausti for washing, there being no launderette. Despite the cold, I make a point of keeping the windows open in the morning for a good half-hour before I go out. I raise my hand to passing cars as they shower me with mud, call out brisk greetings to fellow pedestrians. Most people nod or raise their hands and reply. Of course, there's Christina. And there are certainly a few people who feel guilty about, or embarrassed by, or suspicious of me, or else connect me with their bitter disputes with the Board of Antiquities and the official Lutheran Church. But the majority here listen to a question with interest, and do their best to answer it.

I go out first thing and do my local errands on foot, so as to move my blood around and get as much light as possible. Today, Heikki Seppä's Jeep passed me just as I emerged from the shop. He stopped a few yards ahead, the engine running and the door open, waiting for me.

I explained that I was walking on purpose.

'Five more minutes will make no difference,' he told me, in English.

'No, really,' I said, taking a good look inside the car all the same. He keeps it tidy, with the inevitable maps tucked neatly into side pockets, a rollerball pen fixed with Blu-Tak to the dashboard shelf.

He shrugged.

'I hear you are making good progress,' he told me. 'Is that so? Are you well?'

I told him that his help had been invaluable.

'As for me,' he said, 'I'm having a bad day—' Last night, a long argument on the telephone with his ex-wife. This morning, a flat battery and then late for a meeting with his superiors where he was told that there will be further delays in a number of projects, including the restoration of the church here, making him even less popular with both the religious faction and the new middle-class incomers than he already is—

He shrugged again.

'This is life. But now I am on holiday for two weeks. I am taking Kirsi skiing in Lapland, and then visiting my mother. And meanwhile, I thought you might need to spend some more time in the *pappila*.' He unfastened his seatbelt, dug into the inside pocket of his parka and handed me an iron key-ring. On it, the two large and half-dozen smaller keys that will let me into the main house and anything that's locked up there, alone, as and when I please.

Of course, he shouldn't have given them to me. The *pappila* has been deteriorating for over twenty years, and I shouldn't be allowed in without a hard hat, some kind of supervision—

and, of course, the letter of permission and signed disclaimer, which for some reason are taking ages to arrive. So I thanked Heikki warmly, and wished him a good holiday with his daughter.

It was only after he had driven away that it occurred to me that he might have wanted a coffee or a drink and that I could have risen to the occasion. The wind was behind me as I walked home, angry at my awkwardness, and then angry at him for making me feel it.

# 15

A fat, sunburned man wearing wellington boots and trousers belted with a piece of green twine waved us to a standstill. The trousers had slipped down, showing a broad slice of white skin. Wisps of dry, sandy hair grew from the reddish brown of his scalp, like chaff on a field. Behind him, another lane like the one we were on led uphill to a low stone house and other farm buildings, a windbreak of poplar trees growing behind.



'Harris,' the man said, offering a huge hand through the driver's window. 'Pleased to meet you. It's ten pounds in advance.' He folded the cheque carefully in half and put it away in his back pocket, doing the button up by feel. His movements had an odd, practised delicacy about them, the fat man's grace.

'The ground's dry, it's set fair. I'm up here. My wife'll do eggs and milk any time, plain bottles, brown bags. You can order bread. No fires.' He hitched up the trousers. 'Well—' He raised his hand. 'There's more of you coming.' A blue Imp had stopped behind us.

'Harris,' we heard him say. 'Pleased to meet you . . .'

We coasted slowly down the rest of the lane, stray twigs scraping at the sides of the caravan. A breeze blew through the hedges, bringing a thick, sweet smell that I had no name for. Then, the ground levelled and there it was—a vast and vivid field spreading out across the bottom of the valley, trees marking where the river must be, distant fields, dotted with cattle, rising to the other, steeper side.

Just inside the gates several men strode up to welcome us, gesticulating towards the far corner, where trees offered some shade. We lumbered across the rough ground, Green and Thwaite from Humberside, Mr. Thorn from Suffolk following, and others gathering in the wake. Last of all came a gaggle of ball-playing children and a thin, somehow lopsided boy, Ian McAllister, who had to put his viola on the ground and find his glasses before he could follow the rest.

The Herns and I stood together in the slanting oblong of shade the caravan made. Grasping both of each person's hands and holding them a moment, the Herns greeted each and every person, adult and child... Another family arrived in the middle of this and did the same thing, so it was some time before Barbara could inform the congregation about Mark's silence and announce that I, Natalie, came from a different background but very much wanted to be with them—

'Good,' said the man called Thwaite, not really listening. 'Everyone is coming, but unfortunately Paul Leverson has been delayed—'

'Who's he?' I whispered in Mark's ear, the words coming out of nowhere so that he drew breath and almost answered them by mistake. Thwaite gestured around the field, pointing out blue chemical toilets, for men at the far top side of the field, for women at the far lower; the two taps by the gate, the space at the top of the neighbouring field where tomorrow we would erect a communal food tent, the place below it for meetings. Food would be ready in an hour or so. Was there anything else anyone wanted to know?

'Can I listen to the radio in the car?' I asked him.

'Well, I expect so,' he said, bewildered, seeing me properly this time: the hair, the too-small clothes, the eyes—very green now, in the company of so much grass, fixed somewhere, almost tangible, between his own eyes and hairline—'I can't see why not.'

'There's a transistor,' Barbara said as Mark and his father went to settle the caravan. 'I'll fetch it. We can sit somewhere quiet while I make you look human again.'

I held the radio in my lap, its aerial pointing down the valley, and bent over it, elbows on knees, loose-shouldered. Apollo 11 was beyond the reach of communications, on the dark side of the moon. The men left behind on earth, waiting for news, talked on and on, of degrees and accuracy, timing, computer predictions, gravitational field, velocity.

She squatted on her heels behind me and took my hair in both her hands, buried them in it, squeezed, felt the weight, the damp warmth at the roots, then let go. The hair was tangled and knotted, springy, wilful, matted where it had been slept upon. She separated small sections with her fingers, held them above the first knot with one hand, while she pulled the comb down until it bit. Then it was a matter of ease and tug, ease and tug, small movements with rests in between.



'It doesn't hurt,' I told her.

She leaned in closer. The men on the radio droned on.

'Tell me something,' I said. Barbara reached underneath the hair to where the soft, fine down grew in the warm climate of the nape, combed upwards from there, then carefully down the sides of the head, behind the ears.

'What kind of thing do you mean?' she asked. I leaned further forwards to make the combing easier.

'Something interesting—' Barbara divided my hair for the plait, combing each third over again. Now that the knots were out, and the strands lay next to each other in one mass, the colour of the hair grew deeper, complicated itself.

'Something I don't know,' I told her.

'I expect there's an awful lot you don't know.' She let a smile spread across her face then, knowing I wouldn't see it and feel mocked. The hair slipped between her fingers, fluid, warm, like nothing else but itself.

'I know more than you think,' I said. It was the first time I had made a statement of this kind, a contradiction, and I said it clearly, but very quietly. 'I even know how babies are made,' I told her, 'unless you take the pills. The egg and the worm; I know all that.'

'That—' she said. 'That is a lot to know.' I kept my eyes closed, concentrated on the gentle pulling at the roots of my hair.

'When the baby comes out,' I told her, 'it really hurts.' *Like fuck* was what Sandra said.

'Yes—' Barbara said, simply. In the quiet that followed, was she remembering the labour she had with Ruth? How it was unexpectedly harder than the first, how, in the middle of the worst of it she thought, You, I am doing everything I can. Don't you give up; I shan't—How the pair of them were there, just the two of them, in the universe of their joined but wrestling flesh, and the doctor and nurses, despite the things they did, could only be outside, while mother and child tried to separate themselves so that they could see each other, smile, begin to learn to talk with words—a process as hard to describe as being behind the moon, on its dark side, unable to talk to home...

In any case, the plait grew steadily and neither of us spoke for quite a while.

'Afterwards,' she said eventually, 'that pain is like something that happened in another country years ago. You can tell the story of it, but it is gone... Children are God's gift,' she added.

'So why—'

'Mmm?'

'I mean—' I said, carefully, in a way that seemed to make what I said a question, but not too much of one, more an invitation: 'I mean—you've only got one.' She slipped an elastic band over the end of my plait, and I turned to look at her, fighting those lenses to see what was behind, to be as close as possible, then, and now, still—

'Surely,' she's thinking, 'there is nothing wrong with explaining; the girl is of an age to know that such things take place, though not, of course, the details ...'

'I did have a little girl after Mark,' she says, 'but she only lived for a few months.'

She keeps her gaze steady. She doesn't cry. On the contrary, her lips curl upwards ever so softly and her face softens. It's as if, in the blink of an eye ('In the blink of an eye,' Envall writes, 'a lifetime's faith can be lost, and might take another lifetime to find'), she has grown younger inside, as if something better than ordinary blood flows in her veins and arteries, as if she were breathing oxygen, not air—'Could I tell anyone how I feel right now?' she's thinking. 'I've sat here half an hour with Mrs. Baron's daughter lent to me for a week, my hands sunk into her double-fine-grade red-gold-wool hair, saying this and saying that, listening, then telling her—'



Behind the glasses, Barbara's eyes are bright. She feels alive and open. She can even begin to understand those men hurtling through space, the bluntest of talkers, men in whom the impulse to reach out to others with words seems so reluctant (the earth 'green' and 'brown,' the view 'magnificent') or to be somehow lost between heart and throat. Just as their bodies are wrapped in huge insulating suits which she has heard about but can't really imagine, so their hearts and souls are swaddled inside the experience of being astronauts; they are quite simply at a point where words fail, and they can only hope to communicate with each other.

She takes me by the shoulders and presses her face down on top of my head, breathing in the perfume of the hair and the pale scalp beneath, that intimate, animal incense. Then the radio says, abrupt, but trying to sound calm:

'—there is contact but there are transmission problems... There are transmission problems,' it repeats. We pull apart. For a minute or so there is absolute silence on the airwaves. Then a new voice says:

'Houston,' (you can tell it's from miles and miles away) 'we are in lunar orbit. We had an almost perfect burn back there...'

'There!' I shout at her. 'They're going to make it!'

A few minutes later, when the radio goes boring again, I reach for the end of my new plait, put it experimentally in my mouth.

'Was it a secret that you just told me?' I ask.

'No,' she says, 'just something I don't talk about much.' She stands and lashes out at a cloud of midges that has gathered over us.

'It's time you forgot all these things you say you know about, and went and ran around with the rest of them.'

'I like it here,' I say. I don't move.

She pulls up the corners of the rug, tumbles me onto the grass, then falls on me, working her fingers deliciously between my ribs so that I squeal with laughter. She chases me up the slope.

'Maskelyne... Boot Hill... Sidewinder... Mount Marilyn ... I can see the crater of Aristarchus ... there's a slight amount of fluorescence, a kind of brightness ...' Behind us, the ghost of Armstrong's voice streams out from the radio, which lies forgotten in the grass.

On site, other radios whispered the same and different things. One group of children were borrowing Ian McAllister's viola, another, including Mark, were playing a brisk game of five-a-side football in the meeting-field beyond the hedge: good for him to let off steam, Barbara said. Girls of differing heights waited for their turn to skip a rope turned by two older girls.

'One o'clock, two o'clock, three o'clock, four,' they sing, 'five o'clock, six o'clock, seven o'clock, more . . .' Barbara waited while I ran into the field, hesitated, and took my place at the back of the skipping line, a girl with a plait, just like the rest. But also different. I looked back and waved.

'What are you called?' the girl in front of me asked, blinking in the sunlight. She was plump and short, wore her dark hair in a short, thick ponytail with a fringe as well, which made her face seem even plumper than it was.

'Natalie,' I told her.

'That's a weird name,' she said, angrily, as if it mattered a lot.

'No,' I told her, 'it's French,' and decided not to ask hers—though it was, of course, Christina. Instead, I looked over the top of her head at the girl jumping in the rope. I hadn't done it more than a few times and those a long time ago. It looked hard and for some reason—for Barbara, I think—I wanted to do well.



If the weather held, Barbara thought, the child would need to borrow a sun hat. She walked over to the Thorns' camper, and found Edith setting out to carry a groundsheet and two big bowls of potato salad back down to the river end of the lower field, where supper was to be. The veins on the backs of her hands and thin arms stood out like string, and although she would not hand the task over completely, she was glad of help.

Mr. Thorn had not been very well these past two weeks, she explained, as Barbara arranged the groundsheet and set out the food under cloths. There were pains in his stomach, he just couldn't get up and go—but the doctor found nothing, so it was in the hands of the Lord . . .

They set off back for more.

How was Mark? Mrs. Thorn asked, seeing as one couldn't ask him himself right now. Such a thoughtful boy. So tall now! 'And then,' she said, 'there's this child you have brought along with you, this Nadine—'

'Natalie,' Barbara corrected, glancing quickly across.

They reached the top of the incline, and the older woman, breathing hard, put her hand on Barbara's shoulder, stopping them both.

'Yes, I do wonder,' Edith began, 'whether you and John should have consulted a little, before bringing her?'

'Why?' Something in Barbara's voice made Edith's eyes widen, startled.

'I do think you should be very careful,' she said.

'Of course, Edith,' Barbara said.

But the more careful I am, she thought, as Edith took her by the hands, squeezing them hard, patting at them, running her thumbs over the palms, as if she could feel what was within and stroke it out—the more careful I am, in proportion to the amount I refrain and restrain myself, the more perfectly this thing seems to fall out according to my heart's desire.

When she'd addressed God on this matter, asked what it meant, He was silent. Edith would say that the problem lay in the way in which she approached her prayers. But she did not tell Edith and she would not, and for the first time since she had fought her parents over marrying John Hern, Barbara felt something fierce inside her turn and kick, half terrifying, half delicious.

At supper that evening, over fifty of us sat on blankets on the grass in a rough circle to begin with, then spreading out into smaller groups once Grace had been spoken. Thirty or so more were expected by the end of the next day. The sky darkened to a violet grey, slightly hazy, and then, while we ate, the first shy stars came out, grew bolder, multiplied and drove the haze away. Ian McAllister, standing up with his eyes squeezed shut, played something new that he had been practising, a modern work, full of silent spaces and sudden torrents of notes, and I held Barbara's hand.

# 16



I was watching them. Half-hidden behind the Bryants' caravan, peering around its corner, I could see John Hern, seated on a three-legged stool in a patch of shade at the floor of the steps, while Barbara snipped at his beard with scissors. It was no surprise to see that he was hairy everywhere too. The coarse beard-stuff, mottled grey and ginger, drifted down and away in rough clumps, marooned itself on the towel tied around his neck. Stray hairs drifted beyond the edges of the towel, attached themselves to his bare shoulders and to the neat, sideways-flowing ranks of smaller hairs on the shelf of his belly. When most of it was off, leaving him mottled and grubby-looking, she rubbed a wet brush into a lather. I could see her lips part as she worked at it; she began to smile. She looked quickly up at him, brush in hand, and both of them laughed. He flexed his toes in the grass, tipped his head back and looked up at the treetops and the sky beyond, back down again.

'Come on!' he said. His lips twitched as the brush approached. She covered his face in foam.

'Keep still, now. No talking.' She took his jaw in her hands, turned it firmly to one side, adjusted her position. From a starting-point on the soft pad of flesh just in from his left ear, she stroked the razor downwards, following the line of his jaw.

'Don't move,' she said, 'ssh—' I was very close. If I stilled my own breathing I could hear the wet rough whisper of the blade, imagine its first bite and the slow slide afterwards.

'Okay?' she asked. He widened his eyes to indicate yes, and sat there completely still, silent, obedient. Her face was so close to his that he must have felt her breath play on the newly exposed skin. She worked steadily over the big planes, cheeks, neck, and then, with small, carefully angled strokes, the awkward areas around the mouth and chin. She splashed his face with clean water, dabbed it dry, pulled off the towel and shook it. Mr. Hern caught Barbara's hand, turned it over, kissed the thin pale skin of her wrist and the inside of her arm.

'You look like nothing on earth!' she told him, laughing, while all the time he went on kissing her arm—

So I stepped out from my hiding place, and they stopped it. I got a good look at John's new face: it came in two halves, the eyes and forehead as before, the secret curves of its jaw, the plump, blue-white chin freshly exposed. The crescent of flesh around his neck and the bottom third of his arms were already tea-coloured from the sun, and matched the top part of his face. I looked back to Barbara and said:

'Mark won't talk to me.'

'But you know he's not talking to anyone,' she said. 'Why not leave him alone and try someone else? I thought you were with the girls, helping with the food?'

'Yes, but they don't like me,' I told her.

'Of course they do.'

'What are you doing?'

'We were just holding hands,' she said.

'I want to talk to you.'

'Well, that'd be nice. Go back to the food tent, I'll be along in a while to help.'

'I'd rather do it now, please.'

‘In a little while,’ Barbara insisted. ‘Half an hour.’ The door to the caravan was open behind them; I could see that their bed hadn’t been folded back.

I stood there silently, without moving. I was quite prepared to stand there forever, so what was the point in fighting me?

‘Are you all right?’ she asked. ‘What is it?’ I didn’t reply.

‘Darling,’ she said, ‘I think I had better see what the matter is—’ and John watched us walk off between the caravans and tents, my hand in hers where his had been. I led her at a half-run, pulling at her arm, out between our caravan and the Bryants’, down through the rest of the field, over a stile and diagonally across the slope beyond, past the flat bit where we had eaten supper the night before, along the stream, over another stile—soon, the campsite was out of view. I had no idea where we were going and only the dimmest feeling of what I might say to justify dragging her along like this. I’m sure she had no sense, either, of what she would find herself telling me, and this—the pair of us out of breath as we run in rough grass and buttercups beside the slow stream—is the last moment before everything changes again.

# 17

The wooden steps to the *pappila* are slippery with the dew and thaw but the big key turns easily in a lock that must have been oiled not long ago. Light streams through the windows into the hall, over the paired cabinets, across the striped rug. I turn left, into a long room, also very bright, with lined blue-and-white plaid curtains on the three large windows, blue-grey shutters folded back, plain upholstery and plenty of turned wood. It would be a good place for plants and that must be why there are so many small tables and shelves. There's a huge stove close to the hall wall. On the far side of the room, a metre or so of floorboards has been removed, exposing the partly rotten joists and earth sub-floor below. On the right, towards the back of the room, is a locked door. 

Using one of the smaller keys, I let myself through it into a dark room which smells ever so faintly of damp. I feel my way to the window, fold back the shutters. The room is painted the inverse of the bigger one, blue-grey walls, the woodwork white. As I hoped, it is the Pastor's office. A huge, dark-wood desk takes up the right-hand wall, a vast, overfull bookcase above some low cupboards is on the left. The books are mainly old and leather-bound, here and there a gathering of newer cloth-bound texts, even the occasional paperback. The chair at the desk, I notice immediately, is a rough copy of the one I saw in Tuomas's Uncle Runar's office at the regional museum—a kind of strutted tub to waist level, padded leather seat, rotating mechanism below, a wheel-like circular support sitting on the floor. Surely, then, it is the one Pastor Tuomas Envall used? I sit in it, test the spin. Even the smallest movement or gesture produces an ominous creak, but no doubt that will be fixed during the restoration. And then a cord will be tied across, to stop people trying it out... I really have arrived in the nick of time.

I turn my attention to the desk, which is so large that I cannot reach the back of it without standing. It is wider than my outstretched arms. At the same time, it is rather low. There is a dark-blue leather rectangle set in the top, behind that, just within reach, a blotter and silver inkwells, empty. There are eight small drawers on one side, three large ones on the other, all of them empty and all, except for the filing drawer, lined with some kind of fine baize-like cloth, dark red, rubbed through here and there, and then covered over at the bottom with sheets of thick, cream blotting paper. Some of the drawers are subdivided into little compartments, some of which have little hinged lids, raised by means of a sunken semicircle of silvery metal. In one of these lidded compartments I find a shiny new paperclip, two perished elastic bands and a drawing pin. Then I realize that there are two extension pieces, tucked under the desktop, which (as if more space were needed!) pull out to make more desk to either side. These extensions are decorated with a panel of the same blue leather that is set into the top of the desk, though it's far brighter and newer, almost untouched...

It's not as if I have set out to find anything in particular here, yet something makes me look again, harder, and I realize that these leather panels or inserts are in fact hinged on one side and fastened along the other with tiny rotating metal clips. I pick them open with a paperclip. Beneath each inset is a shallow, hollow space, just bare wood, unlined. The right one contains a handkerchief and an expanding metal bracelet such as men once used to adjust the length of their shirt-sleeves; the left, a thin, leather-bound notebook, dated, on the fly-leaf, 1899: two years before Tuomas died. My first impulse is to push away from the desk and look almost angrily around the room, where book after book stares back at me, and the air is utterly still. The fact that I've been here ten minutes and have already found something seems somehow too much, almost uncanny. Then, as I begin to examine the little book in detail, everything else recedes.

The writing, small and contained in the main but interrupted with sudden, disproportionate upward and downward strokes, is undoubtedly his. Only a few pages at the beginning are filled. I turn over.



'The mind-images that rise up,' I read, forcing the clustered consonants into meaning and translating crudely as I go, 'often at the limits of sleep and waking, are the hardest to judge of, and the hardest to fight with. Oh my Lord, have I not struggled in this respect—'

Again, it's too much. I put the book down for a moment, sit back in the chair. The shadows of twigs outside the window to my left play across the wall in front of me, upon which hang framed biblical texts embroidered in crosses and chain stitch. After a while, I open the window to let in some fresh air. Then I get out my own notebook, pens, dictionary and begin painstakingly to translate what remains.

'And yet sometimes when I wake from my shameful dreams,' he continues, 'it seems to me that the bedroom is less real than what has been taking place in them, and likewise, now, the pen I hold in my hand, the paper I write on, the desk upon which it rests—'

He stops, mid-sentence. Two pages later is another entry. 'My God, but one yearns,' he writes in the same blue-grey ink that he used for the official registers, 'how much even at the end of life one yearns to be fully known by another human soul as I believe I am, whether I will it or not, by You, whose knowing sustains and contains me. Yet (and I do sometimes think this), suppose You are not there? Then no one—'

Clearly, this is not an empty desk.

My hands, I notice, have begun to shake. At the same time, I want to cry, but can't because I'm too tense. Telling or discovering a secret, even being in the vicinity of someone else doing one of these things, is never without ramifications. It must always be some kind of beginning, it can shift you with terrifying abruptness from one possibility to another and, in a few swift seconds, change the entire shape of a life for better or for worse. That's why secrets are kept in the first place, and why letting them go is properly a terrifying thing to do, thought about endlessly before it's done.

# 18



'Natalie—let's stop here,' she says. Her face is damp with sweat and I suddenly feel burning hot as well. There's a scrubby tree by the edge of the stream, a scrap of shade. We sit down there and I pick at the tightly knotted laces of my shoes—once white, now grey, coming apart at the front where they join the soles. Some of the metal eyelets are missing, too, leaving the lace to pass through frayed holes.

'Maybe I can get you a new pair of those?' she says. 'If they have them in the village, then I will. What is it?'

'They don't like me here. They call me names.' Tears come to my eyes as I tell her this, though it isn't the name-calling that makes them come—I know how to deal with that—but the idea of the shoes. One thing slides so easily into the next; years later I'll regret that the conversation began like this in bad faith, but right now, it's the most natural thing in the world.

'Christina Gardner started it.'

'What did she start?'

'She called me a sinner.'

'It's just because you don't go to our services,' she says. 'I'll talk to her mother.'

'Am I one?' I ask, not quite giving in to the embrace. 'I've stolen things,' I tell her, as I prise the shoes off, still laced. I'm warming to my line of enquiry, genuinely curious by now. 'But I did it because I really needed to.' One of the things I've stolen is that twenty-pound note, sitting in Barbara's purse right now—nothing, you could say, to what I would like to take. But very likely Barbara thinks I just mean sweets. The small four-a-penny sweets in boxes at the side of the shop, flying saucers, liquorice, chews. An occasional wrapped chocolate bar from closer to the till—it's just about possible for her to imagine me doing that, walking home sticky-fingered, sugar-lipped...

Of course, she begins, stealing is a sin and it does matter, it matters even if there is a good reason. But at the same time, it is all right too. Her voice goes slow and slightly sing-song, like a teacher's; she continues, explaining how sins are things people do to hurt each other, to hurt themselves, or to hurt God, which happens anyway in either of the two preceding cases. I guess that these are words she's often used to others and my attention wanders. Now that my shoes are off I'm considering whether to dip my feet in the stream, but I somehow can't move. I rest my arms on my legs and my head on my arms. Gradually, my eyes begin to close. Several times I force them back open. 'We are all sinners,' she concludes, 'it's part of being human. So in that sense—yes, you are one too. But the thing is—when we admit what we have done and are sorry, then God just wipes sins away—'

Then she stops, quite suddenly, and I realize that she's looking at me in a particular way. Her dark eyes have settled on mine, where the pale lashes, like careless over-stitching, only just show against the skin. She has given up explaining and is just noticing and waiting for whatever might come next. Her gaze moves fractionally all the time, as if she is reading something very interesting written in tiny print on my face.

'So why?' I ask. 'Why does he just forgive everyone?' It makes everything sound like a waste of effort, somehow.

She ignores this and leans closer. I can hear her draw in breath.

'You know, I'm just like you, Natalie,' she says. Anyone she asked would tell her not to do what she's about to do, to think it through at least. But Barbara doesn't have or give herself (or want, even?) time to think. She lets her secret slip out whole, like one of those women you read about in magazines who go to the bathroom and give birth without knowing what they are doing; ignorant, even, of the pregnancy itself.

'I've got a sin, too.' She pauses, as if half-expecting, half-hoping for a question that will require her to continue. But although I say nothing, just wait, she continues anyway, explaining in a lowered voice that hers was a sin against God, the community, her husband and herself too. She swallows hard, leans forward, as if naming it were physically hard.



'I keep an image,' she says. Her voice is having to stretch itself around a lump in her throat. 'A photograph. I've never told anyone before,' she adds. Slowly, my face cracks open into a huge smile.

'So you see—' Then she just stops, startled-looking as if she has no idea what could follow. Perhaps she wants to say: 'Please don't tell anyone what I've said,' but to ask such a thing would, to her, seem almost worse than burdening me in the first place.

'What's in it?' I ask her. My voice bright, curious, as ever; I really don't know how important what she's said is and will be. 'What's in the photograph? What's it a picture of?'

'The baby girl,' she answers straight away, smiling now. 'I told you about her. The one who died.' She puts her face next to mine and whispers in my ear, all breath and tickle:

'Emma' is what I think she says. Then she pushes her lips together and shakes her head slowly from side to side: I know I'm not to ask anymore. She takes off her glasses; I try them on and laugh as the world swells, rushes inwards, pushing me to the ground. I lie there listening to the summer sounds of insects in grass; the faint trickle of the water; very distantly, the erratic hammering and shouts from the camp where the food tent is being erected.

Barbara sits next to me in a pale, blurred world. What must it be like to have said those words, even in the smallest of voices to a child who doesn't really understand them? To have told a secret and be unable to get it back—like waking up in hospital, knowing some part of her has gone forever: being radically altered by it but unable to complain since she made it happen; tearful, but at the same time relieved. Aware of her surroundings in a way she has not been for years; completely uncertain as to what difference the change will make.

From the direction of the camp comes a ragged cheer, signalling the successful erection of the tent. 'So—' she says, frowning, bringing the conversation back to its starting-point, as if this might somehow obscure what happened in the middle: 'I'll talk to Christina's mother, as soon as we get back.'

'Don't worry,' I tell her. 'I don't care what they think. Not when I'm with you, I don't.'

'I know it's all so very different from what you're used to,' she says, 'but I do want you to be happy here.'

'I am,' I say, and Barbara lies down next to me, puts her arm over her eyes. Drained by the stress and release of her admission, softened by the sun, she quickly falls asleep.

Bored, I make my way back to the camp. The newly erected food tent, sun-bleached green canvas with twin poles, a fringe at the bottom of the roof and an entranceway at each end, stands close to the gate towards the top of the field, where the ground is flatter. Most of the women and one or two men are inside it. Lower down, on a rather disabling slope, a children's cricket game, to be umpired by John Hern in a white shirt and straw hat, is about to start. I glimpse Mark by the far hedge and wave to him; he, of course, ignores me. Then, as I try to decide whether or not to join in, I see Christina, emerge, chewing and sticky-fingered, between two panels of the tent. Partly out of bravado and partly in order to test what will happen, I bite her on the arm as hard as I can.

Barbara would have woken, sweating, with the sun on her face. To begin with, she wouldn't have been able to think why she was there, lying in that field. Then she'd have remembered what had happened, what she had said. It would have taken her a few minutes to find her glasses, which I'd put carefully out of harm's way, on top of a large stone some feet away. And then, once she got her sight back, she could see that it was almost three o'clock.

She hurried, via the camp, to the meeting-field where she was supposed to be helping with tea. The tent was thick with the hum of women's voices. Three trestle tables had been set up along the middle, and a separate one for making tea and mixing squash. She stood next to Alice Cox, who, while buttering, explained in detail about the building of an extension to her house. Barbara spread egg mayonnaise on slices of bread, four at a time, pressed four more slices on top, cut them diagonally in half, piled them on the plate, took more slices. It was comforting. She jumped when Josie Gardner tapped on her arm: they must talk, Josie said, while the children were busy with the cricket match.



They sat on some spare benches by the inside wall of the tent, their faces ghostly in the greenish light that seeped through it. Josie kept her feet tucked under her skirt, her back straight. A fine gold chain, Barbara noticed, was, for part of its length, stuck inside a fold in the skin at the base of the other woman's neck.

Natalie, she said, coming straight to the point, had just bitten Christina on the arm. She pointed out the place on the inside of her own well-fleshed upper arm. Her brown eyes glittered. The bite, she said, leaning forwards and lowering her voice, drew blood. She sat straight again, her hands in the lap of her skirt, waiting.

'Why did she do it?' Barbara asked.

That was not really the point, Josie said.

Some of the children, Barbara said (aware dimly that she was enjoying saying it), including Christina, had been using their faith as a means to attack others.

'I want you to see,' Josie told her.

They went outside, shocked momentarily by the brilliant light, the sharp shadows. As the food tent had taken the flatter patch at the top of the field, the cricket was forced to take place on the more sloping part below, where the prayers had been held in the morning.

Barbara and Josie found us at opposite ends of a row waiting to bat. Christina pulled the plaster from over the mark on her arm, pointed out bloodstains on the gauze pad. I had come up behind her suddenly, she told them, when she was on her own, behind the tent. Her eyes, narrow under straight, fleshy brows, moved steadily from one adult to the other. In that respect, we were more alike than we would have liked to admit.

'You did it to yourself,' I said, carelessly, half-watching the game. 'That's why no one heard you scream: your mouth was full of arm. So you're a liar, and that's another sin on top of what there was before—'

Christina burst into tears. It was because I had said she was fat, she sobbed, by way of admitting that she had taunted me, burying her face in her mother's chest.

'Only after what you said,' I pointed out.

We must both, Josie said, apologize to each other and ask to be shown how to overcome our pride.

'I'm not sorry,' I said to Christina as soon as they were gone.

'I'm not either,' she said. Somehow this defiance bound us together and we stood awkwardly next to each other in the line.

'I hate games,' she told me a while later, as if she had completely forgotten that we were enemies.

'Oh dear,' Barbara said as they walked up the slope, 'oh dear. But it is funny, too.' Josie stopped a moment to get her breath back and tuck her bra strap in. To her mind, she said, it just went to show what a struggle it was to bring a child up, a thing most men had no idea of. But all the same, some were harder than others. Mark, for example, was a lovely boy, thoughtful and hard-working, respectful, sure in his faith. She could see him serving the congregation when he was older, perhaps even taking the long route through ordination and back. There was definitely something special, something of a Paul Leverson about him, even at this age. What mother could want more?



*Oh, Emma,* Barbara thought, as she pushed back into the food tent just in order to get away from the other woman, *my darling. . .* For while the small steel plaque said 'Ruth Hern, three months old,' and she had been happy enough with Ruth before, once the child had been laid to rest, the other name, the one she would have preferred, was the one that came to her. It was soft and simple in the mouth—Emma, Em—and because it belonged to no one else she knew, it could be just between the two of them. The simple syllables carried a feeling far in excess of the nameable facts: that her grip on a finger was even stronger than Barbara remembered Mark's being; that like him, she was a long baby, and that her round eyes, when she was in the mood to look, seemed particularly alert, the tiny beginnings of eyebrows arched high just like Barbara's own, and again, Mark's; that she cried determinedly for her milk, tended to snore at night—which was why as soon as she slept four hours at a time they put the cot across the landing in the back bedroom. But truly, she gave no sign that in the small hours of a Tuesday morning she would simply stop breathing, leaving behind her a terrible silence that woke Barbara, so that she sat bolt upright, listening, then hurried across the landing, twelve steps. There was no sign. There was no sign that her lungs were not properly formed, no sign that she would not just keep growing into herself, even less sign that she would be, as it had turned out, Barbara's last child. Em, what she was, what she might have been. Born May, died September, gone.

She stood for a while until her eyes adjusted. Plates of food had been covered with tea cloths. There was an overwhelming smell of bread and hard-boiled eggs. Most of the helpers had disappeared. She was about to leave herself, when Anna Herrick called out: 'Could you be a dear and cut some cakes up, sixteen pieces from each?'

In the late afternoon she shows me in slow motion how to slip the knitting needle in, carry round, slip off. The important thing is to keep the wool moving steadily over your fingers, not to let it drop, not to pull on it, not really look at it too much, just feel it there and keep track of it with the back of your mind. That way the tension stays the same, and your edges come straight, which is just as important for a six-inch blanket square as it is for a pullover. The people getting the blanket might not notice wavy edges, but then again they might, and there was no reason why they should have second best—

'Barbara,' I interrupt, 'can I ask something?'

'What sort of thing? Well actually, no,' she says. 'I'd rather you didn't, sweetheart, not now—'

'All right,' I tell her. I wanted to know who it was who took the photograph of the dead little girl, but it can wait.

'I don't mind,' I say. The white cardigan she's just started, she says is for me, if I want it.

'I really do!' I say, two rows done, bent double over my needles, the pink thread extra bright in the shadow of my lap.

Later, John washes down using a face flannel and the pale-blue plastic bowl on the table outside the van. Whatever have I done? she thinks, watching him dip the flannel in, squeeze it out, rubbing it over his neck, behind his ears, while he relays the afternoon's news.

Mark got a half century right at the end. Now he's gone somewhere quiet to consider tomorrow's text, he tells her.

Natalie's helping with supper, she says.

He tips out the water, wrings the flannel, pulls the yellow towel from its drying place over the stable door. A shame about this morning, he says, smiling over to where Barbara sits. She's tanning quickly. Her hair is looser than normal, her blouse the worse for a day's wear, her bare feet have grubby soles. She smiles back at him, just as usual. Perhaps it's a rather small smile, but certainly John doesn't sense that his wife has, since this morning, changed: that as she looks back at him she is asking herself which thing, of those she has done wrong, would matter to him most, if he knew.



He comes over to her, squats on the ground by the chair, kisses her lap, offers his hair and the back of his neck to rub. Why not go inside now? he suggests.

While he pulls out the bed, she tugs the curtains closed, puts the latch on the door, then steps out of her dress and hangs it on the hook fixed by the door. Half-clothed, they lie next to each other on top of the covers and stroke and kiss the uncovered parts of each other's bodies.

'I love you, John,' she tells him. She bites, as he likes her to, softly into the muscle between his shoulders and neck. They kiss mouth to mouth and she pushes her lips almost painfully onto his and her tongue deep inside; she presses the whole of her body against his. But when he is naked and makes to take off her brassiere and pants, she shakes her head, separates herself abruptly from him, and lies a foot or so away, looking at him as if she was seeing him for the first or the last time. It is very quiet inside the caravan now, just the sound of breathing, and impossible for him not to see that something is different.

'What is it?' he asks. She watches him watch her slowly shrink, feels her own damp skin grow cool.

How absurd, she thinks—so much thinking, where before there had been none, just the forbidden action, performed in a space of its own, completely separate from the rest of life—How absurd to feel like this, now, after all this time.

Before she spoke it, the secret lay almost peacefully inside her. It was there for her to visit, with due precaution, when she chose. Now it is opposing her; it is trying to tell her what to do. It is making clear that from now on, there will be a price for disobedience. What do I want most? she is thinking. What will happen—suppose I—

'John,' she says, softly.

'Yes?' His eyes shine out of the shadows. She reaches for his hand. There is a kind of peace in the tiny room; she doesn't want to spoil it.

The sun sets behind the hills in a lengthy and spectacular display. We carry rugs and cushions and go to the field by the stream again. I help to serve the food and to clear up. A petition about the passports comes around on a clipboard, with its own pen attached. Barbara watches John test the pen on a corner of the page, sign, then carefully print his name, occupation and address. She writes her own name quickly in rushing rounded script, beneath his small but perfect italics.

'Five pages already!' she says cheerfully as she hands the clipboard on to Pete Anderton to keep for his mother Elsbeth, who has a mouthful of apple and both hands full of stacked cups. 'There must be over a hundred there.'

The boy, his twin brother standing behind him like a shadow, catches my eye, and winks. Then he asks, solemn-faced, in a parody of eager curiosity:

'What do you think the government will decide, Mr. and Mrs. Hern? Upset us—or break with the UN?'

Mark looks up, momentarily, from his book. The point, John insists angrily to the twins' backs, is not what they do, but what we do—

'Surely you see that? I'm talking to you—' he calls out after the twins as they vanish into the dusk. Already the congregation is falling quiet in anticipation of the music.

My head hurts, I tell Barbara. She kisses me on the cheek, squeezes me close, sends me to bed.

The shapes of the land and the branches of trees are black against a violet sky. I wander back through the site, examining the variously shaped Vanguards and Princesses and Imps and Minxes, the newer Cortinas and Wolseleys which gleam darkly beside their paler-coloured caravans and tents, some lit from within, others blank. In our corner by the hedge, I clean my teeth using Barbara's brush, spit the water out onto black-seeming grass.

Inside, the caravan is ready for sleeping. I take off my blouse and pull on the too-big borrowed pyjama top, then turn the radio on and sit, half-listening, on Mark's bed. At last, I climb up. My bed, halfway between bunk and hammock, shifts as I get in, bangs softly against the rear wall of the caravan. I lie on my back with my eyes wide open in the dark and wonder whether you have to be sorry to the person you hurt, or just to God? Suppose it was yes, and suppose you were sorry, but couldn't find or tell them—would that matter or is wanting to good enough? Does the person you hurt forgive you, as well as God? Is it their sin if they don't? But then, how would you ever know, if a person said they were sorry, that they really meant it? What happens if you hurt someone without meaning to?

I let the questions pass through me, enjoying them without trying to find answers, and then I drift into wanting things. How I want, when we get back, to sleep in the pretty pink and apple-green bedroom, the one with the plants, at the back of the Herns' house, and to come down in the morning for breakfast around the table in the kitchen, to sit next to

Barbara, taking up that fourth chair. I want Mark to smile at me. I want Sandra, somehow, as in a dream, to be passing, see us, knock and ask if she could please come in? 'Yes, Mum,' I want to say, 'please do—sit here, next to me.'

I want to always have my hair tidy. I want a cupboard, and in it a tin full of almond biscuits, another of cake. I want to be loved so much that I can be forgiven for anything I might ever do, to anyone, ever, however bad it is. I want to have a wedding. I want new shoes, a white cardigan; I want to see the men walk on the moon.

# 19



At the top of the valley, about a mile across country from the site, is a stone house belonging to a couple called Edward and Angela Baines. He is eighty-six, she seventy-nine and all but blind. They're in their dressing-gowns, his worn plaid, hers pink candlewick, quite new; they hold a small tumbler of whisky apiece and sit in winged, pond-coloured armchairs as old as the marriage itself. A television set (Baird, 1968, bought from savings earlier in the year, its screen fully twelve inches across) casts thin greenish light around the small, dusty living-room. The light reflects from Edward's spectacles, loses itself in Angela's cataract-clouded eyes. A brass carriage clock ticks respectfully on the mantelpiece; there's also an alarm clock, wound and set just in case, on the table at Angie's side. A framed photograph on the wall, taken on their week's honeymoon, shows them as they were, on a windy day sixty years ago. Angela's once fine blonde hair has for years been leaving itself on chair backs, pillows, cardigans and refusing to grow. Now it's all but gone and her pert face has melted, grown larger and less defined. Edward's cheeks have hollowed out and his forehead is sectioned like rock.

They hold hands often. Soon, one of them will be alone, for a short, probably terrible period of time: they know this, but it is at the same time unimaginable; they save shared moments against it the way they once put small sums of money in the bank; and staying up like this, because Edward wanted to, is one of them. Neither of them expected to live to be this old, let alone to be in a world which sends men to travel beyond the reach of the earth's atmosphere to make footprints on the moon itself.

A man, six inches high on the screen, talks in front of them about something scientific, and they are trying to remember the name of a male friend of their granddaughter's, mentioned in her last letter on thin blue air-mail paper, upstairs, too far to get. The name eludes them both and they sit waiting, following separate thoughts beginning from this same point and bound, eventually, to come again to some other similar point—then Angie hears something outside, sends Edward to look and he brings me in.

I've been watching through the window, I tell them, for the last twenty minutes. 'You haven't pulled your curtains,' I explain. 'There isn't any television on the campsite. It's not allowed.' I am very quiet and polite. It's this, perhaps, along with the half-light and generally extraordinary circumstances that makes my appearing unaccompanied like this in the small hours seem less odd to them than it otherwise might.

'She'll come to no harm here,' Angie says. Ed shows me to a footstool and I say thank you, and sit down on it, in front of them, close to the television. We see the outside of the lunar module, a hole on the underside from which emerges a human being, Armstrong, in a huge top-heavy space suit.

'Coming out now,' Ed informs his wife, as Armstrong's booted feet descend nine rungs of the ladder, and tread, at last, on the moon.

'He says it's a small step but a giant leap for mankind,' Ed says.

'It's like fine, powdered charcoal. I can see my footprints,' Armstrong says.

'He's on it. It's just grey. He's got a camera. He's digging. It's in his pocket. Now the other one's coming out . . .' I sit silently, the end of my plait in my mouth. Aldrin comes down next. The pictures are grainy, blurred around the edges, too black sometimes, but still amazing. There are rocks of every kind, they say, dust. There is a low kind of hill in the distance. The astronauts practise their loping walk, try to run. They kick the moon dust and watch it rise and settle in soft, neat unison around their feet. They plant the American flag, begin their experiments, talk to their president on the telephone. They stand still for minute after inexplicable minute, inspecting the outside of their craft.

Angela is asleep, her breath rattling steadily in her throat.

'When you are our age,' Ed says suddenly, 'people will be living up there. There'll be factories and stations for the spaceships to go farther out. Exploration of the universe. What d'you think?' I just look back at him but say nothing. 'You wait and see!' Ed puts his glass down, then forgets I'm there and joins Angela in sleep. I keep on watching until the astronauts climb back into the lunar module, leaving their overshoes behind them in case of germs.



It's light outside now. I go into their kitchen and examine the tins and jars on their shelves, wondering whether there is anything I can eat. I decide against it, just inhale the smell of lemons, tea and uncleaned oven, then push quietly out through the unlocked back door.

Everything is different in the dawn light. It's hard to decide which of the fields ahead of me I cut across just hours ago when it was dark. I guess and set off around the edge of the one I've chosen at a fast walk. I think about the moon, and hope there won't be factories or stations up there, making it just like everywhere else. And I hope the Americans don't go there again, or the Russians either, or anyone else. Even if I could go there myself, I wouldn't, not now. The first time is always the best. And I saw it, that's the thing.

I climb over a stile into another field. It's far later than I expected. I pull the sweater off, tie it around my waist, break into a run. I still believe that I'll just about make it back before anyone wakes up and notices me gone, that I'll be able to slip back into bed and lie there remembering what I have seen.

But at 3 o'clock, sunk in a shocking, wonderful dream, a fabulous beast that escaped him even as he tried to grasp its tail, Mark heard his mother calling his name, as from a great distance. She was standing over him, wearing wellington boots, an anorak over her nightdress. 'Mark—get up and put some things on. Natalie's gone!' she said. 'You've got to help.' Cool night air flooded in through the open door, lapping at his skin. The caravan rocked with the movements and sounds his father made finding clothes, struggling into his shoes in the half-light of the kerosene lamp.

Mark raised his hand and pushed at the underside of the canvas bunk above him; it was indeed empty.

'I've looked in the toilets and the barn. She's taken your father's pullover—' Barbara held up pyjamas, a cast-off skin, threw them back on the bunk. 'It's after three. I've been up half an hour. We've got to find her, so hurry, Mark, will you now.' Her voice was too big for the thinly walled room. 'I'll wake the Andertons. The boys are old enough to come too. Write her a note, in case—' Noticing a half-dry stickiness on his stomach and groin, Mark eased out of his bunk, his limbs fuddled, weak.

Equipped with a torch, he joined the search party in the second, higher field, to the left of Harris's farmhouse.

'Now, where shall we begin?' one of the Anderton twins, probably Peter, asked his twin in a falsely bright voice. In the dark, a brief, mocking smile echoed between them. They stood so close together that they appeared to be actually joined. Their shoulders sloped unathletically, their hands were sunk into their pockets, their faces, with eyebrows like a child's drawing of flying birds, were only just visible beneath the rabbit-fur trim of their parka hoods. They smelled of something Mark didn't recognize, and when he acknowledged them with a nod, their eyes passed, unseeing, over him.

'We must think carefully where she might have gone,' their father said.

'She was with us most of the day,' Barbara explained, 'with me. . . There was a problem with Christina, but I really don't think—'

'Do you know anything, Mark?' Anderton asked, gravely.

'He's not speaking,' Barbara reminded everyone.

'Has anyone else disappeared?' Anderton asked, maddeningly, pointlessly, for surely he can see it is something they can't know without waking the whole site to check. Generally, Mark thought, people just speak too much, without thinking. A waste of time. But his own lips were sealed, like the neck of a jar, with cork and wax. 

They followed his mother up the hill. He brought up the rear.

'Natalie, Natalie!' she was calling, using different intonations and stresses and expressions. She was by turns imperious, pleading, seductive, matter-of-fact—as if it were just a matter of saying the name in the right way: 'Natalie. . . Natalie! Natalie!'

They cast their torch beams around them, picking out in sudden detail hedges and standing cattle, a clump of trees, a drinking-trough and salt-lick. Beyond these things, the darkness grew darker, expanded.

It could still be a dream, he thought. But the chill of a predawn breeze pushed its way between his hastily fastened clothes and his skin, and the insides of his boots were gritty and damp. He wished he had put socks on.

'Is she homesick?' asked Elsbeth Anderton. Her voice was small, especially compared to her husband's chesty rumble, but she strained it to its limits, coming hoarsely and urgently out of silence without preamble, snatching her place in the conversation.

'She's happy to be with us. And anyway, wouldn't she wait until morning? She must know that we wouldn't stop her, that we'd—she wouldn't just leave—' Barbara resumed her calling: 'Natalie! Natalie!'

In the thin starlight they could see only the broad low shapes of the land, the distinction between it and the sky. Solitary strands of early birdsong gathered briefly together in clusters, then fell shyly silent. Small winds shifted through the crops and trees, expired, renewed themselves elsewhere.

Mark switched off his torch. The rubber-covered button resisted the pressure of his thumb, then did the job silently, without seeming to. He looked down at the land below, feeling the landscape with his eyes. The longer he looked, the more detail he could see. The well-spaced caravans and tents, the huge marquee glimmered in the darkness like some strange geological formation. He made out the large tree towards the bottom of the meeting-field. Beyond, at the far side of the valley, he could make out the scattered houses of a village. There were lights on in some of them.

'Perhaps she went into someone else's van,' said one of the twins.

'What do you mean?' Elsbeth snapped.

'I don't know—' Pete or his brother said. 'Well, it is something that happens, you know.' One of the huddle of cows pressed against the far fence lowed; the twins burst into laughter, then stifled it.

Mark's father caught up with Barbara and brought her gently back to the rest.

'There's no point in just wandering about,' he said. Mark sat down on a large stone a few feet away from the rest of them. He remembered how only hours ago Natalie had followed him from task to task, grabbing his arm. 'Talk to me, Mark, now go on . . .' It had been sweet to be able, at last, to deny her. In the past months he had so often wished, hopelessly, that she would disappear. But now it had happened he wanted her to be found. It was not right that she should escape from him, from all of them, like this, leaving them standing roughly dressed in a field at night, not finishing whatever it is that she'd begun with them. And he didn't really believe that she had gone, or would go. From the strength of that disbelief came the notion that if he allowed it, the knowledge of where she was would come running to him, like an eager dog. But what then? What would or should he do?

'Suppose we divide it up,' his father was saying. 'Suppose the twins go along the river and you two go on up the path, and Mark—'

'John,' Elsbeth interrupted, 'there's no point. We've got to phone the police. That's what you do when someone is missing. They will know better what to do than we do.' There was a brief, shocked silence.



'But Elsbeth,' Mark heard his mother say, her throat constricted, all the earlier authority vanishing from her voice, 'I don't know her mother very well. I'd hate her to be unnecessarily alarmed. To have a policeman turn up on the door—if it's going to turn out to be all right in the end—well, surely you see?'

'But is it going to turn out all right in the end?' Elsbeth asked. Her torch was still on; she shone it straight in Barbara's face, blinding her briefly, then gestured with it, spilling the light over chests and hands, suddenly singling out a shoe. 'If something has happened to her, we'd only reproach ourselves—'

'Stop that, please,' she said to the twins, who were kicking in turns at the same stone.

'The police,' Anderton pointed out, 'may have found her already—' The party stood for a moment in horrified silence, considering the full range of meanings contained in that one possibility: Natalie, wearing John's maroon hand-knitted jumper three times her size, picked up in the course of some prank or other and sitting now in the police station at Filey, drinking strong, sweet tea while they worked out where she had come from. Natalie, still at the police station, calmly explaining that she has taken up with a group of religious fanatics, regrets it and wants to be sent home. Natalie, still in the police station, shivering, mud-stained, minus the sweater, huddled speechless in a blanket... Natalie, lying under a bush or by the roadside or in a stretcher or on a hospital bed, with a policeman standing by...

Mark looked out across the darkness to the other side of the valley, and knew in his bones that none of these things was true. They were phantoms, mere possibilities which Natalie cast around herself like a shield... But he couldn't tell the others this, stop them panicking, because of his silence. The silence, ostensibly for spiritual preparation, was at least as much a protection against Natalie. So far it had worked, but now—

What should I do? He asked God.

'If we're agreed,' his father began, addressing the Andertons, 'Barbara and I will go now and check the site one last time. If she's not there, then we'll telephone from the farm—' Barbara, too tall to lean on her husband, stood next to him like some abandoned building, he, arm around her waist, the buttress.

'I'm so sorry—' she said, abjectly, and a pulse pushed through Mark, locked his shoulders and chest tight. Yes: it is all your fault, he thought, but it's even worse that you apologize for yourself like this, to Elsbeth Anderton, for the wrong thing.

'We'll have to postpone Service, won't we?' Elsbeth said. 'Such a shame for you, Mark, I know, and for all of us, of course. We must let everyone know what's going on. Simon and I can do that—'

'Actually,' Mark said, 'I know where she is—' and the huddle of faces turned to look at him. 'Well, not exactly, but there's nothing to worry about. She'll have gone where she can see the moonwalk on television, won't she?'

'Of course!' his mother re-materialized, neither commanding nor terrified now, but simply herself. She looked around at the others, as if expecting to see the pleasure that she felt on their faces too. But Elsbeth's forehead was in furrows, her pale eyebrows tense and prominent.

'Would she do a thing like that?'

'She just doesn't quite understand, yet.'

'It's only a guess. You should still call—'

'I'm sure Mark is right.' Barbara's tone was almost insolent.

'If she's found, she should be sent home,' said Anderton. 'This is no place for someone committed to sin.'



'Exactly,' Elsbeth said.

'But—'

'It can all be discussed later on, in the proper place,' Mark's father said, as they set off back towards the site. Around them, fields and trees emerged minute by minute from degrees of darkness into a textured monotone, faintly washed with colour. They could see mud on their clothes. The skin around their eyes felt tight.

*I'm sure Mark is right,* Pete Anderton said at the last gate, in an exaggeratedly feminine gush.

'You spoke,' his brother Tim told Mark.

'Yes,' said Peter, 'you most certainly did.' Mark shrugged his shoulders, opened his hands, forgave them.

Back at the caravan Barbara began to fill the kettle from the outside water bottle, then abandoned the task and pulled Mark tightly to her, water gurgling wastefully onto the grass:

'I've only just realized. Your silence. Thank you so much, darling.'

'Didn't I warn you, right from the start?' he muttered into her shoulder. The usual traces of soapiness had gone from her scent; she smelled salty, rather like his own skin. He pushed her away and set off for the meeting field.



Now, Mark has carried all the chairs to the meeting-field. The dew has burned away and he's sweating hard. He takes his shirt off and hangs it on an elder twig next to the jacket he put there earlier. A breeze carries the smell of toast or frying bacon from the site. He can hear some children's voices and the clatter of cutlery from beyond the hedge.

He decides on a position close to the west of the field for the table, so that the congregation will not have the sun in their eyes, and then returns to arrange the assorted picnic and deck chairs in concentric curves to face it, with some milk crates at the front for the children. Then he goes back again to the site to get a spade, for it's obvious now that on the day of the Moon Walk the object of contemplation must be earth, a shovel full of a rich, slightly pinkish soil taken from the very field they would all be sitting in. The ground is dry and hard to dig, but by going deep he gets a neat slab, stones, roots, grubs and all. The table is ready and he stands with his back to it, looking out.

It's a good place. The colours of the fabrics of the chairs—plain, broadly striped, canvas or plastic weave, even the whites and faded colours—sing out against the rich green of the grass, as vividly as the yellow cowslips and purple clover that dot the untrampled area higher up. Mark's limbs ache pleasantly from hard work; his sweat stings satisfyingly somehow, in the tiny bramble scratches on his arms. He screws his eyes closed, lets the red light behind them fill his head so that the last traces of school, the remainder of the holidays, the entire rest of his life, cricket, the new bicycle he's intending to build, drop clear away from him... He is following a path that leads to the Kingdom of Heaven on Earth in the Here and Now, given by God out of Love as explained in the Bible, then reinterpreted and properly explained by Tuomas Envall. . . He breathes in slowly and carefully, making himself ready.

When the call comes for Service, Barbara is talking to Mrs. Thorn by the food tent, so she has to sit at the end of the eight brown-haired Gardners, on the edge of the third row, whilst John is right at the front.

Facing them all, Mark stands with the sun on his face and the book ready on the lectern. He stands straight and firm, a huge child now, almost a man, but Barbara cannot keep looking at him nor at the pile of earth on the wooden table, nor at the candles burning invisibly in their glasses, because Natalie still has not returned. Her eyes search the distance, then fix themselves on parts of it, on some rooks pecking at the ground farther up the hill, or the way the heat shimmers on the horizon, or on the yellow tractor slowly coming down the side of a distant field. The tractor sometimes disappears or stops at a gate. It is just a blob of colour but very bright, shining out; she looks at the way the sun strikes the yellow paint, and the way the shadow behind makes it brighter still, and part of her wishes to be on it, or in the aeroplane that has passed unnoticed but has left a white trail in the sky, in some other life but this one—



Her thoughts circle uselessly around the same few matters, in the hope of avoiding those things that are worse to think about, round and round like the small reddish flies that seem to be attracted to her, to her alone, that collect above her head as if there was something about her that they know: that she has not consulted enough and has brought a complete unbeliever with her, a strange girl, to whom she has told a secret that no one else knows, which she has never confessed and even now, will not, cannot stand up and speak of, even though the silence yearns for her to do so. That sometimes it seems as if she loves the strange girl more than she loves her own son; that she has dragged the Andertons out of their beds in the middle of the night to look for this girl who has still not returned—

It's better by far to think of the hundred cutlets, sixty meat and forty nut, not to be cooked in the same pan, but all at once on different stoves, how they must be ready at near enough the same time; the salad already washed and wrapped in cloths, the bread just needing to be cut and buttered, and of course everyone will help with carrying the plates and so on—

Her pulse runs away with her and the sun's on the back of her head and neck. The silence expands, it's as if she has been cast into it, some terrible boundless space with nothing in it at all, except the feeling of fear that fills her up—

Then her son stands, begins to read the Sermon on the Mount, Matthew chapter 6—the whole chapter, as has been agreed. He's reading well, slow and loud. He has practised; the words, in any case familiar, come without his needing to look down: 'But lay up for yourselves treasures in heaven, where neither moth nor rust doth corrupt, and where thieves do not break through nor steal—'

These words are not for her... Or else they are there for her in particular: 'For where your treasure is, there will your heart be also—'

Her ears reject the words just as her eyes did the trestle table and the pile of dirt on it, just as her whole body did the Silence. 'The light of the body is the eye ...' One of the ginger-brown flies, red-eyed, repulsive, settles on her arm and she forces herself to watch it rub its legs. She watches and wills it to go away, because if it does go, she tells herself, everything will be all right. It goes. Everything is not all right. The fly settles again, she brushes it off, another comes—

'If thine eye be evil,' Mark reads out, 'thy whole body shall—' My whole body, she thinks, is full of darkness. She sees the back of her husband's head and his shoulders, often tight with the unarticulated efforts of living, but now relaxed. His hands will be in his lap, his eyes closed over, the jaw she shaved for him still bright white against the tan of the rest of his face, loose. He is not with her, but with the text: 'No man can serve two masters . . .' Can a woman? The Lord is there in times of trouble, John always says to her, He will draw you out of the waters; everything passes, listen and He will tell you—'Heaven and earth shall pass away but my words shall not pass away.' That was what he said to her when she wept and wept and wished she could cry herself to nothing, to die of it. He held her tight, but that was what he said. No miracle, no resurrection, no 'she is not dead but sleepeth,' no 'for with God, nothing shall be impossible.' And now the other girl gone—and it is her fault. She should have known. If she'd thought of it she could have said something—



The yellow tractor, which had disappeared, emerges from behind the hedge of a nearby field; amidst the other sounds around her Barbara finds the soft beat of its engine and holds onto it, a thing not words, not even sound, something like touch.

Mark steps forward. His mouth moistens, just as it did when he first spoke in the meeting all those weeks ago. He closes his eyes.

'This is about the nature of faith,' he tells them, 'and the ways to it.' His left leg begins to vibrate, an invisible movement that nonetheless shakes the whole of him, even his voice, but he goes on: 'The disciples are told that they must go far beyond what they ever thought was required of them, and that most importantly of all, they cannot serve two masters at once. No more, of course, can we—'

He's slippery with sweat but his voice is steadying and the words follow each other out of his mouth, eager but orderly enough. More wait inside him. He can feel them jostle each other, trying themselves out. He squints against the light and waits for them to be ready. He looks into the faces that are looking at him. Even though he feels the chapter is relevant to it, he does not want to talk about the Island, but rather about what lies beneath the desire for it.

'Envall says Faith is a paradox. An inner knowledge of something that cannot be proven except by our knowing of it. Not a knowing about, but a knowing with. That's how he puts it in the Explanations. The means to faith are also its ends. We are being told here about how to open our hearts—' The words begin to ignore whatever has been in charge of them, to make their own way through Mark, gathering silence about themselves, shaping his throat and lips and the pace of his breathing to suit their own rhythm.

'Just a whisper, a hair's breadth, separates faith from its opposite. Remember Saul. From inside it's clear, from outside it's not. Faith is absolute. Utter. Extreme. Demanding. It sets us apart from the ordinary laws and customs of our times. But it is also generous—'

The steady rhythm outside of him which Mark has been half-hearing misses a beat, then stops. He glances to his left and sees the yellow tractor rolling, oddly silent now, down the lane. The words lose direction, scatter. Everyone else is looking too, as the tractor rolls on down past the farmhouse track, spits out something half explosion, half mechanical cough, picks up its rhythm again. It keeps on coming and drives right into the top end of the meeting-field. It comes on down towards them as if it means to run them down, then stops ten feet away from the front row. Harris gets out of one side and I, in my jeans and yellow blouse with John's maroon pullover bundled under my arm, slide down the other.

'Got lost coming back from Saxby,' Harris shouts over the engine, pushing me forwards. Barbara rushes over, hugs me.

'Well, there y'are,' says Harris. No one thinks to thank him. He reverses the tractor, sets off up the slope. The smell of diesel lingers, heady, unsettling.

‘Sit down, please, Natalie, Barbara. Go on, Mark.’ John gestures as he speaks, pointing where we should go as if he were a lollipop man inviting us to cross a difficult road. Barbara and I ignore him, but his voice is brisk and business-like and, for a few moments, it almost seems as if it might be possible to push on past the interruption, as if it had never happened: the seated congregation wait, to see if Mark can perform this feat for them, pick them up where he left off and take them where they were going, as a pilot or a sea captain might steer his passengers around the blustery edges of a disaster and out into the clear blue beyond. But he is only fourteen. It defeats him; he shakes his head and sits slowly down on the wooden chair behind him, checking first that it is still there.

The entire congregation are looking at me now. I look straight back at all of them and my voice bristles with the pleasure of each extraordinary word.



‘I saw the astronauts walking on the moon!’ I tell them. I do know they won’t like it, but I say it all the same—‘I saw it on TV!’

There’s a short, intense silence, then voices erupt. Barbara, appearing from nowhere, takes me in her arms.

‘I was planning to be back before you woke up,’ I tell her; she bursts into tears. Her own suffering has vanished in the relief she feels, but she’ll never forget the sight of Mark, as he sat down on the chair in the field, suddenly becoming a boy again, then a child—

‘I’m sorry,’ I mumble as Anderton gets to his feet, grasps the chair in front of him and bellows out above the rest:

‘Why is this child here?’

‘Because—’ Barbara begins but flounders in the sudden silence.

‘Why?’ Anderton repeats, his colour deepening.

‘Please—stop this,’ says Mrs. Thorn, sitting there in her usual smart skirt, her carefully ironed and packed blouse with the two top buttons undone, the exposed skin blotched and damp. 'Are we or are we not holding Service? Are we going to render unto the Lord what is due to Him, or is this suddenly beyond us?'

Thwaite steps forward then. 'Service is postponed,' he says. 'If everyone goes away and cools down, if we come back at eleven, say, then, perhaps, we can talk this all through—'

It's agreed. The congregation parts around us as it makes its way back to the other field.

'I don't want to come back,' I tell Barbara.

'It'll be all right,' she reassures me, 'you'll see.'

How does she know? I'm the one who started all this, though I wish I hadn't, and I've no idea how it goes from here.

# 20

Back at the caravan, I sit almost in the hedge, head in hands, and wait for someone to start shouting. But no one does: Barbara seems almost cheerful. She washes her face and puts on a short-sleeved blouse, big-collared, pink with white buttons, then bustles pointlessly about. Mark just lies on his back on the scuffed patch of ground in front of the caravan, looking up at the sky. At one point he laughs, then he goes back to looking. Mr. Hern sits in a deckchair, his eyes closed, frowning. 

'We'll be needing milk,' Barbara announces. Mark sits up.

'I'll go.'

'It's my job on the rota,' she tells him. 'Actually, I want the walk.'

'What about me?' I say quietly. 'Can I—'

In the end all four of us set out to get twenty pints for teatime, some sort of expiation, perhaps, for the trouble we've caused. We make our way through the site in a tight group, winding our way around guy ropes and ducking under washing lines, aware all the time of being observed. All of a sudden it feels oddly as if we are something like a family.

'Getting the milk—' Barbara explains to a small gathering of women filling water-bottles at the gate tap. One of them smiles and nods, but the others look past us. Barbara seems to respond to this by standing straighter, and looking back harder.

In the lane, the dusty scent of the cow parsley is undercut with calm, sweet honeysuckle, and the tall hedges make a deep groove of shade, protecting us from observation and the heat alike. By common consent, we slow our pace.

'I'm sorry,' I say, experimentally. 'I am sorry for causing so much trouble.' Am I forgiven? At any rate, it feels quite good to say it like this.

'Thank you, Natalie,' Barbara replies. 'I do know you didn't mean it to happen. But I wish you had told us what you wanted to do.'

Supposing I had, though, what would she have done? I don't ask her that, nor of course do I mention the photograph she told me about—everything here is hanging together by the finest, most frayed of threads, breakable with the slightest extra strain. At the same time, no one is acting that way.

'And I'm sorry, Mark,' I add for good measure, 'that I spoiled your speech.'

'Mark—' Barbara prompts gently.

He inclines his head without looking up.

'It's out of my hands,' he says.

A painted notice tells us to close the gate, a new aluminium one, behind us. There's a distant bickering of chickens, though none are visible and neither can we see the dog barking itself into a frenzy somewhere not far away. The track ground deep by the passage of huge wheels, intermittently cindered, takes us to an open barn with a corrugated roof where the yellow tractor from this morning is parked at a slant. There are several other outhouses, and some long, low sheds. The farmhouse itself is a mixture of old and new, with recently painted blue woodwork. Avoiding the gleaming front door, we follow the concrete flagged path around the side, where a single-storey extension, invisible from the front, projects back onto some levelled ground. It gives onto a large paved area, fenced around with blue-painted picket. There's an empty rotary clothes drier; a row of potted herbs and some tomato plants in grow-bags stand alongside the building. The second of two half-glazed doors is hooked open and music drifts out from somewhere deep inside the house. We knock and peer in at a vast number of egg trays piled up on a large table.

'While we're here, perhaps we could phone your mother,' Barbara suggests; I tell her I tried yesterday and the phone at home still wasn't working.

Eventually a woman comes to the door, wearing tight jeans and a huge man's shirt, nothing on her feet. She has very blue eyes, pale skin and hair that had been dyed pure black, and cut into a fringed bob. There's a bright gold ring on her wedding finger. She examines us, her expression somewhere between curious and amused, nodding sharply all the while to the relentless four-four beat of the music behind her. Harris is coming shortly, she says. Thirsty weather then? she asks. When Harris lumbers into the kitchen, shadowy and huge, she goes away again. The music gets louder, becomes a frenzy of drumming, and then stops abruptly on a low note.



'You again!' Harris says, grinning and jabbing at me with his huge finger.

He leads us across a mud-and-straw yard into a stone-built shed. He has bottled milk; most people prefer it nowadays. He opens a fridge door and gestures at the rows of bottles gleaming dully in the light inside.

'Take it from the top left. Everything all right down there? Got what you need?' Harris sits heavily on an upturned crate, yawns. He has been up since five, cutting hay and finding lost children.

'It's a lovely site,' Barbara says. Somehow, I can't get her to look at me.

'So,' Harris says, rubbing his hand swiftly over his palely stubbled jaw, 'I hear you don't hold with the TV?' John Hern just smiles. He reaches up for the bottles, slipping them two at a time into their compartments.

'I don't have one either,' Harris continues cheerfully. 'I'm holding out. Look at the cost of it, and the time it wastes: you lose twice over. I say to Belinda, if you've got spare time, I can think of something a sight better to do! I suppose it's hard on the kids—' He gestures sideways with his head towards where I am sitting on a crate. 'What do you get out of it, though?'

John puts the two bottles he has been holding down on the dirt floor. He screws his eyes shut for a moment. Harris watches all this, interested.

'God's Grace,' John finally says, looking directly at Harris, his face open, mobile. 'Peace. Confidence. Passion.' A sweet, almost childish smile lights up his face, as if the thing he has spoken of is passing through him right now.

The smell of damp stone in the shed is oddly soothing. There's not much to see in the shadowy light: a pile of empty sacks, a hay fork, some stainless-steel dog bowls crusted with left-over food. We look instead at each other. Mark is leaning against the wall, sucking on a piece of straw. Barbara is standing still, her hands relaxed at her side.

'I don't believe in anything except hard work,' Harris says after a moment or two. He gets up, stretches. 'I have the hippies down here in August, they come from all over, and that's what they want too, heaven on earth, as they see it, music all day and free love all night, and the drugs, of course. Terrible mess at the end of it—mind you, they pay and they come back every year.'

'I have some books with me—' John says.

'I'm not a reader,' Harris tells him. He gets to his feet, offering his huge slab of a hand all around.

Mark and Barbara take one crate, John and I follow with the other, an arrangement dictated by our heights.

'Can I see the books?' I ask John as we leave the farm.

'Of course,' he says. 'Of course you can, Natalie.' The crate bangs into the side of my leg; when I try to hold it away, my shoulder hurts.

We walk past the women left in charge of the younger children, who can't be expected to sit the meeting out: Alison, a thin girl from Berwick, who wears a woollen pullover even in the heat, Gail Vickers, Julia Jowett, who is feeding her new baby. Gail's much younger sister Caroline, pregnant, is in the awning of the food tent, her swollen feet in a bowl of tepid water flecked with grass seed. We put some bottles in the cooling bucket at the back of the tent; they nod their thanks, then glance back at each other—clearly we are the subject of their conversation.

From lower down the field comes the sound of unorganized discussion, a varying density of voices. In the move downhill many people have abandoned chairs in favour of blankets and cushions, so that informal rows of these are broken by the few occasional chairs, with gaps behind. It's the older people, mainly, who have stuck with the chairs, positioning them farther apart than they were before, as if in some vain attempt to encourage a breeze to spring up and circulate between them. Some have shades or small umbrellas that clip onto the framework of their chairs. Anna Herrick stands out wearing a simple shirt-waist dress in a colour somewhere between violet and blue. Mrs. Thorn has changed out of her Service blouse into a sleeveless top, and she's put on some large sunglasses with white plastic rims. Timothy and Peter's grandparents, the Andertons senior, have identical panama hats and seem for a brief moment almost to be twins themselves.

Anthony Thwaite, fresh-faced and dressed in khaki shorts and a white shirt, stands at the front, taking on, by virtue of his role in organizing the camp, a semi-official, chairman-like role. Athletic and energetic, he seems to be enjoying it.

Periodically he dives into the audience to note some question or requirement, or solve a minor practical problem such as the support of a sunshade, the steadying of chairs on uneven ground.

At the river, we sink the milk crates to keep them cool, then hurry back. We take our place in the chairs at the front which have been kept for us, and the murmur of voices in the field dips, then falls away, as if it has rolled over a cliff. Anthony Thwaite takes some folded sheets of paper from his back pocket and studies them briefly.

'The first thing to say,' he begins, 'is that this is an important moment. Let's try to do it justice by—'

But Anderton has already pulled himself to his feet. 'The first thing is,' he interrupts, 'do we have this discussion at all with a non-believer, steeped in sin, in our midst? Answer me that.' I can see the rise and fall of his chest. He pushes a wedge of damp hair from his forehead, looks around the field.

'If so,' he continues, 'is she to participate? If yes, how? How can she? And given that, what is she here for?' He waits a moment, then sits back down heavily, next to his tiny wife.

He's four rows away, but I can smell him, and see the wiry hairs on his arms and in the V of his shirt—a proper hairy-cock, I tell myself, but it doesn't help... All of a sudden I'm way out of my depth. I don't like the way any of them are talking about me, right in front of me but as if I was not here. And I just want to hold Barbara's hand, but Mark is sitting between us, and anyway she's not even looking my way—I grasp the seat of my chair and start kicking my legs, back and forth, back and forth.

'An unbelieving child certainly doesn't trouble me,' says Helen McAllister, nervous but angry, her voice vibrating like a violin string. 'There must always be one or two of us in a state of doubt or sin, and it's never been suggested that they be barred from meetings, not by Envall and certainly not by Christ Himself!'

'Yes!' Barbara calls out. 'And if the person committing a sin doesn't understand that—'

Anderton is up again, raising his hand: doubt within a commitment is an entirely different thing to disbelief. The early Christians, he reminds everyone, when persecuted, met in secret and took steps to avoid betrayal.

'All year,' he says, 'all year, we struggle to live according to our way in a hostile world. Everyone knows how difficult this is. Here we have one chance to be only with ourselves, in the company of the Lord, and renew our strength. But now, Service has been interrupted because a child has decided to go off and watch television—'

'Yes. But Natalie did not realize what she was doing,' Barbara says. It's only half-true, and even she is talking about me as if I was not here. Kick, kick, kick, I bang into the grass with my heels.



'Even a young child,' Elsbeth Anderton counters, 'must learn to take responsibilities. Natalie,' she says, looking over at where I'm sitting, 'should have declined the invitation to come. Or her mother should have done so. Or else, she should, out of respect, have refrained from doing something she knew would cause us distress. But she didn't do this, so how can we trust her now?'

I get to my feet, and tell them: 'Everyone's been listening to it on the radio!'

'Can you understand that we don't mind the journey itself, only the pictures.' It's Simon Thorn who replies, speaking calmly, as if reasoning with one of the children he and his wife would like to have had.

'They were live pictures,' I tell him. 'Anyway, the astronauts couldn't have got to the moon without pictures, they needed pictures to navigate.'

'Is this what we've come here to listen to?' Anderton asks as I sit down again.

Barbara gestures at me in a loose, abstracted way.

'Natalie,' she says, 'told us this morning how sorry she is for what's happened.'

'Is that so?' Thwaite asks.

'Yes,' I tell him, as if confirming a fact known, but which has little to do with me.

'If anyone is to blame,' Barbara says, 'it must be me. I didn't explain things well enough. And perhaps—I should have consulted others before. It's a misunderstanding. I'm sorry.'

Thwaite wipes his face with a large crumpled handkerchief. He thanks Barbara. He pulls out his papers again, clears his throat. 'May we move on?' he asks. 'There are many serious and fundamental issues to be discussed.'

'What,' Anderton bellows, 'could be more serious than protecting ourselves from sin?'

'Well,' Thwaite says, 'why are we meeting here, and not in Elojoki? Isn't it time to get to grips with what that means for the future? What, in the new circumstances regarding passports, does strict observance really mean? Consider the reality of the situation, in terms of human lives: my own predicament, for instance, being engaged to Eija, or that of the McAllisters regarding Alistair's scholarship with Pekka Saarikangas in Helsinki—

'Surely, everyone must ask themselves whether, in the second half of the twentieth century, the nature of which Envall surely could not have predicted, whether the Lord God intended our ordinary lives to be as very difficult, even impossible for us as they are about to become? Surely it is time to open again the whole question of the differences between "making" and "bowing down unto" an image, the related differences between "letter" and "spirit"? Surely we can open up the meaning of "rendering unto Caesar" to include the carrying of such vital documents? Can there please now be a moment's silence, while everyone asks for God's help in addressing these important questions?' He bows his head; others follow suit.

'If that child—' the familiar voice hisses now, rather than booms, '—if she remains among us, then I and my family cannot stay. How many others feel the same?'

'Is that what you want?' Thwaite asks the meeting. 'Is it?' He stuffs his papers back into his waistband.

And now, again without asking me, my legs are still. I can't move them. I keep looking at my knees and hold hard onto the side of my chair. I breathe shallowly, just enough and no more, even though what I really want is to gulp the air in and then bellow it out. When the tears start to fall, I just keep looking down at the grass-stained knees of my jeans because I don't want anyone to know how much this is getting to me.



'All right,' Thwaite says. 'Let's settle it. Those who want Natalie to go, please raise their hands.'

'Mark,' Barbara says, 'let me sit next to Natalie.' It's almost too late. The knees of my jeans are wet through now.

Thwaite begins counting aloud. Higher up the field small girls with bunches and hair slides and crew-cut boys splash in and out of a yellow pool, push a plastic ball down in the water and make it jump up, douse each other with buckets. They shriek and splash, watch the shadows of ripples on the bottom of the pool.

Forty-two people want me to leave: all the Andertons' closest friends, Josie Gardner but not her husband, Adrian Jowett and his elderly father, the Lattens, a block of two large families from the Hull congregation. But, to my surprise, not Mark. He sits there, looking at his hands the way I've been looking at my knees. I guess that he has given up being a prophet.

'And who wants Natalie to stay?' Thwaite asks. Twenty-five people want me to stay. Twenty-seven, including Mark, won't say one way or another.

This isn't what I came here for. Barbara's fingers, gripping my upper arm, start to hurt. 'This is terrible. I'm so sorry—' she says. But she should stop it, right now! I pull away.

'Where,' Thwaite asks, 'is the child supposed to go?'

'With me, of course,' Barbara says. She reaches under her chair for her bag.

'You belong here,' John tells her.

'I can't—' she says, glancing at him angrily. 'The poor child can hardly wander around on her own all day!'

'One of the older girls could take her for a walk—' calls out Josie Gardner.

'I'm not sending her off with someone she doesn't know, after all this. Anyone can see that.'

Barbara squats in front of me now, rubbing my shoulder, holding a hand. 'Natalie—' she continues in a low, soft voice, 'this will blow over. But now, you and I will walk to the village. We will have an ice-cream. Everything will be all right.'

But John Hern gets up and pulls Barbara away from me, holds her tight in a kind of embrace. She struggles, gets her arms free. She holds them, fists clenched, in the air, as if she might rain blows on his back or head.

'Sit down—please, darling—' He pushes into her so that she staggers slightly. 'Stay, please—'

Abruptly, Barbara obeys, sitting down so hard that the chair almost falls back. He takes her hands and looks steadily into her face. His eyes burn with a kind of mad gentleness.

'I love you,' I hear him whisper, at the same time keeping a tight hold of her hands. 'I need you, my wife, to be with me here, now. What happens today will be important.' She stiffens, pulls one hand free, bangs it on her knee—I can see how difficult it is and part of me almost wants to let her go. But only part. And then—

'Mum—' Mark says, 'I can go with Natalie. I don't mind. It's fine now.'

'I don't want to go with him!' I yell at her, then wipe my nose on my arm. 'I want to go with you. I want to go to the village. I don't like it here anymore.' She looks from one to the other of us. Her face is damp with sweat.

'If I stay it will only be because you've asked me to,' Barbara tells John. 'I don't agree with what's happening. Is that what you want?' She shakes her head from side to side as if there was something buzzing in her ear.

'Thank you,' John says, inclining his head. 'I want you to stay.'

'Please understand,' she begins, reaching out for me with her hand and her voice, 'that none of this is your fault. But—'

There's no point in waiting to hear what comes after. I get up and run, up the slope, past Thwaite and towards the gate into the lane. I let it fall back behind me, without once looking back. 

I'm halfway up the hill before I hear Mark: 'Natalie! Natalie! Natalie!' he calls in his silly voice that cracks open at the end. 'Wait! I'm coming with you. Natalie—' It's the first time, so far as I know, that Mark has used my name. I should think that so far even in his mind I've been her, or she, or you. But the three syllables, the sequence of consonants, slip easily from his mouth and I expect they leave behind them an interesting disturbance, like the first mouthful of some complex but untrustworthy foreign food, accidentally taken in and as impossible to spit out as it seems to swallow down.

'Natalie—please! Wait, please!' I hurry on and up, amidst the frenzy of flies and the crickets, smelling the pollen and the sap, my flip-flops slap-slapping against my heels.

# 21

Overnight, the birches are dotted with green and clumps of dill have sprung up in all the kitchen gardens. The air smells of moss and sap. 

Heikki has returned from his holidays.

I've finished using his copier and am browsing through the official parish records and registers temporarily stored in an alcove of his room, row upon row of large leather-bound books with dates stamped on their spines and thick, woody pages: births, deaths, weddings, arrivals, departures, the stuff of our passage through time.

'So, what happened with your ex-wife?' I ask him.

'The usual thing,' he tells me, coming over to where I am sitting at the small table brought in for me to use when consulting the registers.

'What's that?'

Heikki shrugs, pushes his hands down in his pockets. 'Your story would be more interesting, I'm sure,' he says, pretending to study the rows of books.

'Not an adjective I'd choose.'

'I don't mean to be clumsy,' he says. 'You know—' he turns suddenly around to face me, puts both hands on my little desk, more or less obliging me to look up. 'I mean that I would like to know about you, and what I really want to say is that speaking as a man, it doesn't bother me, the way your face is doesn't—'

It's not you that it's here to bother! I almost say. It's me that has it, the memories, the feeling of it from inside. But I do manage to swallow that back, and I stand up because I feel at a disadvantage sitting down.

'Actually, I like it,' he says, and that's really too much—

'That's extremely good of you, Mr. Seppä,' I say, and I make a little mock-solemn bow. I can't stop myself; he ends up leaving his own office, I watch him drive off and then I sit there until I've finished what I came to do. Then, seeing as he didn't ask for the keys to be returned, I make my way back to the *pappila*. It's the place, these days, where I prefer to be.

In Tuomas's panelled and shuttered back room, I have found not only that first notebook but getting on for twenty other personal writings, fragments, mainly on single sheets of paper slipped between the pages of his books, or in one case pushed behind them on the shelves. 'Suppose I had done otherwise. How can one sin be weighed against another? Have I made things better or worse?' he was asking himself, in a private moment in January 1900. 'Perhaps this is the measure. But I cannot judge.' He was always asking, Tuomas, and never quite telling. But at the time, of course, no one knew that he had the slightest doubt. He went on saying the same things (no doubt cowardice came into this, but also a kind of altruism) and so his followers passed on what he had said, across the generations, like runners in a relay race …

I no longer pursue Tuomas. I've got so used to the hugeness of his desk, the gentle dappled light from the window at the side. I like working here, or sitting here to think. I sit in his office with my notebook and pens. It sounds crazy, but sometimes I feel as if I am being visited. At any rate, I am waiting for

Tuomas—for his story—to come to me, and I know that in the end it will.

When bodily discomforts finally get the better of me, I take the little path home. There's a young man in a plaid shirt sitting on the doorstep. Although he introduces himself straight away, I think I would have guessed who he was, not so much from his face, half-hidden as it is in thick brown stubble, as from the expression on it—that particular, suddenly shifting mixture of resentment and need. Perhaps it's a combination that is slightly more attractive in a man, and a young one at that, but it's still not my favourite thing. My own face being so very stuck, I tend to think: if you have a choice, use it. But then perhaps we don't.

'I am Pekka, the son of Kirsti Saarinen,' he says. He doesn't get up, just stays there sitting on the doorstep. 

'She says you are angry with her, so she can't come here herself.' He speaks slowly, but with a heaviness to the vowels and a laziness about the consonants that makes him harder than usual to understand. I shrug, shift my stance to accommodate the laptop and briefcase slung over one shoulder, wait for what might follow. There's a long pause.

'My mother wants to know, what's your business in the *pappila*?' So when I've felt the hair rise on my skin, or found myself suddenly alert, when moments before I was drifting off, it was not the ghost of Tuomas, but one of them, him probably, looking in at me through the window, then slipping away before I saw. Well, maybe that's a relief. I smile at him.

'Research,' I tell him. 'Reading Tuomas Envall's papers and so on. I am trying to decide what made him invent Envallism.'

'It was God's idea, I dare say.'

'So he said, of course. But I'm not convinced. And the *pappila* doesn't have a toilet that works. So I need to get in now if you don't mind. And after that—' He doesn't move.

'My mother has had a hard life,' he says, looking at the toe of his boot. 'Even when my father was here it was hard, harder even, in a different way. I'm the one that looks after her. The others take after him, and are bad-tempered and selfish.'

'Well, I'm sorry,' I say, 'but right now, I do need to get in.'

'May I see what you have in your bag?' he asks.

'No,' I tell him, 'of course you can't.' Actually, I haven't found anything new for almost a week, so there is nothing there he could object to, but that's only luck. When I do find something, I carry it down to the community centre that same day, label it, make a photocopy for myself, and leave the original in a locked drawer of Heikki's filing cabinet. I've no idea who the papers actually belong to or what the legal position might be, and if I think about the rights and wrongs, the various claims on this story that I call the truth about Tuomas Envall, then they are indeed complex and contradictory—but all the same, nothing will stop me doing this. I lean past Christina's son and put the key into my lock.

'What are you finding out?' he asks as I push past. 'Give me something to tell her.'

As I guessed, he is still there, a few metres from the door, when I come out again, with my two brown-glass bottles of beer; he knocks the cap off his while I'm still fiddling with the opener attached to my key ring. How to say to her, via him, that I do not pursue Tuomas anymore? That I no longer want to undo him, but want, more than anything, to understand.

'Tell her to come to the lecture,' I say, taking possession of my back step and rolling up my sleeves—the evenings are just warm enough for this now. 'It's on the second Saturday in June. Tell her,' I say, 'that I like Tuomas Envall far more than I expected to.'

Pekka puts the empty bottle beside me on the step, implying his thanks with a tilt of the head. He would like, I feel, not to have to speak at all, to communicate with expressions, gestures, the odd grunt here and there.

I wait until he has gone, and then I call Heikki Seppä at his home.

'I don't feel that was fair!' he tells me.

'Probably not,' I say.

'What would be the right way?' he asks.

'There probably isn't one,' I admit. 'Shall we have a drink together?'

This, I think, is a date. I am on a date.

The last of the sun warms our faces as Heikki and I sit with our beers by the thawing river, a sawmill screaming in the background, green, actual or reflected, as far as the eye can see. We're in a small bar in a tiny town of pastel-painted wooden houses, halfway between Elojoki and his home.

I have dressed for the occasion in a white blouse and chinos—almost-summery things—but Heikki is wearing track bottoms and one of his traditional patterned jumpers, which looks far too thick for the time of year.



'I think Tuomas Envall was gay,' I tell him. Heikki begins to laugh. 'No one will believe you,' he says. I shrug: it really doesn't bother me. 'But if they do,' he says, laughing more, 'you will be even less popular than I am!' The mill at the other side of the inlet falls momentarily quiet. Light dances on the water. Any minute, night will fall. 'I can't work you out,' Heikki says. You can, I think. I want you to. 'He did believe in what he said, I think,' I tell Heikki, 'until almost the end. And it has to be said, there's no question that many people got something out of it, and they still do. Actually, the avoidance of imagery is a practice with precedent in both the Judaeo-Christian and the Islamic traditions, not to mention ...' I go on and on, drunk on one and a half beers.

'Natalie, would you like to see where I live?' he asks, when I run out of words.

# 22

I was well past the farm before Mark caught up with me. 

'Come back,' he said.

'Why should I? I don't want to.'

'That's the thing about you, isn't it?' he said. 'You don't much think about anyone else.'

I ignored him again, turned left at the top of the lane and went on walking, along the narrow road, onwards from where we had turned off in the car two days ago. He walked sometimes next to me, sometimes behind.

'Where are you going?' he asked. 'You don't know, do you?' he said. A while later, we came to a crossroads, and I stopped to study the names on the sign. He waited too, a few paces away. It was very hot. Despite Barbara's applications of sun cream, the tops of my forearms were going pink, the freckles on them darkening and merging together. I could feel the sweat under my hair, and him looking, the way he always did.

The sign meant nothing to me. I could hardly put the letters together, let alone make them into a sound in my head.

'I want to find the sea,' I told him.

'We're going to the beach on Wednesday,' he said, 'it's miles.'

'Which way is it?'

'Straight over,' he said. I could tell he was guessing as much as I was, but I set off again. On the other side of the crossroads, he stopped and looked back, so that he'd know the place again. We needed to keep the sun to our right, or behind us, he said.

The road, smaller than the last, rose steeply. There was a large, empty-looking stone house, and then nothing. We kept going for half a mile or so, not speaking. The road began to curve insistently in the wrong direction. 'It's this way,' he told me, indicating a left that seemed to cut straight on up a slow hill. 'But it's a long way.'

The air was thick with the rasp of crickets and the busying of flies and bees. The hedge rolled itself alongside us, a kaleidoscope of small shapes, eruptions of colour. We went on and on, ignoring a fork left. I remember a single car passed, suitcase strapped to the roof, buckets and spades on the back shelf. Some time after that, we waited at a gap in the cutting for the lights to turn at a level crossing, watched the train rush past. Then we crossed and kept on going the same way.

We came to a small village, stone cottages and modern bungalows mixed together. A smell of roasting meat hung about the place.

Mark waited outside while I went into the tiny shop. I bought some Tizer, and asked the faded, fat woman who served me the time and the way to the sea.

'It's two o'clock. I've got a pie too,' I told Mark, omitting to say that I hadn't paid for it. 'We'll have it when we get there. We go left, right and then there's a path to the cliffs.'

A stile led into a field of coarse, trampled grass that rose gently towards a fence—wooden posts and wire—at the far side. There was no clear path, but when we were almost at the fence, the sea suddenly came into view, quite distinct from the faded, even blue of the sky at the horizon. Vast and glittering, it moved all the time in small ways, and yet at the same time it seemed still; it seemed to me that it could have been the skin of some enormous, sleeping beast.

We pushed down the wires, holding them for each other in turn, and climbed through. The thin tract of land ahead was dotted with small bushes. Orange and brown butterflies rose as we passed, settled again after us. 'Do not walk near the cliff edge or on the bankings' warned a peeling white-painted notice-board nailed to a stake. But we went on until we could see right over the edge. There were no waves to speak of, just a kind of rhythmical spilling over of the sea, a gentle rustling sound. The cliff stretched in both directions. To the right, occasional jerry-built chalets with asphalt roofs, shingled or pebbled wall panels and brightly painted windows, nestled in the hollows of the cliff approach and, farther away, we could see the white roofs of what looked like several hundred caravans which were arranged in neat, street-like rows in a field far larger than ours. To the left we could see the pastel colours of a sea-front, darker buildings covering the hills behind.



Grass grew right up to the cliff edge. The cliffs themselves were perhaps twenty feet high where we were standing, more elsewhere, and made of a soft-looking rock, almost like soil, browny orange in colour, with a paler band towards the top. They slumped rather than stood, and the beach below was strewn with large, fallen lumps, a muddle of small pebbles and the occasional huge, round boulder. Beyond this, the brownish sand itself was smooth and wet.

'The sea's coming in,' Mark said. It was another guess, of course. We didn't have a watch. It was impossible to know how long we'd been away, how long it would take to get back. Our legs ached.

'We had better stop here,' he said, 'we can't stay long.'

I sat down on the grass, took the small cellophane-wrapped pork pie from my pocket and placed it on the grass between us. I removed my flip-flops and examined my feet. They were filthy, brown from the dust of the roads and fields, rubbed raw between the big and next toe. I pulled the big toe away, and blew on the sore patch. Then I loosened the top on the bottle of Tizer, carefully so it didn't fizz over and waste.

'This is my favourite,' I said and drank steadily with my eyes closed. He was watching me again—catching a glimpse of the paleness beneath the edges of my clothes. The bottle gasped when I took it away from my mouth, and a new crop of bubbles rushed through it.

'Are they going to throw me out, then?' I asked as I handed it to him. I tried to say it lightly, but my voice and the way I kept looking at him, searching for clues, betrayed me.

'I don't know,' Mark said, sipping at the sweet, warm stuff. Clearly, he was beginning to feel in charge of the situation. No doubt that made it easier for him to keep on staring at me like that, taking me in, frowning a bit, as if he was trying to think of a name for what I was: a creature of some kind that hadn't existed before, a name from the encyclopedia suddenly made flesh.

One of my eyes was just a little bigger than the other. There were purplish shadows beneath them. The lids were pale, unfreckled. My lips were cracked, dry beneath the temporary coating of drink, which had stained their margins orange. The corners of my mouth had dirt in them. If looking at me used to frighten Mark, now it was having the opposite effect. The more he looked, the more he felt equal to me, even superior. He was guessing what I might say or do next, getting it right. Nothing I said seemed to surprise him anymore.

'Your mother wants me to stay,' I said, 'and your father. He's going to show me the books. But then, she wouldn't come with me. You didn't vote.'

Mark shrugged. He put the bottle down. 'So?' he asked. A broad grin settled on his face.

'Do you still hate me?' I asked, and regretted it immediately. I could see him thinking how all along I wanted something from him, and now I was wanting it even more. And now that the worst had already happened (or so he thought), my wanting gave him, in exact proportion to its strength, power. He could feel it, a new fluid flowing in his veins. He had no idea what to do with it; it just rushed through him, spread itself everywhere.

The smile stretched farther across his face. He said nothing to reassure me.

'Are you ever going to stop it, then?' I asked, my voice rising. And when he just stared at me, I sprang to my feet. I wanted to hit him. 'You're supposed to love your enemy!' I said. 'You're a hypocrite. It's a sin not to!'

He started to laugh. Soon he was shaking helplessly.

'You're supposed to forgive them!' His laugh, almost without his knowing it, sharpened, but by now he couldn't have spoken even if he'd wanted to.

I turned my back on him, took a few steps towards the ragged edge of the cliff, sat on it with my legs dangling down into the void, perfectly relaxed, as if it were a chair. A gust of wind blew my hair upwards, pulling the remains of the plait with it. I looked down at the drop, more of a very steep slope really, the beach below. Then, with no warning, I pressed down with my hands, eased myself over the edge, and let myself disappear.

# 23

I follow Heikki about forty kilometres, roughly south, and end up in the car-park of some small blocks of flats, which are surrounded with trees. Heikki shows me a small boat which he over-winters under a tarpaulin in the car-park. Then we take the stairs to the fourth floor. The flat, Heikki says, is not his natural habitat: the traditional wooden house they once shared went to his temperamental ex-wife, Maria, who has Kirsi during the week. 

Even so, the flat seems homely enough to me: a large entrance hall, with a coat rack and deep cupboards, a living-room lined along one wall with books. Heikki opens the door to the neat kitchen, a miniature bathroom, and the two bed-rooms, again, small but well-cupboarded. It's like a boat, I'm thinking, full of vital and unexpected things, with everything stowed properly away. Then I remember him showing me Tuomas's house, how he looked inside everything—and I take hold of his hand before he can start. How did he lose his finger? I ask. When he was fourteen. Slightly drunk, gutting a pike.

Impatient—

But now, I think, in the middle of your life, you don't hurry; you seem to be someone who can wait. A man who puts away clothes, replaces implements in their correct places after use, knows how to refold a map, is patient enough to mend things.

He's been waiting a while. Now, he pulls me to him, holds tight.

'Only in the dark,' I tell him, and reach for the switch. 'It's better in the dark.' Of course, I need to hide. To be there and not be seen. But also I find that darkness makes skin the only sense and, invisible, I can live my nakedness from inside.

# 24

I'd taken off my jeans and stood in the watery lace at the edge of the sea, prodding a piece of seaweed with a stick. I watched Mark slither down the cliff, a hundred yards or so to the right. When he was close enough for me to hear him, he stopped and called out: 'That was really stupid! What do you think you're doing? Now come home—'



'No. Not until you like me,' I told him. 'I don't even mind believing in it all,' I said a moment later, 'if someone will tell me properly what it is.' We were talking just as if I had never slipped over the cliff and made him follow me, as if we were picking up on the previous conversation. The breeze and the soft splash of the waves muffled the edges of our words. The thin strip of sand I stood on stretched for miles in either direction, with small clots of sunbathers and swimmers gathered where it made deeper bays and coves. He came a few steps closer.

'You can't just say that,' he said. 'You have to mean it. God comes to you. You attend Service. You study. You practise. You experience conversion. Eventually you make a profession of faith, and then you must share in our communion, bread and wine which is the literal body and blood of Christ. And you have to really mean that too, or it is sin to partake. And then, afterwards, you'd have to be different, really different. But you—' He licked his lips, and I followed suit, tasting salt, 'I don't believe you could be different,' he said. 'I'm not sure,' he added, sounding relieved suddenly, 'that I'd ever like you very much, whatever you did.' All the same, it must have been as clear to him as it was to me that he knew he did not feel exactly as he used to. A wave went over his feet, without him noticing it.

'Your shoes are wet,' I told him. 'There is another thing,' I said.

'What other thing?'

'I can't shout it,' I said. I went over to him. At least, he was probably telling himself, she's moving in the right direction now—if I can just get her off the beach and onto a road, there might be a bus to take us home, or maybe we could even stop a car, get a lift—but before we could leave, something else had to happen, here on the beach where the wind baffled softly around our ears. I knew it and he did too, but he didn't know what. Was I going to touch him? Did he even want me to?

I squatted down next to him, with my back to the sea, and indicated for him to do the same. The damp sand spread about us, interrupted only occasionally by a tiny shell or stone and the depression behind it. 'Mark, look,' I said, and pressed the tip of my finger into the sand by my feet.

Slowly, I pulled my finger along, leaving a furrow of disturbed sand behind. Seawater seeped from below. Did he know what it was? I asked, and he said no, but it was a lie, and even before the line made a little jump and then curved over itself, and began to come back the way it had come, before it could be called, by any stretch of the imagination except his, an image, the thing itself had started to happen in his own body, and kept him there, watching, horrified, hypnotized as I pressed my finger in to make a hole in the top:

'A man's cock,' I said, 'sticking up.'

'That's enough!' Before I could do the woman's parts, he'd grabbed my arm and pulled us both to our feet, saying we must go straight home. But then, of course, we were touching and he was in fact pulling me along with him, at a half run, while he looked for a place where no one would see.

Soon we lay side by side, in a raised hollow where the cliff had collapsed long ago and grass and bushes grew. Mark stared fixedly into my face as if he must not look down, at the rest of me, or at his own crotch, where the man's cock pushed at cotton and twill, yearned towards Natalie Baron, the girl who had drawn it. He must look only at my face, at the landscape of it, at the column of fine, red-gold hairs moving in an elongated triangle from my eyebrows up the centre of my forehead to the hairline, another gathering of them on my upper lip. Back then, there were even tinier hairs, almost white, on my cheeks; it was like a finer version of the ground we lay on, except that when he came to them, my eyes were looking back at him out of it, alert, curious—and there in the dark middle of them, was a tiny picture of himself.



He gripped both my arms: to stop me from doing anything, I suppose he would have said. But by holding me he also stopped himself from moving, especially from moving his legs. He knew he should not lift the left one and push with the right until he was lying on top, which was what he kept wanting, obstinately, to do. So instead, his fingers dug into my arm, and holding on, of course, also prevented him from going away.

'Let go of me,' I said; my excitement was of a different kind. 'I haven't before, but I know what to do,' I informed him.

'So do I!' he said. 'But it's sinful. Stop it. Stop doing this to me.'

'Let go,' I repeated. 'Do what I tell you.' And clearly, his brain told him, siding momentarily with the force that was about to overcome it, we could not stay stuck like this forever. So he relaxed the hands he had been studying hours ago in the meeting-field, and which before that had set out the chairs.

It was useless to pretend, or to try to return to what had been before. Clumsily, he did what I told him:

'Take off your shorts. And your pants. And your shoes!' The laces defeated his fingers and reduced him to something midway between tears and laughter, and all the time, there it was, the new fifth limb of his body, that he could see and I could see; it made him move differently, as if his body was there just to carry it.

I, giving the orders, lay still, my knees filthy, my feet clean from the sea. I propped myself up on my elbows and watched him. His body was muscular and pale. I noticed with interest and relief that hair gathered around his cock but there was none on his chest and not so very much elsewhere, not even on his legs. He wasn't exactly a man, I thought. He probably couldn't make me have a baby. My own legs were plump and white at the top, my underpants were white cotton with pink dots; there was a pale strip of skin between them and the hem of my blouse.

'It has to be good for the woman,' I informed him, when finally the shoes and socks were off, 'or it won't work. You have to stroke me all over.'

'Well, take your things off, or I can't.' For a moment we were both equally afraid. Now it was his turn to watch my fingers struggling as his had done with mother-of-pearl buttons and with the tiny brass safety pin Barbara had fastened where one of them was missing. Of course, my skin was perfect then. Beneath the open blouse freckles scattered away from my neckline and then the smooth glow of it was interrupted only by two nipples, the pale pink of strawberry ice-cream, and the landscape of the body beneath, intricate, soft, completely different from Mark's.

'Go on, then,' I told him, 'touch me,' and then, to my surprise, everything was skin.

I remember I talked all through it, telling him 'like that' or 'not like that' and what might happen next and what his face looked like, and sometimes I laughed. 'Go on then, now, go on!' I told him, and then for a few moments I was in a delicious place, held between desire and the promise of its satisfaction. Then the whole of me gathered together and hurtled away, obliterating everything. Then it was all over for both of us.

'I love you,' Mark told me, in those last, otherworldly moments. He was fourteen. His eyes were shut, his face screwed tight. He was pushed entirely inside me. He meant something by it, certainly, and a few moments afterwards he returned deliciously to himself, to the salty air and the sky above us, so new and astounding, the gold stuff that sprang out of my head and blew into his face and the dappled skin that had frightened him before.

'See?' I told him; I never mentioned love. 'My shoes and trousers are over there on the beach,' I told him, adding that I was hungry. He went to find the clothes. He had been wrong about the tide, which was going out, and now suddenly there were more people, spreading out towards us from the clusters on the bays to either side.



At first he couldn't see the trousers and shoes. Then when he had found them, he began searching the sand for the image I'd made with my finger, but it had vanished. Children's voices shrieked above the splash of the waves as he ran back to the cliff, and worked his way methodically along it. I was sitting up on the grass, with my blouse on, waiting.

'We can get up to the top just over there,' I told him. 'We've got to hurry up. Your Mum'll be killing herself.'

His face fell. For the first time since we had left the camp, he must have been remembering who he was, and what he was a part of. The implications, the consequences of what he had done would have ranked themselves ahead of him like the impossible mountains of a new country, far too vast to take in, let alone approach. But one thing was clear enough:

'She mustn't know. No one must know,' he told me as we set off, scrambling up the gap in the red dirt of the banking, half running, hand in hand, over the cliff-top scrub towards the field and the road.

By the time we reached the village, I was limping. I took my shoes off but my foot still hurt.

'What on earth will we do?' he asked. I had no idea.

Mark banged on the door of the shop and explained to a balding man woken from his afternoon sleep how we had walked too far and everyone would be expecting us by now. Did he sell sticking plasters? We would have to come back and pay for them tomorrow—

'That your sister?' the man asked.

'Yes,' he said. The man called his wife, the one I'd bought the Tizer from.

'They're from Harris's camp,' she said. 'The religious lot, the—' She looked to Mark: 'What are you?'

'Envallists.'

She fetched some sticking plaster, from her own box, she said, adding that Mark was not doing a very good job of looking after his sister. I slipped the flip-flops back on and stood up. It didn't make any difference and I'd never been so tired in my life.

Wasn't there, I asked, anyone in the village who might just happen to be driving towards Harris's farm?

Why would they be doing that? the woman said. She certainly wasn't getting the van out. It was early closing. She and her husband worked every hour of the week, and nowadays they had to get up for the newspapers on Sunday too. But she wouldn't be called uncharitable; there was an old pair of canvas shoes in the shed, too big but better than nothing. We could take those and a pair of socks as well if it helped, and that way we would learn from the experience to prepare ourselves better next time—what was our mother thinking of, letting us out with nothing to eat and wearing such shoes? Didn't our God have something to say about that kind of thing?

We set off again. Mark said that perhaps he could carry me on his back some of the way. I could see that it was as shocking for him to hear himself say this as it had been earlier on to agree that I was his sister. But then, after all, we had seen each other without our clothes, he had touched me all over and felt my hands on him, we had done the thing we didn't have a proper word for, so we were connected by our shared secret and by our desire to get back quickly. On top of that there was the difficulty of the journey itself and somehow it was so awful it was almost funny.

'It is a real pity,' he told me, absurdly, reaching for my hand, 'that you didn't come to Elojoki. It's so much better there!'

# 25



It was mid-afternoon. There was no shade. The congregation shifted in their chairs, fanned themselves with scraps of paper, books, hats; they poured water on their handkerchiefs and wiped their faces, hands, the backs of their necks.

'Anthony Thwaite—you want to remake us all to suit your own circumstances. You are prepared to take everyone else down the path of your own temptation—' Anderton, speaking, gripped the chair in front of him, leaned into it. Damp patches spread from his armpits across his shirtfront, almost meeting in the middle. His face, raw-red, ran with sweat. He wiped it with his wife's tiny handkerchief, returned the handkerchief to her, looked up and around.

'And you—' his voice, rough at the edges, exhausted with its own passion, 'accused Jean McAllister of obeying the Lord's commandments until now only because it was 'not inconvenient.' He pushed the words out, like something painfully but necessarily regurgitated, burning his throat as they emerged. 'Now,' he said, 'you discover that it might entail some sacrifice, and you want it reconsidered . . .' The heat seemed to make Jean whiter, more intense.

'No,' she told him. 'I want it reconsidered because I love my son—' and so Christina's mother Josie joined in: she'd brought up six, so if anyone knew what it was to love a child, then she—

'Not this one—' Jean told her, and then Elsbeth Anderton reminded everyone that it was God's love that mattered—

Jean jabbed her finger towards Anderton. 'Let's say I go into town and have a photograph made, because the law requires it and then I—'

'*Look at it!*' Anderton interrupted. Yes, she agreed. She was bound to see it, but that didn't mean she would—

Here, Barbara leaned in close to John. Her hand was still held tightly in his, damp, almost numb; she put the other hand on top, whispered to him with her lips almost touching his ear: 'I see what Jean means—do you, darling?' *Suppose,* she was hoping against hope, *he changes his mind?* And then—

'Not see, look—' Anderton corrected Jean. 'Slip it in a drawer where you can look at it again. And then think it's harmless and start to want to see other such things: an image is a door for the devil to climb through! How many do we want to give him?' Some cheered at this.

And did any of this matter to Ian himself? Christina's mother was asking when the noise died down. Surely he'd be loved and appreciated by the congregation, whether or not he went to study in Helsinki?

Jean shouted: 'Ask him! Go on!' and pointed up the field to where Ian was lying, halfway between the meeting and the food tent, on his back, kicking one leg rhythmically into the air. Then she sat down, rested her head on the back of the empty chair in front while her husband rubbed the heel of his hand slowly up and down her back.

Barbara turned back from watching this, to John, who was sitting with his head bowed and eyes closed, the thinking position: she pulled her hand free, had to stop herself from shaking him, from shouting out, 'How can you not see—?'

And there was Elsbeth again, talking about the differences between human and divine love, how there were times when earthly love must be put aside, for example—

'Everyone here,' she told them, the faintest flush coming to her damp cheeks, 'everyone knows how we had to lose our daughter—'

Barbara, after years of forbearance and trying to think the best, could stand it no more; she was on her feet before she knew it, shouting:

'You didn't have to lose her! You didn't deserve to have her in the first place! And why did you have to send Natalie away? Why?'

It was obvious that Elsbeth was going to burst into tears, but in the moment of absolute silence that came before she did so, everyone realized, more or less at the same time, that Paul Leverson had arrived. There he was, sitting on the gate to the field, watching and listening. How long had he been there? His blond hair, short at the sides, longer and curled on top, glinted in the sun as he slipped down from the gate and made his way towards the meeting. His loose white shirt was unbuttoned at the neck and his beige trousers, gathered around his waist in a narrow belt, were creased down the front of the legs.



'Leverson!' Anthony Thwaite embraced him, so did John and others. Soon, he was lost in the crowd. An empty chair was brought forward from the back and put, with no discussion, next to Thwaite's. Julia Jowett carried over a jug of cool orange squash, poured him a glass.

Leverson didn't sit down, but set the cup of juice on the seat of the chair, and stood with one hand on its back. 'Who is this Natalie, then?' he asked.

'A child—' Jean said.

'A non-believer—' said Elsbeth, 'brought here by Barbara Hern—'

'She did apologize—' Barbara insisted to no one in particular, sitting down.

'More importantly, it's a matter,' Anthony Thwaite tried to explain, 'of Letter and Spirit—'

Leverson raised a hand for silence. 'Brothers and sisters,' he said, once everyone had stopped talking, 'this is Babel. We must forget the enemy outside and search ourselves inside, each one of us, for what is within.' It was as if he had been brought to them (no one had heard the car), untouched by the journey, from some other, cooler country. The congregation settled again in their places. Their skins had been dissolved, their brains boiled, but already they felt cooler, and waited, calmer, hopeful, while Leverson organized his thoughts.

'Who is without sin?' Leverson began. 'A sin confessed is forgiven and transcended, but an unshriven sin lodges itself inside. Our unshriven sins are stones—to be carried by the sinner alone until the moment of confession. . . Stones, carried inside our bodies or strapped onto them, day and night. They bend us over, they twist us this way or that way, hurting, they force us to distort ourselves in order to support and accommodate them. They bow our heads, they press against our tissues and organs; carrying them takes up more and more attention as time passes. And the longer the sin remains within, the more effort we must make in order to bear the self-imposed burden and to keep it secret. And even if we act in every other way rightly, day after day, we will still not be able, in our hearts, to find God and to know what He requires of us—we are already, you could say, in Hell. . . Yet, if only we can remember or be reminded, all that we have to do is to drop our burdens, to admit them, and, from that moment, we can begin to stand straight and see clearly again, and feel ourselves no longer alone. Surely, brothers and sisters, it is a congregation of such people that now, more than ever, we need to be?'

And at this point, Paul Leverson paused, and let his eyes—famous for their ability to glitter and burn, to melt, soothe, challenge—pass slowly over each and every person there. 'Each one of you,' he said, using his softest, most sympathetic voice, 'knows what he or she is carrying. Each one of you is probably thinking of it at this very moment... Speak—'

Barbara's heart thudded steadily in her chest. Her skin pricked, as she forced herself to meet his gaze. Part of her rushed, like the blood to her cheeks, desperate to do what he asked. But all the same, she found it quite possible to resist, and when Leverson prompted, 'Sister?' she kept her face blank, and looked right back at him. 'Brother?' she heard him ask someone else. Then, blinking back tears, she took John's hand and gently stroked the bone-ridged back of it with her thumb.

# 26

Harris and Belinda's bedroom window gives a good view of both fields. It's the best room in the house. Belinda has taken up the carpet and varnished the floorboards, then bought rugs and hung them on the walls. 

'They've been there all day. Is that earth on the table? What a life! Do you think they screw much?' she asks. It always turns Harris on to hear her use coarse words in her careful southern voice—girls' boarding-school, half a degree in Sociology, then, on the last bit of parental goodwill, the Slade—all of it left behind, for him. A mutual risk, of course, but right from the start he'd seen how it could work. She has her press in the old scullery, dries the work on chicken-wire trays; he gets the prints framed up and sent away to London. Money comes back.

He runs his hands lightly up and down Belinda's sides, pulls her back into him. In the field, they start to sing again.

'No shortage of kids down there,' Harris points out. 'But that girl, the one I brought back, she isn't theirs. And the boy's in a bad way, doesn't talk.'

'Crazy—' Belinda says again, stepping up backwards, so that she's standing on his feet, with her buttocks in his groin. 'They give me the shivers.'

'I like them,' Harris says.

'You just think you can make them pay,' says Belinda, as Harris slips his hands around to the front, one down into her jeans, one up under her shirt: no bra. 'I know you.'

# 27

It is nearly six o'clock when we arrive back at the site, the sun yellow-gold rather than white, but still fierce. The meeting-field is still half-full but the frailer adults and almost all the teenagers and children and their mothers, hungry and hot, have left and are sitting or playing in the squares of shade around the caravans. We go straight to the Hern caravan, noticing little except for Leverson's car. Mark points it out to me: a deep-blue Humber, just a couple of years old, and gleaming clean, parked close to the gate. 

We have cheese-and-tomato sandwiches, sticking them together with mayonnaise from the night before and using almost all the loaf. We eat quickly. My head spins; I think I'm going to be sick. Mark helps me into my bunk. I cover myself, despite the heat, with crocheted blankets and a quilt, pulling at the edges to ensure a perfect seal, then I fall asleep as if someone had turned off a switch.

What has happened? Mark wonders. Is his mother all right? He should let her know that they are back... But a huge weariness presses down on him. Instead of going out into the field he sits for a while on the steps of the caravan, in his father's place, listening blankly to the tap of hawthorn twigs on the roof. Then he goes inside again, pulls the curtains closed, climbs into his own bunk and lies there in the dim, greenish light.

Later, he's aware, very distantly, as from the bottom of some infinitely deep well, of his parents returning, of his mother's soft laughter and the shushing sound she makes to his father. When he wakes properly there is a lamp on the table with a note beside it saying that everyone will be by the river, and 'both of you' are welcome to come; the 'both' is underlined. He finds his torch and goes first to the tap, washes from the bucket without bothering to warm the water. In the distance he can hear the congregation singing Envall's arrangement of the 150th Psalm. Their voices push towards the high notes, gratefully plummet at the ends of each phrase. Softened by its journey across the fields, it sounds almost as it's supposed to, and he hums along to it. It's just as he is tipping the suds into the hedge by the gate that Mark realizes someone is coming up the lane, and then a beam of light seeks him out, so that he has to do the same or be blinded; the four eyes of the Anderton twins gaze back at him, blinking just as he is.

'Oh, hello,' he says. 'What happened then, this afternoon?'

'Well, we should be asking that,' says Peter.

'Where are you off to?' Mark asks.

'Nowhere. You can come if you want,' Peter says. Mark hesitates, then lowers his torch and, leaving the bucket, he falls in with them. They take a stile to the left and are soon in a position where they can see the lights, some moving, some still, down by the river.

Tim says it will do; they all sit down.

'Well,' Peter said, 'Leverson arrived. Shook hands, patted bums and promised great things for the morning...'

'Do you smoke?' Tim asks suddenly.

'No,' Mark tells him, 'of course I don't.'

'Shame.' Timothy lights the cigarette he has been rolling since they sat down and draws deeply upon it. 'In any case,' he adds, after a few moments, 'welcome.' He passes the cigarette to his brother.

'What do you mean?' Mark asks, shortly, blinking against the smoke.

'We were on the hill. We saw you and your redhead coming back. Clear enough what you'd been doing.'

'So welcome—' Pete cuts in, 'to the Republic of Sin. You've left the Kingdom of God behind, and come to a better place.'

'Is that drugs?' Mark asks.

'Sara gets it, at the university,' Tim says. 'All things are possible. For example, Pete and I are going to live in London, as soon as we are sixteen. We'll get a flat. How was it with Natalie, then?'

'It doesn't mean what you think,' Mark says. The twins laugh, choking on their own smoke and trying to push it away with their hands. Below, the singing has stopped and lights separate from the group in twos and threes, proceeding erratically in a variety of directions. The night is very warm. The moon, which Mark had noticed earlier, shining out from behind thin afternoon cloud, has gone.



'What I mean,' Mark persists, 'is that I've got to think everything through, and ask myself questions, and pray, and decide what to do. Everything's upside down and I don't know exactly what it means.'

'Don't know was made to know,' Pete says, slowly exhaling.

'Or maybe it means nothing at all,' says Tim. The smoke, just visible, spreads around them in the dark. Mark has the feeling of visiting a life someone else had told him was his, finding it half-mistaken, half-familiar.

He leaves them there, and cuts back to the van. His parents have still not returned. The van is dark and stuffy. He sees that I've pushed off the blankets and I'm lying there fully clothed, even down to the borrowed socks. I'm breathing with my mouth half open, I lie there like someone cast into a sudden trance, rather than naturally asleep. It is a kind of experiment for Mark to stay there, watching, to see what happens; which is that very slowly, so that he has ample chance to prevent it, but no real sense of urgency until it is too late, the feeling of wanting grows, to the point where, if it felt safe, he would climb into my bunk. But it's not safe. There are voices in the field. Doors open and close, occasional lights jog past the thinly curtained windows. All he does is to reach over, and put the tip of his forefinger in my mouth, rubbing it along the slack wetness behind my lower lip.

What happened in the afternoon did not feel like a sin, and now this doesn't either. That's all he has to weigh against everything he has ever been led to believe, by everyone important in his life. But all the same, weighing it seems worth doing. He stands there, burning, as St. Paul would have put it, and then when he hears his parents' voices outside, slips into his bed underneath.

The car door opens, closes.

'Tomorrow is a new day, my love,' his father says.

'I can't say I'm looking forward to it,' she replies. 'And I really don't know what the poor child will make of it.' Water from their tooth-brushing splatters on the ground as they speak. They are sharing the mug, handing it from one to the other.

'You can't have it both ways,' his father says good-naturedly. 'You must hand it to the Andertons for backing down.'

'It was because they had their way on the more important thing,' she says. Then it goes quiet, while they undress, put their clothes in the car.

She climbs straight into bed. He pushes the latch on the lock of the door. 'God bless,' they tell each other. Mark's father's breathing shifts gears, then slips into the easy, shallow rhythm of solid sleep.

'Are you awake?' his mother whispers some time later. He can see the dim, pale shape of her, sitting up.

'Where did you go? Was Natalie all right?'

She was worried about being thrown out, Mark tells her, leaning half out of his bunk. I am lying just eighteen inches above his head. He and his mother are only feet apart, but in the dark the distance grows and it is rather like having a telephone conversation. Suddenly, he remembers ringing her when he had gone over on his ankle in football practice, and had to be taken to the hospital after school for an X-ray. He must have it, she told him. It would be all right so long as he didn't look at it.

'It was terrible this morning,' she says.

'Yes,' he agrees.

'But good may come of it. You're not to worry. I like Tony Thwaite. Jean too. She's very brave. Are you all right?'

'Yes,' he tells her, 'fine.'



Then he too drifts off, leaving Barbara the only one awake, lying wide-eyed next to her husband in the locked caravan, waiting for the small gusts of breeze that push through the windows, the rustle of leaves outside.

# 28

A cool morning, slightly overcast. Blouses, face cloths, underpants, a tea towel, flutter on the line strung between the caravan and the hedge. John is on the steps again, Mark and Barbara on chairs by the hedge. I have spread a rug on the grass. On my lap, I hold a small leather-bound copy of Envall's sermon The Forgotten Commandment—Finnish to one side, English of sorts on the other. I move my finger steadily along the lines as I read, slowly, trying to make some sense of it. My hair is freshly plaited. I'm wearing a blue-checked dress and a yellow cardigan, and thoroughly enjoying being an Envallist child, and the way that everything has come together all at once. 

'We should make a move,' John says. People are beginning to drift towards the meeting-field, each person or group carrying their own chairs and equipment.

'I need a word with you first, John,' I hear Barbara say.

'I'll carry your chair?' Mark asks me as I shut the book carefully, a blade of grass slipped in to mark my place. He's been annoying me since we got back and I pretend not to have heard. I go inside to put the book away, then linger a moment at the border between our spot and the site in general, looking back. Barbara has one hand on her husband's arm, the other buried in the pocket of her slacks. She gives me a brief but dazzling smile, then waves us children on.

'You go ahead.'

'Are you all right?' Mark asks as we set out together for the other field.

Of course, I tell him. Everyone is being very nice to me now, it's all fine. I look steadily ahead and give no sign of remembering anything about yesterday at all. I'm offering him the opportunity to forget what happened, which is what I want to do, so that I can get on with the new situation. But Mark doesn't want the same thing. He bunches his eyebrows, reaches for my hand, which I snatch away and thrust in the pocket of my dress. He'd very much like to go for a walk with me again. After this meeting is finished, perhaps. There's a lot to talk about. Before tea-time, perhaps? What do I think?

'I don't know,' I say, finally glancing at him.

'Maybe?'

'I said, I don't know,' I repeat, holding out my hands, not to him, but for the chair to sit on.

There's a buzz of excitement in the air as the congregation settles itself in concentric circles around an arrangement of two oil drums with a piece of rough-sawn timber spanning them like a bridge. This is Paul Leverson's doing. The timber is to be a kind of gangplank, along which, one by one, blindfolded, the entire congregation, or as many as can be persuaded, will walk. Each person will carry a rucksack of stones to symbolize their unconfessed sins. At the far end, they will tip the stones out on the ground, naming them for all to hear. Mark says he remembers reading about this in the newsletter, how, on his visit to one of the Canadian congregations, Leverson himself had carried stones in a far more extreme situation: walking along a pine log over a real ravine with a sheer drop beneath; how afterwards, 'the spirit filled him.'

'But of course, you don't have to do it,' he tells me.

'I might,' I say, although anyone can see that the plank is not thick enough and will wobble a lot. 'I might want to.'

'Not about yesterday—'

'Why not?' I ask. 'I'll do what I want. I'll say what I want, and I will, I really will, if you don't leave me alone.'

Elsbeth Anderton has asked if she can be the first.

Another rumour is that Paul Leverson is so thoroughly behind Mark's Island idea, now called Anderton's Island idea, that he is prepared to start the fund with a thousand pounds of his own savings. Anthony Thwaite, on the other hand, is completely against; he and the McAllisters left supper early yesterday to go for a walk together and talk things through . . .

'Someone could fall off and bang their head or something,' I point out. 'Whose fault would that be?'

Everyone is waiting.



When's Barbara going to come?

My legs start kicking again.

Both halves of the caravan's stable doors are closed. The still air inside glows amber from the roof-light. The pale wooden cupboards, flip-down table and orange upholstered benches press into the small central space where Barbara and John stand, perhaps eighteen inches apart. John looks up, curious, and a little afraid, at his frowning wife. Stray hairs of hers touch the roof of the van. She bites on her lower lip. She is still beautiful, unsettling and attractive at the same time.

'What is it, Barbara?'

'I don't want to stand up in the field and say this. I want to tell you, just you,' she says, taking his hands in hers.

The way her eyes shine, he could almost think it was something wonderful she was about to tell him: a pregnancy, a vision. But he knows it's not. 'The truth is, John, that since shortly after she died I have kept a photograph of Ruth, and I take it out and look at it whenever I can—' She says this in a quiet, steady voice that is impossible to mishear or disbelieve.

'It is just the one picture, John. It hasn't made me seek out others. I am sure they're wrong about that.' Then she says she is very sorry, at which he puts his arms around her, pulls her to him. His hand presses into her back, the other cradles the back of her head. She bends down into the embrace, returning it. They pull each other in as close as possible, feeling the push and heave of the muscles that draw their separate breaths in and let them out; the world outside of them vanishes.

You are still there! Barbara thinks, astounded. And it feels, as breath follows breath, his, hers, his, hers again, as if everything might still, somehow, be all right. Perhaps she has after all been wrong, and one thing need not be bought at the expense of another? Perhaps this is the moment when he will change, for her. Perhaps all that was needed was for her to be brave enough? She moves her hands up and down his back, pressing. In a low voice, she tells him over and over how much she loves him.

Minutes pass, and then, gradually, he pulls away. Still holding her, he examines her face, as if looking for some physical sign that he has missed all these years, something that, had he seen it, might have told him that this would happen in the end... He shakes his head gravely from side to side. 'We must go to the field,' he says.

'No—' she tells him.

He takes her hand in his, holding it rather too hard.

'I can't,' she tells him, 'confess. I'm sorry about hurting you, I'm sorry about lying to you, to everyone, I don't mind saying that. But I am not sorry about the photograph itself. That was my daughter! I don't—' She stops, and her face, the whole of her freezes a moment as she realizes what she is about to say: 'I don't want to be forgiven!'

'Where is the Likeness?' he asks. 'Is it here in the caravan?'

'Of course not! John: I'm hoping that you might be able to see—' He sits there like a stone, growing heavier as his rage builds.

'Is it at home, then?'

'Well, yes,' she tells him, 'but listen: I want—' Suddenly she is shouting at him, 'I want you to understand that I needed it!'

'Where is it?' he shouts back. Their voices smash at the flimsy walls of the room. Then it's quiet. They are no longer touching. She sits down, rests her head on her hands. She thinks of her sister-in-law Rose, twelve years ago, outside the crematorium; she stood close with one arm around Barbara's waist, and slipped the envelope into her hand: 'I don't know if this is the right thing to do, Barbara. You needn't look. You can always throw it away . . .' Though when it came to it, of course she could not. And because Rose and probably Adrian too knew that she had accepted this thing, she had to keep away from them and so, too, that whole lazy, honey-scented afternoon in their sunny garden—including the moment when Rose, who'd gone in to get the tea, must have picked up her camera, focused hastily on the baby in her sister-in-law's lap, pressed the shutter and then slipped the camera back into the kitchen drawer, pushing it to, catching her fingertip just as Barbara looked up—that whole afternoon vanished. Only the photograph, in its white envelope, remains. Barbara has risked everything for it—and, it seems, she has lost.



John sits on the edge of the table, too close. 'Well, where? Is it in the bedroom, our bedroom?' he asks. Though it can't be, his voice sounds like someone drunk.

She shrugs, looks beyond him, up through the round-cornered side window, at the washing-line, the glimpse of trees and hills beyond. Above these, just inside the frame, the soft, fat crescent of the waxing moon hangs in the sky. It is quite possible, Barbara thinks, that the two men who have been walking on it are right now looking back at the earth and thinking of the people on it, but she's certain that they would never, ever guess what is happening to her, here in this caravan in Harris's field. In all the vast strangeness of whatever it is that we live in or upon or amongst (with or without God, because He might be there still, hiding in the cracks and crevices of it all, different from what she's been led to imagine or not imagine, but there); in all of it, it seems to her, there is not one single person who could tell her what it's best to do now, or what will happen in the end.

'I don't know,' he says, 'why you are smiling!' Then there's a single sharp knock on the door.

'What are you doing?' I call in to them.

'Paul Leverson wants everyone there before we start,' Mark adds.

Barbara lets us in.

'What is it?' Mark says.

'Your mother,' John tells him, 'has just confessed to keeping a photograph. An image, which she—'

'I look at it,' Barbara says. 'It's true, I do that. But I haven't confessed. I've just—'

'It's a picture of the baby that died. I knew that already,' I say, realizing from the look on John's face that I've made things worse than I meant to. I sit down on Mark's bunk; he sits next to me, and I move away a bit. It seems to me that they are all taking this more seriously than they need to.

'God will forgive her,' I point out.

'She refuses to go to the meeting!' Mr. Hern says.

'It's not a sin,' she says, and you can hear all the small noises everyone is making, their breathing and swallowing and the rub of cloth on cloth and cloth on skin.

'What are we going to do now?' I ask after what seems like a long silence.

'We're going home,' John says, addressing me and Mark. 'To find the photograph,' he explains, as if it was the most reasonable thing in the world.

'I don't want to!' I tell him.

'We must,' he says.

‘Natalie,’ Barbara says, holding out her arms, her face wide open as if she has just returned from a long journey, during which she missed me every minute of every day, ‘come here, darling.’

She and I put the caravan to rights while Mark packs away the outdoor cooking equipment, the water bottles, washing-line and so on. The crowd that's gathered stand a certain distance away, as if that makes some kind of difference. In the main, they just watch, silent or talking in whispers amongst themselves, but Elsbeth Anderton calls out to Mark: ‘Please give your mother my love!’ Her husband comes up, stands close to him as he packs saucepans into a box and insists in a low, confidential voice that he must go inside now and tell his father and mother to change their minds; they really must stay. 

Now, he says, is the point at which everything could change for the better, and if only they will stay—

‘He just wants to find the photograph,’ Mark explains.

‘But really, that isn't important,’ Paul Leverson says, again with surprising gentleness: ‘the photograph will still be wherever it is at the end of the week. . . Whereas to join with us now—’

Mark smiles, shrugs, continues packing enamel breakfast bowls and mugs into their box, wipes some dirty spoons, wraps them together in a cloth.

Barbara allows Jean McAllister in, though she earlier turned down Edith, who kept saying over and over again that she knew something was wrong all the time and only wanted to help.

Inside, the two women embrace and Barbara says, ‘Thank you.’ On her way out, Jean stops, waits for Mark to get to his feet and then shakes his hand, formally, as if they were wearing their best clothes and attending some kind of reception. She wishes him good luck.

He piles the washing-line and still-damp clothes on top of the crockery box and picks it up.

Now, there is nothing left to do but hitch up. Barbara is wearing sunglasses and has changed into her striped dress. She pauses briefly at the passenger door to say that she is sorry for upsetting everyone, then slips inside. Mark and I get in the back. John shakes hands with Paul Leverson, claps Anderton across the shoulders, takes a few of the offered hands and embraces, promises that he'll see everyone at Service in the Gardners' house the next week.

It takes three attempts to get the engine started. More people are gathered at the gate. The twins, their faces open and oddly childlike, bang on the window, signalling to Mark: unwind. He keeps it closed, then they gesture at me, the hand signal for fucking, but I look at them in a way that makes them stop. Harris's yellow tractor is coming down and we have to reverse back down the straight part of the lane to the farm entrance.

Finally, we are on the road.

Twigs slap the sides of the car, insects burst in silent profusion on the windscreen. Behind us the caravan jerks around the bends whilst in front, the engine, still in second gear, roars its protest.

'Please, take it easy, John,' Barbara says.

'Ask your father to please be careful,' she tells Mark, a few minutes later.

'She's got a point, Dad,' he says eventually. 'It isn't worth dying for.' After a moment, John shifts up a gear. We turn onto the main road, where the regular swish of overtaking traffic and the stream of oncoming cars marks some kind of return to normality.

Though things are not at all the same: I sit with my right foot hitched over the opposite knee, to make a bookstand for Envall's Confessions. One hand keeps my place, the other holds the end of my plait, circling the tip round and round my forefinger, or sometimes it cups my chin. Or else I sniff the tips of my fingers, searching for traces of a scent that I wish I could remember. Now, Mark's the one who wants to talk, but I won't let him.

'Shh,' I signal, putting my finger to my lips.

'John,' Barbara says, as he slows down to accommodate a truck, 'Rose took the photograph, without me knowing—'

'John,' she begins again, 'I know you've said, many times, how the faith would help us cope with Ruth's death. Well, it didn't, and I can't explain it, but somehow I'm sure of this—if that photograph had been on the mantelpiece all these years, if it had really been there, instead of hidden, if it had been out there—then life would have been—' he glances rapidly at her while she searches for the word: 'Easier. Better. What can be wrong with that?'



'I can't discuss this now,' he tells her.

'You might try!' she says; then, a moment later, turns around in her seat, smiling brightly.

'Please don't worry, darlings, either of you,' she says. 'It will be all right in the end.' She pushes her sunglasses up so that we can see her eyes, which look sore, but still shine; I still believe her.

'I don't understand,' I say. 'Now that you've admitted it, why aren't you forgiven?'

'It's not enough, yet,' Mark explains. 'She is still attached to the imitation.' His voice has a light, non-committal tone to it, just short of sarcasm. He reaches over, touches the book, pulls a hank of pages towards him, taps with his finger: 'Chapter Five.' His other arm brushes mine. The words are there, but he doesn't need to read them: 'When I speak to you of sin, remember that I do so always as one who has sinned. When I speak of the particular sins involved in the making and worshipping of the likeness of anything that is upon the earth, I have perhaps sinned more than any one of you. Yet, still, I can find myself in a state of grace—'

His voice goes thin, comes back at the wrong pitch. Cars overtake us, speed by. The astronauts hurtle towards earth, asleep. Cows graze in fields. I don't want to go home.

# 29

Because it is handwritten, arrives at the community centre, and is marked 'Lecture,' I open the letter without a second thought:



> Dear Natalie,
> Pekka is delivering this so you can't say I'm not keeping my side of the bargain.
> Thank you for your invitation.
> I want to see this thing through so I will be there, of course.
> I apologize for my handwriting, but my typewriter is broken.
> Yours sincerely,
> Christina

Her letters are in fact very carefully formed, horribly neat. Each sentence, now that there is punctuation, begins on a separate line, as if a lot of thought and effort has gone into making it. I imagine her, sitting at a huge table in a frilly, electric-lit kitchen, bent over the paper with the tip of her tongue between her lips as she writes, the way children do.

'What is the bargain?' Heikki asks.

'I've no idea. I never made one.'

'And what does this mean? What is the thing she is seeing through?'

It could be anything, I tell him, or nothing. It could be a threat to punish me. It could be that she is giving me a chance not to do what she expects me to do—

'And if you do do it?'

'I don't want to think about that,' I say. 'It's maybe something so personal it's impossible to understand. Some little thing...'

'I see,' he says, and must of course be talking about something other than what I have told him, which no one in their right mind could understand. And I am terrified, from the look in his eyes, that he will want to know all the things I am not ready to tell him. Please, I think at him through my turned back, please remember: I am the one who asks the stream of little inconsequential questions that add up in the end (or sometimes doesn't need to: I just get told, as if by osmosis). I am the one who wants all the useless details, who stumbles on the half-forgotten secrets—I always have, I always will. In the end, it's what I do. And until I change the sign, this is a one-way street—

'My ex-wife is a difficult woman, very extreme,' he tells me, in a simple, straightforward kind of tone: proving my point, I think at first. But then, I realize, as he sits down at his desk and ignores me, that he is thinking things I can't know back at me, and I don't know what will come of it.

# 30

In the last of the daylight, we turn left at the lights, enter the familiar sequence of domestic rights and lefts that brings us—all of a sudden, it seems after the long hours of being on the way—home. John Hern gets out, opens the gate, drives onto the paved driveway, keeping close to the right-hand side, and stops again. We look out of our respective windows, feeling the silence between us—already long—deepening now that the engine is quiet.



It must have been raining here: the garden can hardly contain itself. Bushes and flowers are entangled and competing with weeds for space, everything is about to burst from its boundaries. The lawn is dotted with daisies and clover, the joins between the paving-stones filled with moss and grasses. In the midst of all this growth, the house itself stands stalwart, unaffected, its curtains and windows closed. Inside it, the air must be hot and still, there will be a fine layer of dust on the surfaces of tables and windowsills. The fridge will be silent, switched off with its door propped open, the electricity stalled at the meter. The house is resting, gathering its strength. We in the car are exhausted, the backs of our legs numbed and stuck to the seats, yet unwilling to leave; it's as if we might stay here until the extravagant vegetation invades the vehicle itself, and forces us out.

Then I break the spell by leaning forwards, pushing my shoulders between the front seats. The air stirs, alive with the possibilities of words.

'Can I stay?' I ask.

'Oh hush, child,' Barbara tells me, quickly turning around. Her voice is soft as fluff, its fabric finely unravelled. She reaches out and loops a strand of hair behind my ear, the way she is always doing now. 'Now is not the right time,' she says. There will be one, then? John Hern switches the engine back on.

'You'll have to go straight home,' he tells me.

'They won't be expecting me.' I reach through the gap, touch his arm as he feels for the hand-brake.

'No need to drive there. She only has the one bag,' Barbara tells her husband. 'I'll walk her home.'

'I will,' Mark says.

'No,' his father tells him, 'you can help me,' and cuts the engine again. Barbara opens her door. I lean back in my seat. Suppose I refuse to go? When Barbara, now carrying my duffle bag, opens the door, I still don't move.

'You haven't done anything wrong,' she says. 'You mustn't worry. We're all tired... Maybe you can come and see us in the morning.'

I turn to Mark, look him full in the face. I study him hard, my eyes moving minutely from side to side, up and down. The asymmetrical eyebrows still frown at me but they are bewildered now, not hostile. Tired, shadowy eyes, their pupils pitch-black. His lips are slightly parted, the very tip of his tongue just visible. He's changed, though he's also the same.

There's an emotion radiating from me, an intense alarm, a shrill, unvoiced scream far larger than the occasion warrants—this is not my family, after all, not my disaster. He looks steadily back at me.

‘I don’t know what to do,’ he tells me, touching my shoulder. I scramble out of the car, taking with me my panic, but also my warmth, my smell of crushed grass and salt. Barbara and I link arms as we walk back to the gate.

Will Sandra be in? Who else might be there? There is no way of knowing. No way of imagining what it will be like to have the two of them meet, what on earth I can say to either of them to explain my lies—I just push the thought of it away, and take the walk one step at a time, looking at the houses and gardens, just as I did the first time.

John makes his way to the house. Mark is to brace the caravan, take the keys from the ignition, bring the bags into the hall and leave them there, as quickly as possible. He waits in the car a few minutes before climbing into the caravan, pulling open the lockers, dragging the bags out so that they land heavily on the floor; the caravan shakes with each one; he waits for the last vibration of each impact to still itself before reaching for the next bag. His mind is empty: he keeps it that way by filling it with the sounds and sensations of the task. He carries the bags one by one into the house and, bending carefully at the knees, sets them down in a row. His father is nowhere to be seen.



When he has finished the carrying he sets to work on the van, unhitching it, then squatting by each corner for a few moments, moving round every few turns to keep the balance right, giving himself over to the click of the ratchet in the jack. Then, when there’s nothing else to do he walks slowly to the house and counts himself up the stairs. He can hear his father in his parents’ bedroom; he almost knows, before he steps in, that he will see the bed pulled from its place by the wall, roughly but thoroughly stripped, the linen piled on it and topped with his parents’ prayer books and Bibles. The other contents of the cupboards in the bedside tables have been emptied on the floor, as have those of the two chests, the drawers of which are in a rough pile next to a drift of white lining-paper and their mounds of underwear, nightshirts, stockings and socks. His father kneels by the wardrobe, emptying it of shoes. When he sees Mark he pulls himself to his feet, removes an armful of Barbara's clothes from the hanging rail and throws them on top of the bed.

'I am searching it out,' he explains, breathing hard from the effort of his actions, from the greater effort of his feelings. His shirt is unbuttoned, underarm patches of sweat spread unevenly across his chest. The lack of a beard is still momentarily shocking, perplexing in the way it makes his face both harder and more vulnerable. He stands there by the bed, waiting a moment, as if perhaps he wants to be stopped.

'Do we have to do it now?' Mark asks. 'I mean, if it has been here so long? In the morning, maybe—'

'A hidden image has more power than a public one,' his father says, still breathing hard. 'Don't you think so?' and Mark nods; he does in some way agree, though not with the consequence; to save his life, he could not explain why. But during this brief exchange his father seems to grow less alien as he engages in the familiar act of weighing and judging the matter in hand, showing himself to be in some small way right.

'Where do you think she would put such a thing?' he asks.

'I don't know,' Mark says. He has never hidden any material thing, nor anything at all until he began, so recently, to hide the facts of what took place on the beach and the new uncertainty of his belief, by simply not putting them into spoken words.

'You're a good boy,' his father says, smiling now. 'Help me. We'll look everywhere, in all the rooms of the house. If any images are here, we will find them and destroy them. Then, things can begin to return to the right way they have always been... The loft cupboards, your bedroom, the spare rooms—you do those. Be careful. Look under the paper in the drawers, along the edges of the carpets, see if they have ever been pulled up. It could be very small . . .'

Mark stands there. Even if you are right, he thinks, this is wrong. The thought makes him frown.

'What's the matter?' his father asks. I want to defy you, to your face, Mark thinks, but he's scared, without his mother in the house, not quite able to act.

'Please,' his father says, gesturing at the bed, the wardrobe, 'there's so much to look through.'

'I don't know how to,' Mark says. He feels the weight of his father's hand on his shoulders, guiding him through the door and into the smaller spare room. The pink curtains are open; the electric light sours all the colours and sets the fragile, man-made objects against the inky sky outside. The plant on top of the paraffin heater is dead. The lid has not been replaced on the sewing machine and two long white threads dangle from bobbin case and needle, as if a piece of sewing has been hastily removed: something he has seen his mother do countless times, biting the threads because picking up the scissors will take too long.



'Just open everything,' he is told.

But there's nothing in here! he thinks back.

Yet there is something, and it's surprisingly easy to find. He sits on the bed. Two books lie on the wicker table beside it. He reaches for the one underneath, not the prayer book but the leather-bound Testament. He doesn't even have to shake the pages, because the corner of an envelope pokes carelessly out, and inside that, he knows, is the photograph. He holds the envelope long enough to notice its thinness, that the flap is merely tucked in, and that the edges and corners are scuffed. Then he slips it back inside, closes the book and begins to unmake the bed. As he removes each layer: the green candlewick spread, the pink Witney blankets, the paler pink brushed-cotton sheets, he folds them and puts them on the chair. When he has finished, he puts the two books on top of the linen, in the way his father had in the other room. He lifts the mattress, leaves it propped against the wall. He notes, as if he were someone observing his own behaviour, that he is leaving evidence of a pointless search and that he has not yet called his father. Will he? He's not sure what he will eventually do, but clings for now to the fact that it is possible, at this stage, to say that he hasn't seen the photograph. He hasn't seen it. He knows it is there, but he hasn't seen it. His father would make mincemeat of this and he could do the same if he chose, but he does not choose, because from a certain, limited perspective not seeing makes a difference. It makes a small shelter, a scrap of gentle shade in the glare of what is happening. He puts it to himself that it is possibly necessary to finish what he has been asked to do in order to know what to do next.

So he goes to the cupboard, mechanically removes the ironing-board and the iron, then the cover from the ironing-board and the loose piece of carpet from the cupboard floor. His father comes in as he is doing this and announces that he is going downstairs. If Mark finds anything, he says, he should turn it face down, call him immediately: has Mark heard? He's encouraging now, almost tender. There's a smell of work about him, salt, heavy. His voice is rougher.

When he's gone, Mark sits on the floor with his back to the wall. From this angle just indigo treetops and violet sky are visible through the window. He gets up, opens it, sits down again. From below comes the sound of drawers pulled open, furniture being dragged from its place, books thumped to the floor in chest-wide piles. Between these abrupt noises are bouts of concentrated silence, during which, presumably, his father leafs through the books, or looks quietly into the spaces he has made. If he lets himself, Mark knows, he will either retch or faint. It's tempting to create his own emergency, but he suspects that, short of suicide, he could do nothing big enough to distract his father. He leaves the room and wanders into the next, then the bathroom, ruffling their surfaces without any serious intent. Finally he shuffles though the folded towels and sheets in the airing cupboard, noticing only too late, because he's not really looking, that his hands are filthy. He returns to the bathroom, washes them. The water is cold because his father has forgotten to put the immersion heater back on.

He goes back to the pink and green room. It is, he can see now, a girl's room, the colours intended to be both bright and delicate. And also, he can see it is a kind of idolatrous shrine. The ironing-board, the geraniums in winter are superfluous to its deeper purpose. He wonders, exactly how does his mother look at the photograph? Does she sit down on the bed at some quiet time during the day? Does she even kneel on the floor, the testament open, the picture on the page? How often does she come? In the day or during the night, perhaps  when everyone else is asleep? Has she ever looked at the picture while he and his father were close by? How often does she open the envelope? Every year? Every week? Every day?

He walks quickly over to the bedside chair, removes the envelope again, and puts it into the pocket at the back of his shorts. It fits exactly. He fastens the button and leaves the room.

The landing is dark now, only a faint shred of indirect and dusky light coming from the half-open doors of the rooms. The stairs are a kind of limbo: he goes down them quickly, into the living-room. There are more things downstairs, and despite knowing what to expect, the sight is even more shocking than it was in the bedroom. The armchairs and sofa lie on their backs, cushions off, springs exposed. The alcove shelves are empty. The shiny LP records are out of their plain white sleeves, stacked, heedless of scratches. Balls of wool from his mother's sewing box have unravelled. And everywhere are buttons, scattered like confetti or fallen petals on a lawn. He remembers that first day when I came and said that the carpet was like grass, and even now in the midst of the dismantling of his home, his skin bristles at the thought of my skin.

'Well?' his father asks. He's trying to pull up the carpet at the fireplace edge. Dust has stuck to the sweat on his face. One of his hands is bleeding. Without answering, Mark leaves the room, goes back through the hall and through the front door, just in time to see his mother unhitch the gate. He runs towards her.

'He's rolling back the carpets,' he tells her, 'undoing the beds, chucking stuff around!'

'Something's not right there,' she tells him, pushing his news aside. 'Her mother didn't seem to know anything. There was a terrible mess in the kitchen. I tried to explain—'

'Barbara!' John Hern shouts from the porch. He is holding a vase, one of the pair with the pale glaze that came from Elojoki. 'Barbara, can you not save us all and tell me where it is—'

'I don't want it destroyed,' she calls back.

'You'll not come in this house until that image is found.'

'I don't want to come in!'

'Mark—' he calls.

'I'll stay with her, Dad,' Mark calls back, closing his ears so hard against any answer that he doesn't know whether there is one or not. 'We'll get in the van, Mum,' he tells her.

They sit on the fold-down seats in the caravan and watch lights go on and off in the house.

'He won't find it, Mum,' Mark says, groping for a box of matches.

'He might,' she tells him. 'But it's that poor child I'm thinking of. "So you're back, are you?" the mother said. "Who the hell are you?" she asked me. I think she'd been drinking. She obviously hadn't got the letters I sent. The man she lives with isn't Natalie's father. He wasn't there, in any case. I should do something, but I don't know what—' She stares intently out of the window. From the direction of the house comes the sound of something shattering, dropped or thrown, broken in any case.

'Your father will never get over this,' she says. 'You know you can go in the house if you want. I don't want to come between you. I'm looking for my knitting—'

'I'll be all right,' she says once Mark has found it in the locker under his own bunk. 'I don't mind being on my own.' She pulls the needles from the ball of wool, makes a few busy stitches. Then her hand finds a steady rhythm and the needles begin to click relentlessly on, only the faintest variation, not enough for a pause, at the end of the row.

'Your father is such a strong-willed man.' There's a catch to her breath as she inhales.

'But he could have made an exception.' A few tears slip under the rims of her glasses, over the planes of her cheeks, turning inwards and down towards her mouth. In an oddly childish gesture, she pokes her tongue out and licks her upper lip. 

'I found your photograph. I found the envelope.' Mark says. She looks up at him to check what she's heard.

'I don't think he should have shouted at me like that,' she says. 'After all, in the end they'll decide to give in over the passports.'

'It's in my pocket,' he tells her.

'Truly?' she asks. 'Which one? No, don't tell me. I'd rather not know!' Her voice lifts, gathering them both up into some kind of release: 'So he won't be coming out for a while, then!' she says. She puts the knitting down.

'Maybe by now he's digging under the floor!'

'Maybe he'll get to Australia!'

The caravan shifts as his mother moves over to the kitchen area. 'We can have tinned supper in here. I'll see what there is. BB?' she calls out, holding the shiny, label-less tins aloft one in each hand, wiggling them at the wrists, 'and CB? After, there are peaches. There's probably some of that cream.'

Mark loves her for her gaiety in that moment, however false it is. He helps to reconnect the gas bottle and they stand side by side at the tiny hot-plate while baked beans heat up in the pan and the slices of meat warm under the grill. At some point, he knows, he will see the photograph inside the envelope that sits in his pocket, stiffening the cloth just enough for him not to forget it. At some point, all of this will be over, and they will live a different kind of life. He spoons the steaming beans next to the slices of heat-softened corned beef.

'I'll close the curtains,' his mother says. 'I'm going to put the latch on, just in case.' They sit opposite each other, and eat hungrily.

'Natalie didn't tell her mother the first thing about us, nothing at all—' she says after a while, 'that's what I think. Can you believe it?'

'What will Dad do when he can't find it?' Mark asks.

'I don't know,' she says.

Sandra is sitting upright on the sofa while I, buried in the farthest armchair, finish my toast and jam. 'I should have known,' she says. 'I went like a fool and reported you missing yesterday. I knew you weren't really gone but Luke made me. Now I'll have to tell them you've turned up. But it can wait till morning. In fact, you can bloody well go yourself, and tell them you're back. That'd be a laugh—they won't ask you whether you're married or not.'

'It was supposed to be for a week,' I say. 'But there was an argument so we came back early.' I'm still very hungry; it's a bottomless kind of feeling. I return to the kitchen, search the cupboards and find an open packet of ginger biscuits. Suppose, I think, tipping them onto a plate, the person you want to hurt just doesn't seem to feel it, but they might just be pretending? How will you ever know? How could you ever forgive them, even though it was that you most wanted? What is left to do, now?

'You could have said,' Sandra continues when I'm back. 'I wouldn't have stopped you, for heaven's sake. Did she do that to your hair? It's tight enough to cut your circulation off. Come here, I'll get it out.'

'No,' I tell her, sitting back in the armchair. A loose spring digs into me from underneath. 'No thanks, I like it this way.' I'm damp and chilly and look around for something to cover up with.

'No thanks,' Sandra repeats, raising her eyebrows, studying me a moment or two with the beginnings of curiosity. 'Well, the TV broke, but we're getting it fixed, and you can have it in your room. There'll be a bigger one for down here come Friday.'

'I don't watch TV anymore.' I know even as I say this that it is not a position I'll be able to sustain, not here, a place which somehow, despite the pitch of my desire and the ingenuity of my efforts, I've neither managed to leave behind nor to make any different. It's fortunate that the spent bulbs in the front room have still not been replaced; there's just the lamp with a scarf draped over, so it doesn't show when the heaviness that has been filling me up all the way down the A1 and into the increasingly familiar landscape spills over, a little, at the eyes—oh, Mum, I'd like to call out, raising my arms blindly, and let that be the end of it.



'What was it like, then?' Sandra asks, pushing her hair from her face and lighting another cigarette. 'What did you do all day?'

'Just cooking and things,' I tell her. 'Cricket. We went on a long walk to the beach—' Briefly, I contemplate telling her what I did with Mark, which might interest her, decide no, continue instead with 'Singing, praying, and stuff like that.'

'Praying?' Sandra says. 'Christ! I thought there was something odd about that woman. Praying! What for? More pocket money? Which reminds me, that twenty quid you took out of my bag—' I pick at a loose thread on the check dress.

'I gave it to them for my keep,' I explain.

'Well, you can get it back,' Sandra says, 'that's another thing you can do in the morning. You can go around there and ask for it back and I'll come with you to make sure you do.'

I huddle in the depths of the armchair, saying nothing.

'Where do they live?' she asks, and when there's still no reply, she picks up the ashtray she's been using, a bright-yellow one from the pub, empties it over the coffee table, then leans forward and hurls it across the space between us: it misses me by a long way, but all the same I flinch when it hits the wall, and then the floor. This isn't something that's happened before. It's a path I don't want to take. I get up, leave the room.

'Go to bed,' I hear her say as I close the door behind me, which somehow makes it impossible, despite how exhausted I feel, to climb the stairs. Instead, I slide back the latch on the front door, close it noiselessly behind me. No doubt she's still sitting there, glowering at the wall while I do the same with the gate. I start to run, and keep it up all the way back to the Avenues.

The Herns' front door is open, just as if they were expecting me, but the only light on is a lamp in the front room, where Mr. Hern sits with his hands on his knees and his eyes closed, though clearly not asleep, amidst a sea of buttons and records. It's none of my business and anyway, everything will be all right in the morning, when we will all get up and have breakfast together, just as I've imagined it... I climb the stairs and turn at last into the room that I've wanted, since that first afternoon, to be mine. I pull the door almost closed behind me, take the sheets and blankets from the pile on the chair, make up the bed, climb in. It's soft and cool. There's a light pull above the bed, and I plunge the room into darkness. I have the feeling of being suspended in something between water and air, almost exactly the temperature of my skin. It's a pure and perfect, utterly physical happiness, something I'll remember always, and need to. A few more breaths, and I'm completely dissolved.

# 31

At eight, the sun is still high and shines through the trees so white and bright that it could be lunchtime. We have to close the venetian blinds on two sides of the community hall. I am to speak from a raised platform, on which stands a chair, a lectern and a small table for my papers and water. Seating is arranged in rows of ten, four blocks of three: I can't see us filling them—but, as Heikki points out, a party of students is coming from the university at Oulu. Then there's the historian from Helsinki, at least eight from the Board of Antiquities, plus, very likely, some partners. At least three ministers of religion, then the town itself—'It adds up,' he says. 

And we stand close, though not touching; perfectly proper, but as unlike colleagues as it is possible to feel. My mother, on the phone, keeps asking me, 'Has something happened?' She, of course, is not coming to hear me speak: 'Just get this over with, Natty, and come home!' And my Dean of Studies has cancelled at the last minute and couldn't find a replacement, so I'm here all on my own... I've been warned that even if they're not actually hostile or indifferent, the audience will probably seem that way: this is a cultural thing, not to be taken personally. And of course, though no one has said this, leaving aside any reaction to the content of what I say, they still have to deal with the way I look.

And now they're starting to come in; they choose wine or juice or water from the table at the side, then take their seats.

The ordinary villagers and the guests, by virtue of dressing up and dressing down, and my own ignorance of how to read appearances here, seem oddly indistinguishable.

Heikki goes to the door to greet his colleagues; I slip onto the platform. I watch the rows fill up: Mrs. Lohi wheeled in by a young woman who might be the granddaughter she mentioned, several other of the older people from her flats; the friendly woman who runs the daycare and chats to me over the fence, Maria and Tuomas, the couple who have just bought a derelict farm to renovate, Katrin from the supermarket, her husband and oldest girl. Christina and Pekka and a small group of hangers-on, an odd mixture of elderly and teenage, come in and sit at the back, and then, to my surprise, the room is over two-thirds full.

'Just a few words of introduction,' Heikki says. I have the feeling of blushing, though I don't, of course. 'Many of you here will have met our speaker, Dr. Natalie Baron, from the University of Durham, England. She is the author of many articles dealing with interesting aspects of religious history—' So says the man I've pressed myself against, touched all over, let inside of me, cried out to, held. Three times now, but always in the darkest dark we can make, blinds, curtains and eyes closed tight.

'I believe this is her first proper visit to Finland and it has come about as a result of the generous support from institutions in both countries—'

My head's so light, I could float away.

'One day will we do this seeing too?' he asked me two days ago, stroking the palm of my hand in the darkness. . . 'Why,' I whispered back, 'why risk spoiling such a very good thing?'

And the kiss that followed was an answer, and also not one, and I fell asleep by accident so that I had to ask him to leave his own bedroom in the morning while I dressed, then follow him into work, fully visible to anyone who looked—

Behind me, someone is fiddling with the blinds. And now Heikki has done with the credits to funders et cetera and is winding down, pointing out that in order to pursue my interests here I have had to get used to Finnish ways and, of course, the climate... There's a polite spattering of applause, as he goes to his front-row seat, and I begin.

'The subject of my enquiry here has been the life of Tuomas Envall, a nineteenth-century cleric and the founder of a sect utterly opposed to visual representation of all kinds. More exactly, as most people here already know by now, I have wanted to discover what made Tuomas Envall invent this particular faith, based supposedly on an extreme, over-literal reading of the second commandment, but clearly emanating from some other, deeper place in his psyche or understanding of the world... Why did he do it? That is the question which has brought me here to Elojoki, and I will share my answer with you tonight.

'It should be said first that Envallism is a sect which, against all odds, continues today, albeit now broken into a series of rival factions, some of which bear little resemblance to the original. The First Envallist Church is the most traditional of these. In 1980, they purchased several small islands to the far north-east of Scotland, and most of this group either live or aspire to live on the larger, habitable island, or else on the 'mainland' nearby, using Middle Skerry as a site of worship. The weather is very harsh and this is a lifestyle not without discomfort and risk. Perhaps surprisingly, this far from liberal church has a growing membership. Their summer meeting attracts a wide variety of people, especially the young. During

July, this remote archipelago is, in terms of roads and accommodation, acutely congested. The hardier visitors camp or stay in caravans, and people on the neighbouring islands make a sizeable income from this and from offering bed and breakfast and boat trips to the harbour on Midskerry.

'As it happens, the First Envallist community owes its Island existence to the initial purchase of the islands by businessman Bob Harris. It could neither have sustained itself nor repaid its debt to him without the revenue brought by visitors. The summer meeting is free; as is admission at any time to the peculiar but splendid modernist church, with its wall of huge, round windows and asymmetrical roof, designed and built, apart from specialist masonry and lead-work, by the community itself. Donations are encouraged, and the fees charged at other times during the year for attendance at courses or retreats are substantial. A copy of one of Envall's essays, just twenty pages long, hand-set and printed on the Island's press, costs nearly twenty pounds.

'Nonetheless, and largely for reasons they cannot articulate, "looking for something" or "drawn to it, somehow," a steady stream of people do make long journeys to this obscure and windswept place where images do not exist. Again, why? The answer to that question is a complex one; I will leave you to consider it while I speak . . .'

The paper rustles in my hand as I move the first sheet from left to right on the lectern. I force myself to take a couple of deep breaths.

'To return to Tuomas: the only remaining likeness of Tuomas Envall, painted when he was fourteen or fifteen, can be seen in the Maakuntamuseo. It shows a thin, dreamy boy: rather wistful, not very strong, you'd say, and looking at it you would never guess that within a decade he would be inciting the residents of Elojoki to pile their most treasured possessions in a heap and set them alight . . .'

And of course, I'm thinking as I speak, you'd never have guessed, from a portrait of me as I was at the beginning of that summer of 1969, what I would be like by the end of it. This is the oddest thing: I'm realizing, literally as I speak, that I've come, in an oblique sort of way and on the very slightest of grounds, to identify with the man I set out to vilify.

'Of course, biography is not a science,' I tell them as I think all this. 'Imagination is a part of the process as much as research is.'

I tell them about Tuomas's conversation with Runar in the study. I tell them about Tuomas's arrival in Elojoki, where the minister was dying but refusing to admit it; how he wasn't wanted but refused to go away. I tell them how he found his paints at the bottom of his bag. How the bishop ignored him. How he painted for some of every day and then for most of every day, and so time passed until summer began, though the old pastor, gaunt and pale, still wore scarves wound around his neck. It's a story, more than a paper, but then this is a community hall, and not a university.



'By now,' I continue, 'it was high summer. Like now. The air was filled with every kind of sound, birdsong, the whispering of leaves, the whine of mosquitoes. Night hardly existed ...' For two months it had all been brown, but now that was forgotten and everything was green. The tendrils of garden cucumbers wound themselves almost visibly around the sticks and strings that supported them.

Tuomas had made a log-and-plank table and an easel so that he could work outside. He read virtually nothing, just worked continuously at his pictures. Now, he could give a sense of depth to objects, a feeling of weight. He could match colours, or create the sense of them, show how the light fell. He could paint a picture of a forest that you might almost walk into by mistake, but as soon as it was achieved this lost its satisfaction. He found himself wanting to depict things he could only just see, moments of extraordinary harmony that vanished before he could mix the first colour, colours that existed only while things moved, the vibrations of light, the unseen essence beneath the appearance. "So far had I gone away from Him," he wrote long afterwards in his Confessions," that had the pastor at that point come to the door while I was engaged in this pursuit, and called for my help in God's work, I would have been angry with him for taking me away from what I did..." His hair grew long and his eyes were wide with looking. Although he always went to the *pappila* in the morning, sometimes he forgot to go during the day, and sometimes he was awake all night, painting or seeing what he might paint in his mind's eye...'

I drink a little from my glass of water, setting it carefully back on the table with no trace of a shake. I look around quickly: the audience seems attentive enough, their faces slack, their eyes alert, though one of Christina's elderly companions, I notice, has fallen asleep.

I tell them about the portrait: a well-known story, but always lacking in certain crucial details, which I supply:

'It must have been mid-August,' I tell them. 'The nights would be returning. Let's imagine Tuomas wore a jacket when he sat outside at his table in the evenings. One evening, when he's returned to the small house to get a pair of fingerless gloves as well, he looks up from his work and sees Jaakko, the boy who sometimes helps the housekeeper Ulla with heavier work at the *pappila*, standing there on the path, looking straight at him. It's a look, not a stare, not hostile. The boy doesn't stop when Tuomas sees him.

'Remember,' I tell them, 'that Tuomas hasn't heard a friendly word since he arrived in the place. "It's late, Jaakko," Tuomas says, when the boy comes a few steps closer, and puts the small cloth-wrapped parcel he's carrying carefully on the table. "Are you making a picture?" he asks, edging round.

'Tuomas gestures at the board propped in front of him, the mess of green, the thin but inky blue. Several nights in a row he's been trying to capture the quality of summer light at dusk, the way the colours and the simple shapes of trees sing together in flat but plangent voices, those long moments when the shadows lose their edge, dissolve. It's an impossible project; he half hates and half loves it, can't stop, finishes and dismisses each effort with increasing speed.

'"Trees," Jaakko tells him.

'"Well done!" Both their faces break into smiles. Now the boy is at Tuomas's side. He smells of sweat, smoke, milk. His clothes are dark, his face, forearms, hands and unshod feet glow cleanly in the dusk.

'"It's no good," Tuomas says. The boy appears indifferent or to reserve his judgement.

'"Can you do a cow?" he asks.

'Tuomas leans back in his chair, stretches. Five months of unspoken words inside him shift and loosen, ready to slither and rush out of his mouth all at once. He braces himself carefully against this. He knows he is half mad with loneliness; he doesn't want to scare the boy away. Jaakko is twelve, thirteen at the most. Since March, he has grown so that now his trouser hems float around his calves. Is there perhaps a bit of a shadow on his jaw? Hard to tell.



'"Can you? Or a heron?" Jaakko is asking. "An owl?"

'"Why, yes, I can." Tuomas's eyes are bright. "Even a fish."

'"Me?" Jaakko's hand briefly grips Tuomas's arm, his face is split by an enormous grin—"Paint me!"

'"It's night," Tuomas says, "Run on back now, say your prayers and get what sleep you can –" But of course Tuomas longs to do such a thing, to paint not the hugeness of God's creation but a small part of His humanity, this part, who speaks to him like this, stands close and makes him feel warm, who, so long as he painted, would not go away—

'"Please –"

'"I turned back to the board," Tuomas says—again, it's right there, in the published Confessions—"and seeing that it had failed so completely that nothing could spoil it, I darkened the sky, put above the trees the blob of a moon that did not exist, and painted on in the last moments of the light, a man possessed, trying to make a likeness of the figure leaning against the trunk of a tree."

'That, in the *Confessions*, is all he says about the painting. But the brush strokes, I'd guess, were sometimes free and fast, sometimes intimate, lingering, and not so much thought about as felt, each one a response to a particular glance at Jaakko, who stood as still as he could, and was disappointed to be told that the picture was not finished, that he would have to come back another time—'

'What is it that you are suggesting?' someone in the back row of the audience calls out.

'Please,' I say, 'let me go on.'

'Questions will be at the end,' Heikki booms out from the front row.

'It was the very next morning,' I tell them, 'that the old pastor finally knocked on Tuomas's door, and gestured back to the *pappila*. They went together into the study, and the pastor, his huge, swollen neck wrapped in cloths smelling of juniper oil, his voice finally gone, handed Tuomas a sheaf of papers: the sermon he had planned to deliver that very day.

'Tuomas stood in the lidded box with his hands shaking, the minister in the front row, staring, grimacing, straining forwards, as if by sheer effort of will he could make clear what he had meant by the blotted, thick-nibbed script which Tuomas was struggling to decipher—as if he could make what he heard inside his head come out of someone else's mouth. It was a mockery and a humiliation, but Tuomas was discovering in himself all over again a capacity—almost a desire—to bear something unpleasant until it ended, and he continued sound by sound and word by word, as a child might read a primer, while the pastor banged his fist on the seat next to him, making the faintest of thudding sounds, and now and then mouthed words with absolutely no noise coming out, and the congregation made of it whatever they could, and then hurried away.

'Afterwards, Tuomas led the minister slowly along the short stretch of road to his house. It was hot. Some of the birches were beginning, just, to turn yellow, and small gusts of wind blew up fine dust on the road. He felt the minister leaning increasingly on him, so that by the time they reached the house it was clear that he should pick him up and carry him in, through the dining-room and to his room at the back of the house, calling for Ulla as he did so.

'The old man was easy to carry. He revived slightly once he was lying down and was able to suck at the wet cloth Ulla provided. He still did not want a doctor. He indicated that Tuomas should stay with him, and now his eyes were fixed on the younger man seated by his bed just as they had been in church, though the task now was more difficult still.



'"In silence?" Tuomas asked, "or should I speak? Are you afraid? Is your soul quiet? Do any sins trouble you? For you know that repentance is the dew that comes in the morning and forgiveness the sun that dries it up. Prayer is as the air we breathe; we will pray—" and he began to do so in a low, gentle voice, beginning with the familiar and appropriate, and moving on from these to things half remembered and words he was not sure if he had invented. As important as the words, he felt, was touch, to take the cold hands of the man who was no longer a minister in his own hands as he spoke the words that tradition and intuition gave to him, and to look back into the eyes that were looking into his. He knew that he must keep looking until the other man could no longer see him, and when, with a slow shudder, the old man allowed the last of life to escape him, Tuomas knew the exact moment of its passing, for the eyes he was looking into suddenly stilled, as water does before it knits into ice. Tuomas stood, and made the sign of the cross. He felt that something had taken place between himself and the old man, and he felt as if something divine, "a kind of white heat that did not burn," had passed through him, leaving an immense aching calm in its wake. But it was impossible to know—even as it happened, and even more so afterwards—what the old man's experience had been.

'Ulla was not in the kitchen, but he found her, to his surprise, in the sitting-room, waiting with her hands, raw-looking, too large for the rest of her, in the lap of her skirt. They returned together to the room, and looked for a few moments, unspeaking. The old man's white hair was flung about his head, his jaw had dropped, his cheeks sunken. His shirt was unbuttoned, but his neck was still bandaged, a misshapen bridge between body and head. It was hard now to imagine that he had so recently lived.

'Then, as Tuomas was about to offer prayer, Ulla said: "Leave me with him."

'And Tuomas asked, his voice quiet but bright as he began to understand that here was a story of some kind of earthly love, guilt, betrayal: "Did you want to be with him before?"

'"Yes," she told him, "had the former minister also wanted it."

'Walking out into the hall, Tuomas felt Elojoki, two hundred souls, all this time impervious to him, begin to open and melt, revealing itself as the land had after snow. He walked out into it, found the churchwarden and his son, sent the boy, Jaakko, to the bishop with the news, suggested that the wife go to help Ulla. By then, the light was failing, and he returned to his own house.

'The table outside was as he had left it the night before, and he sat at it a moment and looked at what he had painted. There, roughly done, but oh so clear, was the boy he had just been looking at, leant against the tree, his hips at an angle, his shoulders back, his eyes looking straight at Tuomas and wearing an expression they had never worn at the time, insolent, inviting—"I saw it was a terrible thing, full of awful desires, which I had not felt in me until I had painted it and then looked at what I had painted, and these were not things which God intended to exist but rather—"

'Tuomas says that he took the brush he had used, broke it, then went inside and knelt for hours in the dark with his elbows on his bed, as he used to when he was a child. When he had finished praying, he began straight away to write the document that became his first sermon and then the essay, *Close the Devil's Window* (1870). Here he coined the phrase that has come to sum Envallism up: "An image is a window for the devil to climb through."

'The passage continues:

> From then onwards I began to truly see that 'the heavens, even the heavens are the Lord's, but the earth hath he given to the children of men': we are being told here that the making of what exists and its ways of being is God's work and our work is to live on the earth as best we can. The beginning of which, clearly, is to accept the Glory of Creation, and not to substitute for it devious imitations of our own making.
>
> Of images and idols the psalmist says: 'They have hands but they handle not, feet but they walk not, neither speak they through their throats. They that make them are like unto them, so is everyone that trusteth in them …'
>
> Imitations bring to our minds that which no longer exists or that which was never created, when it is God's will that it does not exist or was not made, was not meant to be. They lead to a contemplation of ourselves and our own powers which estranges us from the Divine. They open up a space for sinful thoughts and actions to enter in, the Devil's window, which we must close tight …'

'Well,' I tell them, 'there he sits at his table in the small house where I have been staying, a young man of his time and place, who has just given the last rites for the first time, adrift in a sea of trees . . .'

It's at this point that I decide to stop, even though a couple of pages elaborating and justifying my theory remain. I have come to love Tuomas Envall and I have finished with him at the same time. As far as I'm concerned, you could say it's all over and done with, just like my love affair with Armstrong, Aldrin and Collins all those years ago.

'Thank you,' I say, as I step away from the lectern and look up at my audience.

Most of them are looking back at me, or at the light streaming through the blinds behind me. Perhaps, indeed, they can't see me very well? Quite a few moments pass. No one claps. I sit down, and let myself look at Heikki, who smiles broadly back.

In silence, I pick up my water glass, drink what's left of it. Then I fill it up again. While I'm doing this, two of the pastors in the front row get up, nod in my direction, and hurry out, leaving one remaining. He studies his fingernails; the academics lean into each other and murmur inaudible observations. But at the same time, they are all still looking at me. I finish my second glass of water, put down the glass.

Heikki clears his throat and says:

'Are there some questions?' and still no one speaks. Perhaps the problem is that those who don't know about 1969 will be thinking: *But what happened to you?* While at the same time, those who do know will be wanting to know: *What was it like?*

# 32

I slept on, serene in the pink and green room. Mark woke, suddenly alert, just after midnight. There was something in the air, a faint, dirty tang. He pulled his curtain open, and even though the window faced onto the road, it was obvious that something was wrong: it wasn't dark and it wasn't daytime but he could see every leaf on the Avenue trees, glowing gold. He clambered over Barbara to reach the window at the back, shouted her awake: 'Fire! The house is burning down!'

The door handle burned his hand. The whole house side of the caravan was buckling, the air hot and rough with smoke, hard to breathe. The fire roared, spat, pulled everything good in towards it. Through the open front door they could see the banisters igniting one by one. The living-room glowed, filled wall to wall with flame.

John Hern was standing on the lawn.

'Have you phoned the fire brigade?' Mark shouted at him. But his father, the tang of petrol in his nose, didn't reply, wouldn't take his eyes from the fire.

'I hope it's gone,' he told Barbara.

'What do you mean?' she asked him, as if her memory had been vaporized by the heat of the fire.

'The image!' he yelled at her, as if, likewise, he had forgotten that they were at war, 'I just couldn't find it!'

By the time Mark returned from the next-door phone the stairs were a sheet of flame. As he watched, the strings of the blinds in his parents' bedroom exploded briefly into rows of tiny lights. Neighbours gathered, handkerchiefs over their noses and mouths, just outside the front fence. Sirens screamed up the hill, the engine, larger than life, disgorged men who landed at a run. 'Anyone in there?' the leader called out. 'Any pets? Count your blessings—' They dragged fat hoses over flower-beds, set two up at the front. Water arched up in orange plumes, thickening the existing smell with steam, laying a fierce hiss over the cracking and stumbling of the burning house, the roar of the fire itself. Two firemen broke through the side gate, the key to which must have been glowing, red hot in the flaming kitchen drawers—

Imagine—or rather, don't, just don't imagine what it is like to come to, choking, and think Where am I?, then see the flames at the end of the bed of that pretty green and pink room. I can't move. Then I am crammed onto the windowsill without knowing how I've got there. The far window is open already, air rushing in—good to breathe but also fodder for the blaze. Flames behind me, an immense heat pushing up from below, I grip the upright of the window-frame. I see the fire crew rush into the garden, and then for some reason—pure folly, blind fate, damned curiosity—I turn back to have one last look at what I am about to escape from. As I do this—the only thing in my entire life that I will wish I had not done—as I turn, the paraffin heater goes up. There is the crack of an explosion, right in front of my face, inside my head, and in an instant I am blinded, consumed, flayed and welded to the sill. Then, somehow, I jump—

# 33



My first question: it's from the thin man who interrupted me ages ago. He's someone I've passed in the street once or twice, sitting now towards the end of Christina's row:

'So—you are saying that Tuomas Envall lusted after a young boy?'

'Yes,' I tell him. 'That particular boy, who like everyone I've mentioned, did exist and was very probably the one. But on the other hand, I don't think he ever did anything about these feelings, and certainly we do know that Tuomas went on to marry and have a family. What I think Tuomas did was to create another sin, in order to avoid even naming what he had felt that night.'

'Yet nowhere does it say so, categorically—'

'The Confessions mention only "a figure." But among the fragments I have discovered during my research are some remarks that must relate to the same incident. For example: Fragment 18, found on the fly-leaf of a Bible which was given to Tuomas by the congregation in Helsinki, in 1898: "Even now, that youth can appear before me as he did then, standing not as he actually did, but as the devil made him seem to me—"'

'And where is this fragment?'

'I have handed all my discoveries over to the safekeeping of the NBA. I understand they'll form part of a special archive, when the museum is built—' At this, there's a murmur of mingled dissent and disbelief from the back row. 'Whose past is this?' someone asks. But, to my surprise, Christina, appearing very calm and collected, silences her followers. She gets to her feet and says:

'Natalie Baron, I'm afraid I have to say that I believe you.' She smiles, and then bursts into tears at the same time. Pekka, next to her, puts his arm around her shoulder and whispers something in her ear, but she shrugs him off, and sits, the tears more or less under control, her eyes glued to my face. It is no longer as if she could burn me up by looking, but as if I could somehow say something now that would pull her clear of her entire past life and set her on a different course. But of course, I can't. And I only ever wanted a hearing, not belief. So I nod briefly, say 'Thank you,' and then look past Christina and say, smiling and nodding in a general kind of way: 'I must say it has been wonderful to have such an open-minded and attentive audience. And I must say that I am surprised no one has put all this together before.' All the while, I'm thinking: *Will someone please ask me something else?* and I have to be rescued by Heikki.

'Would it be right to say that you seem very sympathetic to your subject, this rather misguided Reverend Envall?'

'Oh, I do like him a lot,' I say. 'Far more than I expected to.'

'But,' Heikki continues, 'according to your theory, he led people badly astray—'

A woman in the middle row interrupts: 'What bothers me more is that this is a man who had feelings towards children which no one can condone—'

'One child, actually, and under particular circumstances—' My voice is tired. And, in any case, the students have joined the fray.

'Setting himself up as a moral authority—'

'But if he did not act upon those feelings—'

'The fact is, you have to consider the historical context—'

'Actually, that kind of relativism is a choice, not a given—'

They're off.

I gather my talk together and replace it in the recycled-paper document wallet I bought from Oulu, where Tuomas got his paints. I step down from the platform. A young man in a rather shabby jacket and expensive spectacles comes up to me and explains that he is from the local newspaper. What in the first place gave me my interest in this minor historical figure? he asks—It's a question I'm saved from by Mrs. Lohi:

'A very enjoyable evening,' she says, holding out her hand, chill to the touch, despite the hand-knitted woollens she's dressed in. 'I am glad you came to see us.' She leans into her lap and fumbles with the catch of her handbag. 'The spoon—' she says, 'you remember? Here.'



It's a tiny thing, just bigger than a teaspoon, no use for soup. A child's spoon, in juniper or birch, the twisted handle worn smooth. I find myself oddly tearful as I walk to the door with her and her niece, and then back into the room, papers in one hand, spoon in the other.

Heikki is pulling up the blinds. Then he opens a pair of sliding glass doors so that the smell of summer can come in and people can drift out into the trees. The academics from Oulu decamp en masse, their glasses refilled, their voices growing loud. Others crowd about the refreshment table, where platters of cheese and smoked fish on crispbread have appeared. The room is awash with movement and there's a steady buzz of conversation, not much of it, so far as I can work out, connected to the talk.

I should find Christina, I think, and talk to her properly. But she seems to have gone, and before I know it I've had three glasses of wine.

Heikki and I drift away from the rest, beyond the playing field, right to the edge of the real woods.

'So—' Heikki says suddenly, taking my wrist in his hand. 'So—what happens now? I know all about Tuomas Envall. Do you tell me a bit more about who you are? Or do I just wave you goodbye on the plane? Or maybe not even that? Perhaps you're pleased enough with the outcome and want to move on?'

'You're holding me too hard,' I tell him, twisting my arm away.

'It is hard,' he tells me, letting go. 'It is hard not knowing anything. Being in this damn dark all the time. What am I supposed to do? If you trusted me—' and now he's smoothing the fabric of my shirt front with one hand, slipping his fingertips between the buttons, pulling me into him with the other, 'we could make love right now, here, outside: feel better, celebrate, as the case might be—'

'I can't!'

'I know,' he says, falling still. 'It's because of your face, your skin. The accident you had. But can't you even tell me what it was? Not all of it, just something, to start with? For example, where did it happen? How old were you?'

It's ten o'clock, and still midday-bright. Nowhere to hide.

'I was thirteen—' I tell him. And it strikes me that one of the reasons I've thought so long and hard about The Story of My Face must be so as to be able to tell it to someone else, to the person who needs to know it and will see what it means. But the moment I do so, it will change again.

# 34



I've talked and drunk and talked and drunk. It's late, the sky is the rich blue that passes for dark at this time of year. Countless stars. We sit together on the grass, the empty bottle between us.

'Barbara came with me in the ambulance,' I tell Heikki. 'The first hospital sent us straight on. We had to go to Billericay, two hours perhaps. I know it started to rain; I heard it on the roof. Sometimes I was there and sometimes I wasn't, but I did hear her, telling me all the time in a calm voice how it wouldn't be long, how everything would be all right. Then we were somewhere bright and hot where no one said anything about all right. She was gone, and I never saw her again, even though she did once try to visit. No further contact, the social workers said. Start over.'

Heikki takes my hand again. He listens well. I can feel the heat of his touch, even though I've more or less drunk my body out of reach.

'I don't remember anything very clearly for quite a while. Just the feeling of the anesthetic closing over my head. Sinking deep. Then it's just bits.' Now that I've begun, I do want to tell him everything. I want to finish, but at the same time I am so very tired and my lips seem too clumsy for some of the words I need to use.

I'm in Billericay Burns Unit: the door invisibly opens and closes, and in other rooms beyond mine people talk with blurred voices, and right next to me clothes rustle and rubber wheels and shoe soles peel themselves from the floor; something huge—like a pump, the heart of the hospital—is humming all the time.

'Natalie, my name is Caroline,' she tells me, as my breath goes in and out, in and out. 'We're very hopeful that you will be able to see again,' she says. 'Can you tell me if you're feeling any pain in your hand? Your chest?... Have you ever had an operation before? —'

Of course, I can't move my lips. I signal my replies with a faint grunt, from the very bottom of my throat. I go away and come back, but she's still there, talking in her soft, low voice: 'Your mother,' I think she's just said, 'your mother will soon be here—' And then I'm not sure and in any case can't prevent myself from sinking back into nothingness.

Some time later, I think I hear Sandra herself, hoarse, almost sharp: 'Natty, can you hear me?' But I still can't be sure, and there's something new wrong with me and I can't even make the throat noise I was using anymore. But she might be real, and the possibility is enough to make me want to cross whatever is ahead of me that I can't possibly imagine, just in case. Hope—not a singing bird or a gushing spring, as poets would have it, but a man with a whip, driving you on.

Whatever they're giving me begins to wear off and the pain drives me into the centre of my body. I drift on under the skin of darkness, borne up by the tides of my medication, half of one world, half of another. Days pass. I manage to raise my eyelids. And now I am sure: masked and gowned, blurred, Sandra sits in a chair to my right, her head tilted back, her hands lying still in her lap. She's asleep. I watch as her chest rises and falls, rises and falls, just as I can feel mine doing. I keep my eyes open for as long as I possibly can. I have lost almost a third of my body weight, which, they say, will come back soon, and I have lost one and a half fingers on my right hand, which obviously will not. But I have Sandra back. She watches over me while I sleep; she observes my every movement. She follows every upturn and downturn in my progress, and feels her well-being bound inescapably to it.

'I stayed in Billericay almost six months. I screamed when they moved me at all, every day, for weeks. But the thing is, my mother came,' I say to Heikki. 'She came every morning, exactly like the mothers of the other children there, but of course she was far, far better than they: prodigal, penitent, but gorgeous still in her heels, makeup and jewellery, even though her hair was different, cut in a short bob to save time in the mornings. Sometimes she'd go off and spend an hour on the payphone. Sometimes she'd flirt too much with the doctor. To begin with she needed Aunt Sue and the social worker to keep her in line. But even so, I knew she wouldn't ever leave me and I didn't care how much knowing that had cost me. In the end, I still don't, even when she's at her worst. I got her back. She's a part of me now.

'Now you know!' I tell him. It's not just drink, the lightheadedness I feel, but a bewildering absence. 'Feel better?' I start to laugh, haven't got the strength to carry it through.

'Come inside, now,' he says, helping me up. One foot has gone to sleep. I'm shivering. 'We must go home.' But first, we share the stewed coffee left in the machine, and, when we put the cups down, hold each other tight in the empty hall. While he stacks the last few chairs and locks the windows and doors, I let myself into the Jeep, plug in the belt and lean back gratefully into the big bucket seat. Heaven knows, I think, what will come of all this.

Heikki touches my knee when he gets in, and then the engine coughs and shakes me right awake.

'It's okay,' he says, 'sleep if you want.' We pull out, turn left into the village, where everything is dark except the minimart. I watch Heikki as he drives; his hands relaxed on the wheel, the grey eyes shifting, in textbook fashion, from mirror to road and back again, and just occasionally meeting mine.

'I couldn't live around here,' I tell him.

'Really?' he says, in mock surprise, grinning. 'Are you sure?'

But I don't want to go back either.

We're soon out of Elojoki proper and passing the first of the outlying farms. I'm wondering how my mother will take all of this—will she come around to the idea, can she let me go, and how should I best begin to tell her?—when Heikki jams on the brakes. The belt cuts into my chest, then the seat thuds into my back. We come to a halt just a few yards beyond Christina's farm.

'Idiot!' Heikki yells at the figure standing in the road. It's Pekka Saarinen, ghost-faced, fumbling now at the door of the Jeep.

'It's my mother!' he tells us. 'I've called the ambulance. They said to keep her awake but I can't!'

# 35

The farmhouse sitting-room blazes, every light and lamp switched on. Christina is on the floor, unconscious, lying on her side. She's soaking from the water Pekka has splashed uselessly on her face. 

'The others are all out drinking. She knocked a vase over and it woke me up. Once she went under I just couldn't hold her up—' he says. 'How long can it take them to come?' A Swedish DJ gabbles away on the radio; Heikki turns it off. 'Please!' Pekka says. 'Do something!'

So I go over and kneel on the floor next to Christina. She is still breathing, very shallowly, her face sickly and blank, her lips drained of colour. Her jaw sags open. A trickle of saliva is running out on the lower side. A swatch of hair is stuck to her cheek with sweat; I scrape it away then grab hold of her shoulders with both hands, dig my fingers in and shake as hard as I can, knowing it'll be no use.

'Christina!' I shout. 'Wake up, damn you! How dare you do this!' *So what if you think you've been mistaken, so what if you've wasted a few years*, I'm thinking. *What about the ones you've got left! What about your children!* My heart's a runaway engine in my chest as I stop shaking, shove her over onto her back and slap her cheek as hard as I can. My hand stings. Her head lolls from side to side a few times, taking up the impact. I do it again, again, this side then that, quite a few times. Then I grab a handful of hair and pull—

'No—it's too much!' Heikki shouts.

Actually, it's not enough. I make a fist and punch, right in the middle of her body, the softest part.

There's a kind of rippling echo of the blow in her neck. She splutters in her sleep; a gobbet of thin fluid comes out of her mouth. Breathing hard, I stop to watch.

'On her side!' Pekka says, pushing me away.

'Sit down, Natalie!' Heikki orders. And when, just minutes later, the ambulance arrives, he stops me from going with them: 'No—' he says, putting himself, it seems, between me and my past. 'Look. They'll pump her out. She'll probably be all right. It's not your business, is it?'

# 36

We've come to Savo, where the trees are far taller and stretch up to a peerless pale-blue sky. We have eaten our picnic of bread, cheese and cucumber; we have drunk the first two of our small green bottles of beer, and now we walk on, sometimes separate, sometimes hand in hand, along a path that we believe or hope will lead us to one of many lakes, still as glass, ice-cold, bottomless, teeming with fish and mysteries: a destination which gives shape and pretext to the journey. Heikki, wearing his pale-blue tee-shirt and track pants, carrying the bag of provisions, sweats heavily. Half of me can't sweat anymore so I am hotter still. I dab at my inner arms with a wetted cloth, and every hour I re-coat my face and neck and left arm and hand with sunblock. Even in the shade here, I can feel how the ultraviolet wants to burn me. But I know how to protect myself. I've bought yet another pair of sunglasses, the wraparound kind designed for cyclists. And although the sun is fierce, there is plenty of shade. Everything is dappled. The air is the cleanest I have ever breathed.



'You'll like the winters here,' Heikki tells me. 'December, you could miss the light entirely ...'

'I can smell water,' he tells me, smiling. 'I think we will see the lake quite soon.' We leave the path and begin threading our way through the last of the trees, pushing branches aside, clambering over fallen trunks. Soon I too can smell the water and I'm thinking to myself: *Look how far I have come! I am in a new story now. And yet, at the same time, must I still be sitting on my bed in Billericay?* I'm thinking of that particular grey and windy morning when I had, following Caroline's instructions, put on my best turquoise blouse. Caroline was to one side of me, Sandra, who I now called Mum, was on the other; the mirror, pink plastic handle and back, oddly foreign in its domesticity, lay face down on my skinny lap. I'd been in the hospital about fourteen weeks, endured daily the agony of having my dressings changed. I'd had half a dozen operations to my face, neck and chest and ahead of me was a potentially infinite number of further procedures.

And now it was time for me to see for myself what had happened to my face, rather than catch mere glimpses of it in other people's eyes and expressions. It was hard for me to see how this knowledge would improve my life. It was the third time we'd tried.

Through the mattress, I could feel Sandra shake.

'Not if you're not ready, Natty,' she said.

'Just for a short moment,' Caroline encouraged, softly, from the other side. 'You're a very brave girl,' she added, shameless. 'I'll count to ten—'

The lake, a huge blue rent in the inky green of the forest, spills itself ahead of us.

'There. I told you,' Heikki says, dropping the bag, which has left a dark print of itself on the pale blue of his tee-shirt.

'Here, then,' I say, and hand him the camera, my little semi-automatic. There's a pause, long enough, I'd say, for him to appreciate the nature of the request and its probable consequences. I watch him weigh the camera in his hand, check to see that there is film inside, what kind, where the shutter is.

'Sure,' he says, looking up, bright and eager. 'What about the boulder there?' It seems as good a place as any. I climb up, undo the top buttons of my shirt, sit cross-legged, hippie-style, one hand on each knee. Heikki gathers his bulk around the tiny silver machine and then, at the last minute, I remember to remove my glasses. Because I do, thanks to Mr. Arthur Boyes, have perfectly good, albeit lashless, eyelids, and because I do want Heikki to be able to record those along with everything else that is me: the many different textures and thicknesses of skin that make up my remade face, most notably the anomalously uniform swathe of soft skin, freckled, as all of me once used to be, over my chin, jaw and neck. It comes from my back and was grafted as a skin-flap, still joined to its source between my shoulder blades, in a process lasting several months. This loosened up the scarring under my chin so that I could stop looking at my feet. Beneath the smooth patch, the skin on my neck and chest is of a far rougher texture, thickly ridged and dipped. Well below where they should be are the nipples I allowed them to replace, just in case... That was my last operation, because after it I decided I'd rather not. They've moved again since, and don't line up. The picture will show the finely done seams around the big planes of my cheeks, the messy patch above my right eye, which for almost a year wouldn't heal and then for another year pulled my face entirely out of even the loosest notion of symmetry: Heikki, it is all there: my nose, perfectly functional, though with a somewhat rough-hewn look to it; my two ears, not matching; my mouth with its proper pink lips, not rosebud, not bee-stung, not even entirely horizontal, but sensitive all the same; my eyes, different in shape to the originals and to each other, but still green; my hair, which, as luck would have it, grows as thick and bright as ever. Here is my skin, my face, which is nothing like what it was or would have grown to be, but nonetheless, is mine:

'Are you ready?' Heikki says.

The lens is a door. I hear the wheeze of the zoom, blink at the click of the shutter's fall, and find I have passed through.

# EPILOGUE

My name is Natalie Seppä. I made this story, and it made me.  Now I live in a new country, vote in its elections, speak, write and even dream in its languages. I look at my face each morning in the mirror, curious as to how age will take a skin like mine; vain, still, about the colour of my hair.

But although I move further and further away from my past, and the thread between then and now grows thinner and thinner as it lengthens, it is still strong. It will always be there.

I know some things about what happened afterwards. I know that John Hern was charged, but got off when things came to court. Then, not long after, he was run over, wandering the lanes near the Thorns' farmhouse at night: it served him right, Mum said when she read of it.

I know that Mark turned out all right, because—it's the strangest thing—I've seen him several times on television. He's grown into a big man, slightly overweight, but comfortable with it, articulate, easy in his movements. He's done two series on modern art, several books. It says on the back of the one on Jackson Pollock that he went to Winchester Art School. I expect he's married and so on, by now. Does he remember me as I was then? Does he remember the sweat and toffee smell and the wild, first-time excitement? Has he ever turned, terrified, from the question of what I've become in all the years since, what I might be like now? Or has he buried me completely away? I don't know.

I know that charges against Barbara were dropped. I know, of course, that she made sure some of the money left from the sale of the house plot and sawmill was put in trust for me. I expect she and Mark went to stay with Adrian and Rose while the aftermath of the fire took its tedious, painful course. I hope that somehow it came out all right, but I've no idea how. Of course, it's Barbara that I think of most. How many grandchildren might she have? Does she still keep the photograph of her lost baby?

Would she like one of me?

Heikki thinks that I should leave well alone. And of course, I don't want to upset my mother. But I know Barbara is still alive. I know where she lives: 193 King Street, something Christina found out for me quite easily via Jean McAllister. And look—there are so many pictures to chose from now: for example, this one of us outside the wooden house we've built ourselves. Or this one, which my mother took, of us on a family holiday in the Aland Islands—Heikki and I holding hands in front of the summer cottage, Kirsi dripping wet from her swim. Surely she would like to see that? I want her to know that she was, after all, right; I would like to show her how very glad I am that she unlatched the blue-painted gate and let me in.

Kathy Page is the author of ten previous books, including *Dear Evelyn*, winner of the 2018 Rogers Writers' Trust Fiction Prize, and *Paradise & Elsewhere* (2014) and *The Two of Us* (2016), both of which were nominated for the Scotiabank Giller Prize. Other works include *Alphabet*, a Governor General's Award finalist in 2005, and *Frankie Styne and the Silver Man*. First published in 2002, *The Story of My Face* was long-listed for the Orange Prize. Born in the UK, Page moved to Salt Spring Island with her family in 2001, and now divides her time between writing and teaching at Vancouver Island University.